D1591294

To The Tall Timber (Buckskin Chronicles Book 2)

By

B.N. Rundell

Chapter One: Journey

JEREMIAH AND SCRATCH stood tall in their stirrups and stretched as high as their legs allowed, striving to gain as much of the long-sought fresh air as their lungs would hold. They were starved for the smells of the woods and streams of the wilderness having just left the stench of the sewer strewn streets of St. Louis. Scratch was the first to sound off, "Whooooeeeee! My lungs wuz beginning to complain so much, I thot they wuz gonna just up and leave me breathless! 'n muh nose weren't much happier with me. If we'd stayed thar much longer, I swear my whole face woulda melted right off my skull!"

With a barely muffled chuckle, Jeremiah responded, "Well, I know whatcha mean, but ain't you spreadin' it on a little thick?"

"Not a bit! I swear it's the gospel truth! I'm gonna hafta scrub every pore in muh body at the first water hole just so's muh buckskins will know they didn't git on the wrong body. Course, there ain't no other body as fine as mine, but you know what I mean."

"Yeah, I know, and I'm powerful glad I'm upwind of you!"

Although the two men acted like they had been partners for many years, it had actually been less than a year on the calendar, but a lifetime when measured in miles and adventure. Jeremiah had been on a vengeance quest with his two Arapahoe friends from the Wind River Mountains in Wyoming and hot on the trail of the renegade band of slave catchers, cutthroats, exiled Indians and ne'er do wells.

The three friends had already exacted vengeance on two of the Indians and one of the slave catchers when they caught up with the four remaining renegades on the bank of the Missouri River across from Fort Union in Montana. It was there that Scratch introduced himself by dropping one of the outlaws that had leveled his rifle at Broken Shield as he fought the remaining renegade Indian. With only two remaining slave catchers, one had made his escape on the *Yellowstone* side-wheeler headed for St. Louis and the remaining one willingly giving up the leader that had absconded with all the stolen gold.

Scratch teamed up with Jeremiah and the two had traveled down the Missouri, caught the remaining slave catcher, retrieved the gold and used it to fulfill the promise made to Jeremiah's mentor and friend that had been killed by them. That promise was to free his family from slavery where they were kept in Kentucky. Now they were returning from that successful adventure.

"Course, you know doncha boy, that if you'd made up yore mind to do this when we wuz in Kentucky, we coulda just headed North and probly been thar by now," observed Scratch.

"Yeah, you've only said that three times so far, too. I toldjah I didn't really think about it till we wuz in St. Louis, and just bein' there reminded me of when my father and I were there the first time, and that was right after we left Elizabeth with Aunt Sarah up in Michigan territory. Just bein' there reminded me of her. Ain't seen her fer 8 – 10 years and this'll probly be the only chance I git."

Both men were quite capable of speaking without the easy vernacular of the mountain man, and had readily carried off the

charade of wealthy farm owners shopping for slaves when they
bought the freedom of Ezekiel's family, but now the
comfortable confab of the mountain man unhindered by social
restraints came easy to mind and mouth.

After returning to St. Louis from the Kentucky plantation
country, the men had outfitted themselves at the Hawken
brothers shop with ample powder, lead and some additional
gear. Jeremiah had an early model Colt Paterson revolver, and
traded it for the newer model .36 caliber with the built in
loading ramrod that made it possible to reload without having
to almost completely disassemble it as the older model
required.

The two men were already equipped with .54 caliber
Hawken rifles and both had Bowie knives. Scratch refused to
surrender his long-tom .54 caliber flintlock Kentucky rifle and
his Walker flintlock pistol, "Cuz, ya just might run outta them
little caps and then whatcha gonna do?" as he referred to the
caps used by the Hawken and Paterson. The remainder of their
gear was picked up at the nearby general mercantile.

After emptying his bank account earlier in the day, trading
his several bags of gold dust panned in the mountains and
deposited on the outbound trip, for gold coin, the men went
first to the livery at the Southwest edge of town at the end of
Market Street. This was the place with the best selection of
horses and tack to outfit them for their long journey. Settling
on a steel-dust grey gelding for himself and Scratch picking a
soft-eyed blood sorrel mare, the two agreed on a pair of bay
geldings for their pack horses. With the dickering finished, the
men saddled the horses, rigged the pack-saddles to the pack
horses, and headed back to the mercantile to load up for the
trip.

They didn't get out of town until late morning and now,
after pushing hard most of the day, the sun was dropping into
a pool of orange behind them. The shadows lengthened from
the tall Sycamore and Tulip trees that sheltered a few smaller
Oak and Cedar. All the trees were starting to bud out and green

up in this early spring and the travelers were glad to be back in the woods and away from the crowds of the cities. Both agreed they had seen enough city life to last a long time, but they also knew they would be visiting a few more before they made it back to their beloved mountains.

After visiting with many men of similar ilk at the Hawken brothers shop, which had become a buckskin hangout of sorts, Jeremiah calculated the extended trip they were facing would probably take all summer and they would be lucky to be back in the mountains and with his beloved Laughing Waters by the start of winter.

Laughing Waters, the thought of her brought a smile to his face as he rocked along with the steady gait of the steel-dust. They had practically grown up together, after his father was killed and he'd been taken in by the escaped slave, Ezekiel, who lived with the Arapaho in the Wind River Mountains. She was just a year younger than him and the little sister of his best friend, Broken Shield. She had proven herself to be as skilled a warrior as either Jeremiah and Shield and a better archer than either of them. This competition and companionship had slowly grown into more between them Waters and it was that connection that drew Jeremiah back to the mountains.

In the approaching darkness, the light splashing chuckle of a stream drew the travelers a bit closer to the bank and a cluster of trees that provided a good campsite for the night. Dropping to the ground, both men stretched as they surveyed the area with the usual wariness of seasoned mountain men.

They didn't expect to have any problems or company but just because none was expected, didn't mean there wouldn't be any, as only friendly company announced itself but the unfriendly kind didn't bother to make itself known, whether it be man or beast.

In short order, the horses were tethered, unsaddled and unpacked and the camp began to take shape with bedrolls and a fire ring. It had been a long day and both were more concerned with sleep than food, so only a small hat-sized fire was sufficient for a few strips of salt-pork hung on green branches for supper.

Both men were light sleepers, and they turned into their bedrolls and cradled their Hawkens nearby, pistols under their rolled-up blankets used for pillows. Their first night on the trail ended with the snores of Scratch competing with the distant questions of the great horned owls.

To The Tall Timber

Chapter Two: Reflection

THE USUAL EARLY START saw the two well on their way. Scratch led the way for the two-man, four horse caravan. The plan was to travel East to the Kaskaskia river, cross it and continue East to the Wabash. The Wabash river would lead them North to Fort Wayne for re-supply and from there they would continue North into Michigan territory and hopefully the reunion with Jeremiah's sister, Elizabeth.

Scratch was what most would describe as a "grizzled" mountain man, hardened and wizened by the many years survived in the wilds of the Western mountains of the Rockies. He had lived with Indians, trapped with the American Fur Company, and explored with the likes of Jim Bridger and others of their time.

The only surprising revelation came on their recent trip to Kentucky when Scratch revealed his momma was a slave and his daddy was a white plantation owner in Kentucky. When his daddy threatened to kill the child, his momma had begged the noted black pastor in Lexington to take him. Pastor London Ferrill and his wife took him in, named him Lucas, and raised him as their own until the mountains called the young man to a life of outdoor adventure. The recent trip was the only time Scratch returned to his roots in Kentucky.

Not an overly big man, Scratch filled out his buckskins with what would be called a "wiry" frame, but his lean figure was not to be mistaken for weakness. He was quick of mind and faster of limb whether it was to be fleet of foot, or sudden of reaction, Scratch was not one to take for granted. His full beard and bushy hair shot with streaks of grey framed high cheekbones, a dark complexion, and penetrating dark brown eyes that hid under the bushy eyebrows that hung from a bold brow. When he stretched out, he stood just shy of six feet and weighed in at about 175. Astraddle his sorrel mare, her casual gait and fluid movements continued in his frame as if the two were one. That was his way, easy, smooth movement that belied his quickness.

By contrast, Jeremiah, about 10 years Scratch's junior, had filled out his once youthful frame in just the last year the two traveled together. Before he started the last trek to fulfill the promise to his mentor and adopted father, Ezekiel, Jeremiah Thompsett showed his youth in his enthusiasm and endless energy. Full of optimism and idealism and thinking himself immortal, he had initiated the vengeance quest that resulted in the promise fulfilled.

But more than that, he had benefitted with a mature judgment beyond his years and experience that would benefit him the rest of his life. That arduous trek had also resulted in physical growth and a physique that showed the man he had become. Now standing a few fingers over six feet, his frame held over 200 pounds of hardened muscle.

His light brown hair was long and fell almost to his shoulders and mingled with his wavy full beard that gave a look of maturity beyond his years. The piercing green eyes held both a glint of ever present suspicion and a sparkle of mischief and humor. Even his voice had matured and was now a deeper bass with a mellow ring that caused any nearby to turn and listen.

Quick to show himself friendly, he always held back that part that cradled any trust that might be given until that trust was earned. His agility was unusual for one of his size and frame, but his quickness of action and judgment were his strongest traits.

His mount, the steel-dust grey, was just over 15 hands tall and well-muscled with plenty of bottom. The two bonded by the end of the first day and now moved with a confidence born of friendship and trust. Jeremiah had learned well from Ezekiel and his Arapaho family how to handle a horse and the treatment the mount deserved before the trust would be given from horse to man. He now leaned down and ran his hand along the neck of the grey and spoke, "So, Dusty, how ya doin' today. Gittin' used to the trail are ya? I shore like your gait, boy. Nice and smooth, easy goin', shore makes ridin' easy. You and me are gonna be good friends, ya know that?"

"No, I didn't know that!" Scratch chuckled as he straightened up. He had seen Jeremiah lean down to stroke the neck of his mount and figured he would be talking to him, so Scratch had dropped back and leaned down so his response would seem to come from Jeremiah's mount.

He had achieved the desired reaction. Jeremiah straightened up with a start and looked back down at his horse as if expecting him to say more. When he realized the stunt pulled by Scratch, he stretched down with his long arm to grab a stone from the ground while holding the saddle horn with his other hand. Successfully grabbing a stone, he playfully threw it at his partner and scored a direct hit in the middle of his back.

"Owww! That ain't no way to treat the best durn partner ya ever had! Just fer that, I think you need to cook supper tonite!"

"I already had that figgered out. Cuz after chokin' down some 'o yer cookin' I figgered if we were gonna survive this trip, either I had to do more o' the cookin' or you'd need to learn how ta cook!"

9

The easy banter continued off and on as they made their way eastward. They hoped to make it to the Kaskaskia River before nightfall and that meant maintaining a steady gait along the way. Usually they would stop for an hour or more for their noonin' but with the mounts still fresh on the trail, their noon stop would be a quick one and back on the trail.

It was easy to settle into the steady rhythm of the horse's pace and with this being new country to the both of them, they didn't waste the opportunity to survey the countryside and take in the varied terrain. This was flat country, at least in comparison to their home in the mountains. Lots of vegetation, plenty of grass for the horses, trees galore and of a variety of types unknown to the men filled their eyes.

It was early spring and the grasses were green and the trees were budding out. Bushes were sprouting leaves almost as fast as the breezes rattled their skinny branches. It was a beautiful day with mostly blue sky and a spattering of puffy white marshmallow clouds. The light breeze kept them from dozing in the rocking saddles that had the to and fro motion of a baby's cradle.

The warm sun on his chest coupled with the steady sway of the horses on the trail soon lulled Jeremiah into a state of reflection. It was easy to bring forth the image of Laughing Waters and be reminded of their many happy times together as they numbered the days of their youth. Seldom could Jeremiah or White Wolf be found without the nearby presence of both Laughing Waters and her brother Broken Shield.

The three were inseparable as they participated in the many games of the younger members of the Arapaho village and even invented their own games that were exclusive to the trio. As they grew older, the games became competition of warrior skills with the bow, knife, and riding as well as the hunting skills of tracking and outwitting their quarry. The competition continually sharpened their skill until the trio always excelled in any of the events shared.

Those skills had become practical when together they pursued the renegades that slaughtered Ezekiel and stole their stockpiled gold. But through it all, the bond between Laughing Waters and Jeremiah had grown stronger and when they finally acknowledged their mutual feelings, they had to part with Waters taking the wounded Shield back to the village and Jeremiah continuing on the trail of the renegades with Scratch. That parting was wrapped in the promises of Jeremiah to return and Waters to wait, promises that Jeremiah anxiously sought to see fulfilled.

His random wandering around in the halls of memory also brought forth the image of Ezekiel, his mentor and adopted father. Although much of his youth was spent in the company of Laughing Waters and Broken Shield, he actually lived with Ezekiel, also known as Buffalo Thunder, and his mate, Walking Dove.

It was Ezekiel that gave the much needed guidance and instruction in life's challenges and obstacles that made Jeremiah the man he became. The image of the big black slave's body crumpled in the corner of the burned cabin had been seared into his mind to stay forever. The years they spent together in the cabin were the most treasured of his life. It was there they panned the many bags of gold that were used to free Ezekiel's family from slavery and it was there that the plan was formulated and the promise made that would accomplish the almost overwhelming task. Although the trek had been long, life-threatening and challenging, the promise had been fulfilled and that gave Jeremiah the solace he needed.

The clatter of the horse's hooves on the rocky trail brought Jeremiah to a renewed state of awareness. Looking around at the scattered willows, he realized they were approaching a small stream, the chuckling of the water over the few rocks were the dead giveaway. It was a small stream that crossed the trail and left the scattered stones on the bank for the horses' hooves to clatter about.

Scratch, on his little sorrel mare, casually stepped forward to the trail crossing of the stream, the mare dipped her head for a quick drink of the clear water, then continued across the shallow stream. They were closely followed by the packhorse trailing behind Scratch and then by Jeremiah aboard his steel dust gelding and his packhorse following. Each horse copied the little mare in dropping their head for a quick slurp of refreshing water as they crossed.

It was a combination of actions that caused the explosion. First, Jeremiah's gelding let out a startled whinny that caused Scratch's packhorse to jerk his head back to see what the alarm was about. The sudden jerk on the lead rope unbalanced Scratch, then the Massasagua rattle snake that was sunning himself on the flat rock on the riverbank was scared to wakefulness and automatically sounded off with his rattles.

The fight or flight reaction of Scratch's sorrel tripped the bear-trap springs in her four legs and catapulted her and Scratch straight up in a valiant attempt to hang his hat on the nearest passing cloud. With her front legs to the left and the hind legs to the right, she twisted in the middle trying to unseat her now unwelcome burden. She tucked her head between her front legs and appeared to scratch her belly with the bit in the bridle.

A sudden kick with her hind legs stretched her body out parallel with the ground, and then she broke in half, all before coming back down to earth for her second record-shattering vault back into the air.

Scratch had swapped his grip on the lead rope for a death grip on the saddle horn as he valiantly grabbed his horse with every limb, hand, foot and anything else he could as he only saw blue sky where he thought his saddle should belong. He didn't realize how easy it was to fly as he tried flapping his now unloosed arms to make his landing less traumatic. With his legs churning as he tried to run without his feet yet on the ground, he looked for the horse he had just been astraddle of a few seconds ago, but his search was in vain. The sudden stop to his descent pushed all the air from his body from every opening he had and he gasped as he tried to recapture that which he had lost.

"Scratch! Move, you're on top of that snake!" shouted Jeremiah.

With an automatic reaction that caused every part of his body to move in what seemed like opposite directions, he fulfilled his nickname and scratched his way up the trail faster than Jeremiah could ride after him. Looking back at his landing spot, he saw a now squashed coil of grey brown spotted reptile that vaguely resembled a rattle snake.

"Well, I guess we don't have to hunt for meat for supper. Most folks say they taste like chicken, so I reckon we'll find out. Course, ya didn't have to squash him so flat, didja?" drawled Jeremiah.

Scratch sat up, tried dusting himself off, and reached to his back as the pain reminded him of his one-point landing. He looked around to find his mare and the trailing packhorse and noted they were in a nearby clearing and munching on the new spring grass as if nothing had happened.

He didn't know whether he was mad or relieved, but he knew he was in no condition to go chasing after a couple of loose horses. Feeling like a man twice his age, he struggled up and went to secure his horses as Jeremiah, having tethered his horses to the green branches of the willows, walked back to gather their evening meat. At Scratch's suggestion, they made camp for the night.

To The Tall Timber

Chapter Three: Wabash

THREE DAYs on the trail brought them to the Wabash river, the point of their course change to head North. So far, they had successfully avoided the many small villages and the main roads that held more travelers than they necessarily wanted to confront. Both men were more prone to isolation than association. The so-called civilized people were too "civilized" to suit the two buckskin-clad mountain men.

They knew they would have to deal with enough people who couldn't be avoided without seeking more "knot heads and dimwits" as Scratch called them. It was evident there was a considerable village on the East bank of the Wabash, so Jeremiah sought out the usual trail that paralleled the river on the west bank. There was still plenty of daylight for them to continue their travels and get them further on their journey to the Michigan territory.

The few days on the trail had allowed Scratch to heal up from his rattlesnake mishap, although he continued to complain about his mare's spring-loaded legs and he was always careful now to take a deep seat in the saddle before he brought his heels to her ribs. Jeremiah enjoyed the scenery and often took note of the many spring flowers scattered across the hillsides and to the edges of the thick trees that bordered the river.

He especially enjoyed the clusters of the violets with their small blue blossoms and what looked to be the closely related phlox with their smaller star-shaped purple blooms. Many different flowers were coming on so thick they appeared to carpet the sun-drenched hillsides. Of course there was a variety of blossoms- from the lacy and tall white hyacinth to clusters of the bright yellow, daisy-looking ragwort. Jeremiah didn't know the names of the many flowers, nor did he care to know. He just enjoyed the green-up of spring and the new life that put on its spring-time best to show the many colors of the Creator's hand.

"Ya know, Scratch, this country ain't got no mountains, but all these here flowers and such shore are pretty. Why, even the bushes and many of the trees are bustin' out in color. I ain't never seen so many different blooms all at oncet!"

"Yup. I know whatcha mean. Fore I made it to the mountains, I wandered all 'round this hyar country for a year or two. There shorely are a bunch o' dem flowers an' sech. Course, I still like the look and smell 'o pines more'n anything."

"Yup. Gotta agree witcha dere. My nose's been searchin' for that pine smell fer some time. I seen a couple them pines here, but, ain't 'nough of 'em to suit me."

A small clearing in the trees caught their attention and they headed to their stopping place for the night. Just off the trail and set back from the river, it was evident this was a popular stopover for many travelers. A fire ring of stone in the middle was framed by three large logs for seats and there were a few pieces of firewood stacked by the ring of stones. As they removed the tack from the horses, Jeremiah said, "I think I'm gonna take a walk over near the river and see if I can't find a little fresh meat. We've got a little time 'fore dark and I could use some fresh red meat, couldn't you?"

"Yeah, you go 'head on. I'll take my time and git camp set up, maybe git a little more firewood."

Jeremiah slipped the Red Willow bow that had been a gift from Black Kettle, the Arapaho Shaman, from the scabbard on his packhorse. With a handful of arrows dropped into his belt quiver, he headed out through the thick timber. Few could match his stealth through the woods, a skill he had mastered in his many years with the Arapaho and from his constant competition with Laughing Waters and Broken Shield, his childhood, lifelong friends.

As Jeremiah disappeared into the dense foliage, Scratch set about arranging their camp for the night's stay. He gathered up loose firewood from nearby downed timber, returned to the fire ring and placed the wood with the kindling and tinder. Striking steel across flint, the sparks quickly ignited the tinder with a spark and emitted a bit of smoke.

Crouching down, he blew lightly to spread the flame and ignite the kindling. With a few waves of his hat, the fire caught and began to grow. He filled the coffee pot with water and set it on a flat stone near the fire. Placing the bedrolls on the opposite side of the fire ring and far enough away to prevent a spark-started fire, he used a small shovel to turn the soil and make the bed sites a bit more comfortable. Now he sat back against one of the logs with his legs outstretched and watched as the fire began to flare to life.

The click of the hammer on a rifle is an unmistakable sound that when unexpected, brings a cold chill of fear that can only be allayed when it is accompanied by a friendly voice.

"Sit real still," commanded a stranger from behind Scratch, "I might want to join you, and then again, I just might want to relieve you of your burdens." A large, bearded and scruffy figure stepped around in front of Scratch and pointed a long, flintlock Kentucky rifle at Scratch's midriff. "It's been a while since I had some coffee, and if that's what yore brewin' thar, I think I'll just have me a cup."

"Tain't ready yet. All that's there is just the hot water. I was just gittin' ready ta put the grounds in when you interrupted me," stated Scratch.

17

"Well git with it, then," demanded the man, his dark eyes peering out from under the bushes that passed for eyebrows. The mass of matted hair and bush of a beard made it possible for the man to pass for a black bear, only he was a mite bigger. The clothes were on the ragged side and it was difficult to tell where the patches ended and the dirt began. His patchwork coat looked more like a filthy bed quilt than a coat. "What's one man doin' with so many horses? Whatcha packin' that cha need so many?"

"Oh, nuthin' special. It's just a long trip I'm headin' on and need plenty of supplies. Course one of 'ems a spare that I was gonna trade when I git to the next settlement. He ain't nuthin' special and don't like packin'." Scratch was trying to bide his time until Jeremiah returned.

"Yah, I think yore lyin' to me. You probly got a bunch a trade goods or sumpin' pretty special in thar. I might just have ta take all that off yore hands. Whatcha think 'bout that, huh?"

"Not much." Scratch dropped a handful of grounds in the now boiling water and moved the pot back a little from the flames. "I'll git us some cups," he said as he headed to the packs.

"Watch yoresef," the bear growled. "I'd just as soon shootcha right now, as not." The big man seated himself on the opposite log and held his rifle across his lap with the barrel in Scratch's direction.

Bending over the pack with his back to the fire, Scratch called out loudly, in an effort to warn Jeremiah, "Do you need some sugar in that coffee? I'll bring some…"

"What fer ya put sugar in coffee? Coffee's coffee, don't need nuttin' else." The big man began to look over the camp site, first at the packs and saddles, then at the fire and finally at the bedroll at the end of the log by Scratch. As he looked, he turned and noticed behind him the second bedroll. He started to turn around when an arrow whispered past the fire and buried itself in the big man's thigh, pinning him to the log. With a yell of pain, he started to fall back and grabbed for his rifle but it had fallen from his lap just out of reach. As he tried to stretch for it, the arrow held him fast to the log and the pain increased.

"Don't move or I'll pin the other one down too!" growled the tall buckskin-clad man standing beside Scratch.

"I won't, I won't. Just git this'n outta here, I'm gonna bleed ta death!" whined the big man in a high, squeaky voice. His voice sounded more like a scared girl than the mountain of a man he appeared.

Scratch stepped by the man and grabbed his rifle, then pointing it at the thug and ordered, "Now, just put any other weapons you got right down here in front of us. You know, like that pistol under your coat, and that knife in yore boot, and anything else like that. Come on now, I git nervous when I have to go too long without my coffee."

One pistol and two knives found their way to the indicated spot in front of the man. Scratch dragged them away with his foot, then stooped to pick them up without taking the rifle off the man.

"Come on, come on, I'm bleedin' here," the man squealed.

"Well, now thatchur hands are free, pull it out yore ownself," instructed Scratch.

With hands bloodied from trying to stanch the flow of blood, the big man grasped the arrow and succeeded only in breaking it off underneath his leg. Then, with another quick pull, his hands sliding the remaining length of the shaft to tear the fletching off, he finally managed to extract the arrow from his leg.

He looked up at Jeremiah who was still holding the fully drawn bow with a notched arrow, then his eyes rolled back in his head and he fell backwards off the log and lay still.

"He's a biggun ain't he?" observed Scratch, as if they had uninvited visitors like that all the time.

"Yup. Guess we oughta try ta fix him up fore he bleeds ta death."

19

Without the need for more words, both men set down their arms and went to help the man. They stretched him out alongside a log, used some leather thongs to bind his wrists together and tied him fast to the log. Jeremiah laid his knife with the tip in the flames while Scratch tore the man's pants away from the wound both front and back. The wound was bleeding with a slight pulsating and Scratch said, "I'm not so sure that doctorin' him's gonna help. I think that arrow got his main blood spot here," he said as he pointed to the growing pool of blood.

As the knife blade began to glow a bright orange, Jeremiah grabbed the handle, walked to the man and laid the tip on the wound. He held it while it seared and smoked and the man tried to set up as he screamed. When he fell back, Scratch rolled him to his side enough for Jeremiah to cauterize the exit wound. Then the two men stepped back to the fire as they looked at the still unconscious man. Jeremiah said, "If that don't do it, he's not gonna make it. Too bad, I was just gittin' to like him." Scratch jerked his head around and looked at Jeremiah with a startled and questioning expression.

"Like him? Ya didn't even know him."

"Yeah, but there at the last, he was nice and quiet. That's my kinda man," stated Jeremiah with a droll expression on his face. Then he stepped away and said, "Come on and help me with this little buck I shot. I'm gittin' hungry."

Shaking his head in wonderment, Scratch followed Jeremiah to fetch the deer.

Chapter Four: River Trail

AS NIGHT LIFTED her grey hemmed skirts of darkness to reveal the pink petticoat of the new dawn, Jeremiah and Scratch stretched to wakefulness in anticipation of their campfire coffee.

The older man with shots of grey streaking his mussed beard and hair rolled out first and staggered his way to stir the embers to life and he threw a couple of small sticks onto the pile of now glowing ashes. He reached down to get the coffee pot in anticipation of refilling the smoke blackened pot with fresh water, then stood abruptly to look past the larger log to the now vacant site of the wounded would-be camp robber.

Neatly coiled strands of rawhide bindings sat complacently atop the log as if they were nothing more than camp decorations. Scratch quickly turned to look at the nearby tree that had been the resting place of the big man's Kentucky rifle and possibles bag with powder horn only to be disappointed at their absence.

"Jeremiah! He's gone, plumb gone! Lemme check ta see if he took anythin' else," muttered Scratch as he scampered toward the packs and tethered horses. Sliding to a stop he began to take inventory of their gear and supplies as he pointed and counted aloud. "Well, I'll be snookered! He didn't touch a thang, but he shore did skedaddle like a scairt injun in the night!"

Jeremiah now stood near the rekindled fire and reached for the forgotten coffee pot. As he stood erect he said, "Well, if he's gone, guess we don't have ta worry 'bout him no more. Let's eat us some vittles and git on the trail. It looks like it's gonna be a good day for travelin' and we got a long ways to go."

The men made short work of breakfast and were soon on the trail with each leading their respective pack horses. The days were already becoming routine, fair weather, blue skies with scattered clouds, occasional showers and the trees, spring flowers and field grasses turning green.

The early spring weather was typical for this part of the country, but it wasn't what Jeremiah longed for as he much preferred cool breezes off the still snow-capped mountains whispering through the tall timber of ponderosa pine and towering fir and spruce trees. But the vast green fields that were occasionally marred by some settler's plow had their own kind of beauty and he enjoyed the variety of colors wrought by the Creator's hand.

Mid-morning of the second day after their run-in with the would be camp robber, the men were making their way to a copse of brush with some shade trees atop a small knob just North of the trail when they heard a considerable ruckus coming from further up the trail.

They gigged their horses past the shrubs and found a nice little clearing to do their noonin' and make a little fire for coffee. The slight elevation of the knob also provided a view of the source of the ruckus. There appeared to be some type of construction going on with a large number of workers and several piles of fresh dirt.

"Now, whatta ya spose that's all about?" inquired Jeremiah.

"Just what is there 'bout me that makes you think I'm supposed to know the answer ta that question?" responded Scratch as he busied himself with a small fire for their coffee.

"Well, you're the man 'o the world, that's been ever'where and done ever'thing. Ain't you supposed to know ever' single thing?"

Scratch stood and walked to the edge of the clearing that afforded a view of the tree-lined meadow beyond. He stood with his hands on his hips, then moved one hand up to stroke his beard and mumbled some unintelligible gibberish. Then turning to Jeremiah, "First, I thought they was buildin' a railroad, but they's diggin' down a ways and 'less they's buryin' that railroad, it must be sumpin' else," he concluded. Then he returned to the task of making coffee.

Jeremiah continued to watch the workers in the distance in a vain effort to deduce the answer to his own question. He occasionally turned to watch the horses grazing on the nearby grass as they stretched their tether ropes to the full extent of their length, assuming the grass just out of reach was somehow tastier than that at their feet. Scratch said the coffee was ready, and with one last look at the workers in the distance, Jeremiah turned to partake of their luncheon repast.

Shortly after their noon break, the men approached the worksite and stopped their horses away from the hub-bub. A lone man sat on a nearby rock observing the work and looked at the newcomers, then said, "You feller's lookin' fer work?"

Scratch replied, "The last time I looked fer work, it found me and I been runnin' from it ever since!"

The rock sitter chuckled then asked, "So, what are ya'll up to?"

"Just a passin' thru. So, what is all this commotion about, anyhow?" inquired the mountain man.

"Why, they're diggin' a canal. Cain't ya tell?"

"A canal? What fer?"

"Well, ya see," began the observer as he turned to face the visitors, ". . . they started way up at the Erie Lake above Ohio,

23

and they're diggin' this all the way to the Mississippi river. They plan on usin' it fer shippin', you know, usin' them flatboats loaded with goods from back East and carryin' 'em all the way to the Mississippi, and from there on down to all those places on the river."

"Seems like a mighty lot a diggin' ta me," observed Scratch.

"They been diggin' for nigh unto 6, 7 years now and I'm sure it's gonna take a mite longer."

"Wal, we're headed up to Ft. Wayne. How much farther ya spose it is?" inquired Scratch.

"Ya got about 2 mebbe 3 days. If ya stay this side of the Wabash and the canal, the only thing ya gotta cross is the Eel river, it's just a little ways on down the trail. Course, this time 'o year, what with the Spring runoff and the showers we been havin' lately, it might be tough goin' so don't try it at night."

With a nod and a bit of a wave, the two travelers continued on their way, watching the work of the diggers as they passed. The many workers, several hundred of them, ignored the passing travelers and bent to the work of digging the six-foot-deep and twenty to thirty foot-wide canal with the picks and shovels while many others pushed metal wheel barrows to carry the dirt to the banks. Most of the workers were shirtless and all were covered with dirt and sweat, prompting Jeremiah to say, "I hope they're gettin' good pay for that, cuz it shore looks like back breakin' work."

"Yup. And it's men like that doin' the work of the big money men that're leavin' their tracks all over this country and makin' so it ain't fit fer man nor beast. I'd just as soon they go back to their stinkin' cities and leave the rest of the country alone," groused Scratch.

Jeremiah held his silence. He had learned that silence accomplished more with Scratch than entering into one of his "perils of civilization" tirades. As they continued on the trail, the numbers of workers dwindled until the canal work was minimal and mostly completed.

It was a massive project and at least provided work for a lot of men. Jeremiah thought it best to have something to keep the men here as opposed to having this many people wandering through the wilderness with no means of supporting themselves and unable to live off the land. He thought it would be best if they just made farmers out of themselves and settled this likely looking country that seemed to beg for farms and crops. *At least, that would keep them out of the mountains,* thought Jeremiah.

As they approached the banks of the Eel river, they could hear the rushing water lapping at the sides and eroding the soft earth and grass-covered banks. There were occasional pieces of trees and other driftwood carried on the swift running current of muddy, angry waters.

They turned upstream in search of a likely crossing point that wouldn't be quite so dangerous. After making about a quarter of a mile, the riverside timber cleared and revealed an apparent crossing that had been used by the construction crews. Both banks sloped to the water's edge with rocky roadways entering and leaving the river. Although the river was not a necessarily large one, the fast moving flood waters made it dangerous.

The water here seemed to be moving steadily but without excess rapids revealing an apparent smooth river bottom. Because it had been used as a crossing many times before, they were sure the bottom would be solid and provide good footing. As the men looked at each other, then at the raging water, Jeremiah said, "Well, we ain't gittin' anywhere just lookin' so I'll lead out. Why don't you wait until I git across before you start, just in case."

"Just in case a what?" asked Scratch.

"Well, I s'pose, just in case I don't make it. Then you can figger out some other way." With that, Jeremiah kneed his horse into the water. He dallied his lead rope around the saddle horn and prepared for the current. Shortly, the current took the horses off their feet and they began to swim for the opposite shore. They dipped and struggled to keep their heads above water and pointed to the goal of the bank with their noses.

The current began to push them downstream and the pack horse slipped further down and was brought upright with the tethered lead-rope. Jeremiah slipped from the saddle and held to his horses tail and let the horse have his head and swim to the bank. With a little more bobbing in the current, the Steel Dust finally found footing and struggled up the opposite bank to safety. Once on solid footing, he shook so violently the saddle slipped a bit to the side as Jeremiah led the two horses to the level landing above the water. He stood and turned to wave to Scratch on the far side. He then stepped down near the water to await his partner.

Aboard his sorrel, Scratch started into the water. His crossing was much the same as Jeremiah's, and as the current threatened to take his mount, he too dropped to the side and let the sorrel have its way to swim the fast-moving current. He paddled alongside and looked to the opposite bank to see Jeremiah waving his arms and pointing upstream. Scratch fought the current and looked through the splashing muddy water upstream to see a large snag of flood ravaged timber racing toward him and the horses!

He paddled his feet in fear as he loudly urged his little sorrel to hurry. The dallied rope on the saddle horn gave the pack horse a measure of stability as he, too, paddled against the mad waters. Scratch looked at the oncoming snag and saw that it was headed directly toward the pack horse. The mountain man swiveled his head to the horse and back to the snag, and in that instant he knew he had to free the pack horse from the dallied lead rope if it was to have any chance of making it across.

Reaching forward to the saddle horn, he loosened the dally and let go the rope. The current caught the now struggling packhorse and turned it downstream, but the effort was too little too late as the huge snag of a tree reached out with skeletal branches and swept the packhorse under, carrying it out of sight downstream.

Scratch and the sorrel found footing and struggled to the shore and the outstretched hands of Jeremiah. As they made their way to the level landing above the waters, both men fell to the grass and sought to catch their much needed breath. The horses stood with legs splayed out and stomachs sagging as they too sought to fill their water slogged lungs with much needed air.

"Wal, ain't we a bunch a sorry critters," observed Scratch as he lifted himself to his elbows to survey the remnants of the traveling crew.

"I sure didn't expect it to be that bad, but at least we're all in one piece. Sorry about that hoss but at least we didn't lose nuthin' that can't be replaced, so I guess we're all right," answered Jeremiah.

After a short time of putting things back together, they continued their trek on the river side trail Northeastward. They welcomed the coming dusk and eagerly made an early camp to try to dry out their gear and equipment. After a short jaunt into the timber, Jeremiah returned with two rabbits for their evening meal which was downed quickly as both men sought to turn in for a well-earned night's rest.

To The Tall Timber

Chapter Five: Resupply

THE LEATHER APRON did little to cover the paunch that hung over the big man's belt. A large handlebar mustache drooped below his chin line and his bald head was framed with a bushy growth of graying hair. Thick eyebrows shaded a pair of bright eyes that brimmed with a glint of mischief and a broad smile pushed back fat dimpled cheeks letting a hearty laugh escape his cracked lips.

The liveryman and blacksmith for the largest livery in the growing village of Fort Wayne, who also served as the mayor, spoke to the visitors with a deep bass voice. "Well, you two look like you just escaped from yonder mountains. Ain't seen the likes of you mountain men in some time, what with all these ditch diggers hangin' 'round here for the last couple years. What can I do ya fer, gentlemen?"

Scratch spoke up with, "First thing, ya can quit callin' us names like 'gentlemen' and then ya can show us whatcha got in the way of pack horses," explained the wiry mountain man with a broad smile underneath laughing eyes. He knew right away that this was the kind of man he could spend some time with and enjoy swapping lies.

"Pack horses, 'eh? I got just the thing fer ya, but they ain't horses."

Scratch and Jeremiah gave a quick glance at the liveryman and then at each other, as they followed the big man through the large building that smelled of horse, hay, and a bit of smoke from the forge fire. As they stepped into the bright sunlight, the liveryman put a foot on the bottom rail of the pole corral fence, then turning to the travelers said, "My name's Joshua, but most folks just call me Smokey," and extended his meaty paw for a handshake.

Grasping his hand in his, Scratch said, "I'm called Scratch, and this here's Jeremiah," as he pointed to his younger partner. "So, what's these pack animals that ain't horses?"

"Right there they be," he stated as he waved to the two mules standing together in an attempt to take advantage of the bit of shade in the far corner of the corral. Both animals stood with heads erect and eyes focused on the noise makers that just exited the building. They appeared to be a matched pair as both animals were a mix of splotches of red and white that blended together with faded lines in random patterns over their bodies. If they were horses, most would think they were mixed blood of pinto and appaloosa, but the two mountain men just saw them as colorful but strange creatures.

Jeremiah spoke up, "We only need one. We lost one of our pack horses crossing the Eel river back a ways, but we have one and just wanted to replace the other'n."

"You won't find a better pack animal than a sure-footed mule. They can pack more, they're smarter and don't get into trouble from bein' stupid like a horse, and they're even broke to ride. So if ya need to, you can ride 'em out of whatever trouble your horses get you into. But, they gotta go as a pair. They've been together since they was borned and they wouldn't stand bein' separated," the big man informed them. "But, I'll tell what I'll do, I'll take your pack horse in trade and make you a deal you can't refuse on these two."

The dickering continued until a deal was reached for the two mules and additional packs and tack for the second animal. After receiving directions to the nearest general store/mercantile, the men got their first experience with mules as they led the pair behind their horses just a short ways down the main street to the Fort Wayne Mercantile. They had been on the trail less than two weeks, but the loss of the one pack horse and the supplies carried, as well as the supplies used, dictated the full replacement to continue their journey.

The supply list consisted of the usual staples, flour, beans, sugar, coffee, salt pork and bacon, and miscellaneous other items. As usual, while waiting for the clerk to fill the supply list, the men gravitated toward the gun rack and knife case. They added the usual galena bars, a couple of new bullet molds, patch ticking, and powder.

The Paterson colt pistol, at .36 caliber, required a smaller mold than the rifles that used the .54 caliber, and Jeremiah asked for an additional mold of the smaller caliber. They noticed the gun rack held a Hawken rifle, which was unusual as they were not in plentiful supply as yet, and after their inquiry, they decided an extra rifle would be beneficial. After settling the bill, the men readily loaded the new supplies in anticipation of a departure that would enable them to soon depart from all this "con-sarned civilization" that seemed to bother Scratch.

With lead ropes dallied around the saddle horns, the gentle tug from the horses brought the speckled mules in line as the road led the way North out of Fort Wayne. It was unusual for the men to travel on the road as their custom was to usually parallel any roadway to avoid any contact with other travelers or the occasional ne'er-do-well or would-be highwaymen. But traveling the roadway made the experience of leading the mules behind horses that weren't real excited about their new companions, seemed to be the wiser choice for the remaining hours of the day. Whenever the roadway led to a village of any kind, the men made it a point to swing wide and make their way around the settlement. As they approached an intersection of two roads, they learned by the road signs that the roadway they had been traveling was called the Coldwater road, because it led to the settlement of Coldwater in what was known as Michigan Territory. Although this had been recently admitted to the union as the state of Michigan, it was still referred to by many as Michigan Territory.

As the sun reached the treetops to the West, the men drifted off the roadway in search of a camp spot for the night. Crossing a stream that meandered alongside a nearby copse of brush and trees, they turned up a slight grade to the shelter afforded there. A small clearing presented itself just inside the edge of trees, and it was immediately apparent they were not the first to find this natural campsite.

The usual routine was followed; camp was made, their meal and coffee prepared and finished and the men turned in for the night. Both men had long ago developed the ability to sleep light, the slightest difference in the usual night sounds bringing them instantly awake and watchful. With this confidence, the night began peacefully, the only sounds being crickets, distant frogs, an occasional owl or other night bird and the occasional shuffling of the horses and mules.

It wasn't a different or unusual sound that brought Jeremiah awake, but rather the absence of sound. The night is seldom silent unless something has caused the sound-makers to cease. He lay still, only opening his eyes enough to peer straight ahead to the edges of the clearing that was slightly illuminated by the dying embers of the fire.

Without moving, he searched the open spaces around him until his eyes rested on a figure near the ring of stones around the remains of the fire. It appeared someone was sitting on the log and staring at the prone figures of Scratch and Jeremiah.

He didn't move, but in a quiet voice asked, "All right if I drink some coffee?" A slow nod from Jeremiah gave the visitor permission and he picked up an overturned cup and filled it with the remainder of the black liquid.

Jeremiah looked for a nearby weapon but saw none and he slowly rose from his bedroll. With a nonchalant stretch, he turned to pick up the now empty coffee pot and said, "Guess I might as well make another pot." He turned to get more water from the small spring-fed stream nearby and upon his return, he kicked Scratch to wakefulness as he passed his bedroll. He continued on to the fire and the bag of coffee beans. As the water heated, he busied himself crushing the beans on the stone and watched his visitor for some indication for the reason of the unannounced visit.

Noticing the stirring of the second man in the bedroll, the visitor said a little more loudly, "I am called Long Runner. I am Potawatomie and this was my home," he indicated the surrounding area with a sweep of his arm. "All my people were chased away and sent to what they called Indian Territory in Oklahoma on the other side of the big waters. I have returned."

"I can see that. But why have you returned?" asked Jeremiah.

"My family all die here. I will die here."

"What are you plannin' on doin'? Goin' on the warpath or sumpin'?"

"No. I will just live out my days here. This is my home," the visitor stated again.

Scratch had rolled out and quietly came to the fire, cradling his Hawken. Now he put in his two-bits worth, "Well, we ain't a'gonna live out our days here, cuz our home's in the mountains yonder," as he indicated by pointing his chin whiskers to the West. "But you shore got us outta bed sooner'n I 'spected, so I guess we might's just as well have our breakfast and hit the trail. We got some 'o dat cornpone left over from last night, ain't we?" he inquired as he made to sit on the opposite log by the fire.

Jeremiah took the hint and dragged the frying pan with the left-overs nearer the fire. Left-overs are always better when served a bit warm. There was just enough for each to have a

33

small biscuit size of the corn patty and Jeremiah passed out a good size piece of jerky to each man.

Long Walker gratefully accepted the offering and nodded his thanks to Jeremiah. As the two travelers were packing up to leave, the young mountain man prepared a bit of jerky, beans, and corn flour in a rag of his old shirt and tied it into a bundle and offered it to the now standing Long Walker. "Ain't much, but it'll keep ya goin' for a while," said Jeremiah, as he turned to climb aboard his mount. The tall Potawatomie looked at the white man with a surprised expression on his face and said, "May the Great Spirit go with you," as he stepped back from the horse and nodded his good-bye.

Chapter Six: Michigan

JEREMIAH WASN'T CERTAIN where he would find his sister, Elizabeth. All he really remembered when he and his dad brought her to stay with his Aunt Sarah, was sitting horseback on the bank of the Kalamazoo River when they turned to wave their last good-bye. Aunt Sarah was married to a farmer named Hamilton and she had two girls of her own when she agreed to take in Elizabeth.

Now, two days after their early morning visit by the big Potawatomie, Jeremiah and Scratch were once again on the bank of the Kalamazoo. They sat their horses on a slight rise overlooking a small village on the North bank of the river. "Doesn't look like much," the younger man murmured, "but maybe there's a post office or general store or something where we might get a little information."

Jeremiah's voice was soft and low, almost as if he was talking to himself. With no response from Scratch, he clucked his tongue to start his mount down the slight incline on the way to the bridge that stretched across the narrow stream.

The main street was lined on both sides with several businesses, the first and largest building they passed being the livery stable. Just two doors down from the livery was a large two-story stone building with a big sign reading, *Marshall Mercantile*.

The two men turned their horses to the hitch rail, stepped down and hitched the horses and pack mules to the rail and stepped up on the boardwalk. A couple of local citizens passed them before they reached the front door, and both Jeremiah and Scratch nodded in greeting, receiving nothing more than a grunt of disapproval in return.

Scratch said, "Well, howdy doo! Guess we don't quite measure up to the local standards. Course, it's probably you, more'n me, I took a bath just before we reached St. Louie!" He grinned as he stepped in front of Jeremiah to enter the store. Both men paused to let their eyes adjust to the lesser light of the interior, then Jeremiah stepped to the counter where a matronly woman with a clerk's apron over her simple grey dress asked, "How may I help you?"

"Mornin' mam. I just need a little helpful information, if you don't mind. I'm lookin' for my sister, her name's Elizabeth Thompsett, or at least it used to be, she might be married by now. She'd be a couple years younger'n me, little thing, light brown hair. She lived with my aunt Sarah Hamilton," he added with a hopeful expression on his bearded face.

"Hmmm. Let me think. I don't know, the only Elizabeth I can think of is an elderly woman."

Another woman standing near the counter and fingering some material, stepped nearer and said, "Martha, what about Dr. Robinson's wife, isn't her name Elizabeth?" then looking to Jeremiah said, "I'm sorry, young man, I couldn't help overhearing."

"You know, I think you're right. I do believe his second wife's name is Elizabeth. And she'd be the right age and his description... does sound like her," replied Martha.

Jeremiah asked, "Second wife?"

"Yes, his first wife died and left him with a young son. The way I understand it, he was tendin' to the farmer Hamilton when he met his Elizabeth," but it's so sad.

By this time Jeremiah was getting pretty perplexed and asked, "Sad?"

"Yes, Dr. Hamilton died just over a week ago, and left his son with Elizabeth. Course, she's the only mother he's really known. She's been his mother goin' on about seven or eight years now."

"Uh, can you tell us where they… er, she lives and how to get there?" impatiently asked Jeremiah.

"Well, now young man. Don't go gettin' in any hurry to go out there. Several folks around there have been struck down with a plague, Typhus, I think."

Jeremiah couldn't have been hurt harder if he had been hit square on with a charging buffalo. All he could say was, "Please?"

With both men listening intently, the ladies conspired on the best directions and wished the men, "God's speed!"

The directions took them west of town about an hour's ride to a log farm house set back from a sizable meadow and an adjoining corn field with young cornstalks just popping out of the ground. There was a one-horse wagon in front of the house with the horse tied off at the hitch-rail.

The men walked their horses to the house and Jeremiah stepped down and handed the reins of the grey's bridle to Scratch. He walked to the door, hesitated a moment with bowed head, then lightly knocked on the door and stepped back. Almost immediately, the door swung inward and revealed a blonde headed boy of about nine or ten, attired in bib overalls and shirtless with bare feet peeking out from too-short pants legs. "Who're you?" he asked with a scowl on his face.

"Uh, is this the Robinson place?" asked Jeremiah as he dropped to one knee to be face to face with the boy.

"Yup. Like I said, who're you?"

"Is your Momma's name Elizabeth?" asked Jeremiah.

"Yeah. So what?"

"Well, I'm . . ." The sudden appearance of a black woman behind the boy stopped Jeremiah in mid-sentence. She was wiping her hands on a hand towel, and a few loose hairs fell from the bun at the back of her head. She appeared to be in her mid-thirties, was somewhat attractive and had a commanding presence about her as she asked, "Yes?"

"I'd like to see Elizabeth, please," asked Jeremiah.

She looked askance at what appeared to be some type of wild mountain man that stood before her, and then she noticed the other one standing by the horses. Distrust showed in her eyes as she said, "And just who might chou be and why do you wanta see missy 'Lizbeth?"

"I'm her brother, Jeremiah."

"Oh. She's mighty sick. She's got Typhus, and it's catchin', so don't git too close," she commanded as she stepped back from the door to allow him entrance.

As he stepped inside, he nervously ran his fingers through his long hair, pushing it back from his forehead. He walked quietly to the door the woman indicated, tapped lightly and entered. A frail figure lay on the feather bed, propped up slightly with extra pillows, and covered with a patchwork quilt. She turned her head to see her visitor and fear filled her eyes as she caught her breath bringing a doubled fist to her mouth.

"Elizabeth, it's me Jeremiah, your brother," he said quickly to stay her fright.

She dropped her hand, scowled with her eyes as she furrowed her brow, then motioned him nearer. He knelt beside the bed and brought his face close to hers as she examined his countenance. "Jeremiah, is it really you? I thought I would never see you again. Oh, thank God," she choked as tears filled her eyes.

He gently reached for her hand, afraid he would hurt her. She looked so frail, almost like a skeleton with thin pale skin stretched tightly over exposed bones. He dropped his head to hide his own tears. As her hand rested in his, he lightly stroked it with his other and lifted his head to drink in the vision of his long, lost sister. Memories tried to crowd in, but he pushed them back to savor the moment.

Elizabeth asked, "And Poppa?"

He nodded his head negatively and said, "No. He was killed by Indians shortly after we reached the mountains. I was taken in by an escaped slave named Ezekiel and raised by him and his Indian wife, Walking Dove. I've had a good life. But, enough about me, what's with you gettin' sick just when I come to see you?"

"I'm sorry Jeremiah, I'm plumb worn out. Could you get Maizy for me, please? We'll talk later, O.K?'

Jeremiah stood, still holding her hand, and said, "Sure, Lizzy, sure," then turned to get the woman named Maizy. She was waiting outside the door and nodded her head as he exited the bedroom, walking into the room without waiting for instructions.

Jeremiah went outside to talk to Scratch and decide what they would do for the night. He was afraid, afraid in a way that he had never known before. It was different when Ezekiel had died. By the time Jeremiah had gotten to the big man, he was already dead and Jeremiah could do nothing to help.

But this was different… he felt he had to do something. It was his sister in there, the girl he had played with, protected, pestered, and the only family he had left. There must be something he could do. But first, he and Scratch had to make arrangements for the night and maybe a few extra days.

He walked to the horses, looked at Scratch, gave a nod of his head for Scratch to follow, and they walked, leading the horses to the woods set back from the rear of the house. They heard a small stream just after entering the woods and walked a short way into a small clearing that looked as if it had been used for cook-outs or camping.

Neither man spoke as they prepared their camp, hobbling the horses so they could graze on the grass on the stream bank, and arranging the packs and tack. Jeremiah sat on large rock by the previously used fire ring and stared moodily at the dead, black coals. Scratch could tell that the young man had dropped into a melancholy mood and would be of little help in the final preparations.

Looking for firewood, Scratch took a short walk through the nearby trees and returned with an armload of broken branches and dropped them near the fire ring.

Jeremiah absent-mindedly built the fire, used the flint and steel to spark the tinder, bent to blow it to life and sat back, gently fanning the growing flame. Scratch was digging out the utensils, coffee and other necessities and was slightly startled when the tow-headed boy said, "So, whatcha doin'?"

"What are *you* doin' out here boy? Ain't you s'posed ta be in there wid yer ma?" replied Scratch.

"Nah, Maizy is takin' care of her. I'm not sposed ta git too close, cuz that Typhus stuff can git ya, and Ma don't want me gittin' sick."

Jeremiah had heard the boy and joined the two by the gear as Scratch continued to gather the fixins' for their evening meal.

"So, just how old are you anyway, and what's your name?" asked Jeremiah.

"I'm almost ten and my name's Caleb. Are you guys really mountain men?"

"Yessiree Bob, there ain't never been two more hellacious, rag-tag, Indian chasin', bear wrestlin', wild and wooly mountain men sech as us'ns!" boldly bragged Scratch with just a little braggadocio.

"Did you really rassle a bear?" asked the doubtful boy.

"Why, course I did. Won too, and skinned him alive and used his hide ta keep me warm!" chuckled Scratch with a straight face.

"Ahhh, I don't believe you. You're funnin' me. But I'd sure like to be a mountain man. My pa and I, he died just last week, we used to sit around this heah fire and talk about someday goin' to the mountains," boasted the boy, then with a lower and sadder voice added, ". . . but I guess we won't do it now." The tow head dropped his chin to his chest and reached a small paw to rub the tears from his eyes. "I better git back to the house. I'll talk to ya tommora if you're still here, okay?"

"Sure, it's O.K." chimed the two mountain men together. Both men turned to watch the boy make his way through the tall grass and back to the front of the house. They stood watching the emptiness as their minds filled with thoughts of a young boy, soon to be all alone.

To The Tall Timber

Chapter Seven: Caleb

THE MANY TREES around the campsite were budding out with a variety of leaves, many of which were new to Jeremiah. But even with the encroaching trees and branches and the new buds and leaves, it was the star-studded sky that filled Jeremiah's sleepless eyes.

Many were the times that he had lain beneath the stars and enjoyed the many constellations Ezekiel had taught him about and he remembered that each star-gazing night began with his search for Orion and his favorite star at the tip of the hunter's upraised sword, Betelgeuse. He recalled the fun he'd had with Ezekiel when he pronounced the name as "Beetle Juice."

But tonight he wasn't thinking as much about the stars as he was thinking about his sister. He knew about Typhus and understood that most folks that came down with it, didn't survive. If Elizabeth's appearance revealed anything, he was certain she didn't have long to live.

It seemed so long ago when the two of them had run away when a band of drunken renegade Potawatomie attacked their home and their Mom had sent them to their secret hideout. It had only taken a few minutes to get to their cut-away cave in the river bank near the big old oak tree.

Dad had always said they were to hide there if danger arose and to stay there until he came and got them. It was late that same day when they finally heard the voice of their dad calling to them and lifting them up the bank to join him.

When they returned to their house, there was nothing but smoldering timbers and their Mom was nowhere to be found. When questioned their Dad said he had to bury her before he came and got them and that they were going up North now to see their Aunt Sarah. Until that terrible day, the years together with his sister had been good and he had many great memories.

Now, he wondered uneasily, *what's going to happen?* His mind was going in too many directions to really figure anything out and the lack of resolution kept him tossing and turning most of the night.

As the first streak of grey light forced its way through the trees, Jeremiah kicked off the blankets, rose and put a few sticks on the still hot coals, then headed for the cabin. He rapped lightly on the door, pushed it open and stepped inside.

Maizy stirred in a rocking chair near the fireplace and looked at the tall man entering her domain. She quickly rose, went to the stove and opened the small door to put in some fresh wood, using the poker to stir the coals. She refilled the coffee pot and put it on the soon-to-be hot stove. "Just sit down there at the table, coffee'll be ready in a minute or two," said Maizy. "Sides, we gotta talk," she continued without looking his way, ". . . some things needs ta git settled."

Jeremiah obediently pulled out a chair and sat down, placing his elbows on the table and folding his hands under his chin. He watched Maizy as she puttered around the stove with complete confidence from years of practice. He wondered about the relationship she had with Lizzy. *What is she, a friend, a neighbor, does she work for Lizzy?* Before his mind wandered any further, she said, "Missy Lisbeth is my best friend an' she ain't got long for this world and she wants you ta know that. This Typhus stuff is horrible bad. Just sucks the life right outta person, gits so bad, it even takes their mind sometimes 'fore it takes their body. Missy Lisbeth's husband, the doctor, once he came down with it he didn't last no time a'tall."

"Where'd this stuff come from anyway? How did it just get these folks and nowhere else?" asked Jeremiah, desperate for some answers to questions that really weren't the ones that had bothered him all night.

"That blasted Erie canal has had so many folks comin' from those big cities back East and many of 'em carryin' all kinda disease. They was a couple came here and were sick when they got here. The good doctor took care of 'em, and then he and a couple others that those folks stayed with, they all come down with it. Now it's Missy Lizbeth."

"What about you. Can't you get it, you've been around her a lot and takin' care of her."

"Nahsuh, not me. I don't git nuttin', my dead husband said I was too blasted ornery to git sick," she smiled at the memory, ". . . sides, wouldn't make no nevermind, cuz Missy Lizbeth's my best friend and I'd still help her anyways."

"She's lucky to have a friend like you."

Maizy heard a faint call from the bedroom and rose to tend to her patient. After a few moments, Jeremiah heard his name called by Maizy and he rose to obey the summons. As he walked into the bedroom, he hesitated a step, and took a quick suck of wind to give him time to control his emotions as it appeared that Elizabeth's condition had deteriorated since he left her side just hours before.

A frail hand motioned him to her bedside and he quickly moved to be with her, dropping to one knee on the rag rug at the bedside. She dropped her hand into his and forced a smile at his bearded face. She struggled to speak and with a raspy whisper she said, "You look so different with whiskers, but I'm glad you're here. I've been prayin' for days and it looks like the good Lord has brought my answer right here to my bedside. I thought I'd never see you again."

45

"Many a time I've prayed for you too, but I must not a'been prayin' hard 'nough," he replied.

With a deeply grave look, she said, "Jeremiah, I need you to do something for me. . ."

He interrupted her, "Anything, Lizzy, anything for you."

"Now don't go jumpin' the gun on me. Let me finish. I want you to take Caleb."

"Sure, I will. Where do you want me to take him, his grandparents or somethin'?"

"Will you hush a minute? I want *you* to take him. He doesn't have any other family. His daddy, my husband, was all the family he had after his ma died. I've been his ma for the last 8 years, even before the good doctor and I were married. Now, he's got no one, 'ceptin you. I need you to take him and raise him as if he were your own. Promise me? Please?"

Jeremiah was so flabbergasted he couldn't even move, much less talk. The thoughts swirling around in his head actually knocked him to the floor and he had to kick his one leg out from under him before it broke. He was propped up with his arms stretched behind him with his palms flat on the floor and he was gasping for air. His face revealed a fear akin to an attack by a grizzly bear. Stuttering he said, "You want me to do what?"

It had been some time since Lizzy had anything to laugh about, but the sight of her big tough mountain man brother flailing on the floor caused her to start giggling and laughing so much she started coughing and that brought Maizy running to her aid. The negress looked at the man on the floor and her friend choking on the bed and she threw a scowl at the man and bent to the bedside with an arm around Lizzy to help her more upright and to catch her breath.

"What'd you do to her? If you hurt her, you scalawag, I'll beat you with a broom till you can't stand!"

Her response just started Lizzy laughing and coughing again, and with a wave of her hand, she brought peace between her two care-givers.

"Oh, Maizy, did you ever see such a silly lookin' lummox as my brother?" asked Lizzy.

Forcing a smile, Jeremiah rolled over to his knees, and from all fours, stood and turned to chuckle along with the two making fun of him. With a mock dusting off of his buckskins and looking down at his moccasins, he said, "Did you say what I think you said?"

After struggling to suck in a couple of big breaths, and letting out a long sigh, she replied, "Yes, Jeremiah, I did, and before you answer, remember you already said 'anything, Lizzy' remember?"

"But Lizzy, I live up in the mountains with the Indians. My best friend is Broken Shield and his sister Laughing Waters, and there ain't a white man within days of where we camp."

"I thought that man you're travelin' with was your best friend. What'd you call him, Scratch?" she asked.

"Well, he's like my partner. We've been through a lot together and we'll be stayin' together, but I was raised with Shield and Waters." His voice went a little soft when he mentioned Waters' name and it did not go unnoticed by his sister.

"Jeremiah, Caleb is a good boy, he learns fast and he loves the outdoors. He'd rather sleep under the trees than in a bed and has done so many times. I know you would take care of him, just like you did with me, and you're the only hope I've got." She dropped her head to her hand and tried to stifle another cough. Then she looked at Jeremiah again, "Please brother, promise me? You're the only hope we have left!"

Maizy chimed in and said, "You'll have ta git outta here now, Missy Lizbeth needs to get a little rest. You come back later."

"Promise me, please," pleaded Lizzy.

"I promise," growled Jeremiah as he turned to leave. *What am I saying? I can't take care of no kid, I can barely take care of myself!* Stoop shouldered, he left the house and made his way back to their campsite and his traveling partner. Walking up to the campfire, he noticed Caleb sitting on the log opposite Scratch and it appeared the two were in deep conversation.

". . . and that ole bar had his teeth tangled up right chere in my beard and was shakin' me sumpin' fierce, so I's seen muh chance and I's up and poked both my thumbs in his big brown eyes. He started caterwauling' like one of them mountain painters and fell to his back a'grabbin' his face. Since he let me go, I turned tail an run, with nary a look back! And that's how I was nose ta nose with the biggest grizz in the mountains and never got a scratch. So, the only scratch I got, is my name." Scratch took a deep breath and leaned back, feeling satisfied with himself for telling such a tall tale.

Caleb painted his face with a frown of disbelief and seeing Jeremiah return, he looked to the younger mountain man and said, "Yore partner here has more hot air than my momma's chimney," then crossed his arms across his chest as if he had won an arm wrestling match with a windbag.

Jeremiah had to smile and said, "You got him figgered out pretty quick, you did. By the way, I think Maizy wants you to fetch her some more water, if you're up to it, that is." As the boy headed back to the cabin, Jeremiah took his place by the fire and looked at his partner, who sat with his hands at his sides on the log and a smug expression on his face that was the usual giveaway after he had told a whopper.

"That boy's quite a young'un. Smart as a whip, he is," observed Scratch.

"I'm glad you've taken a liking to him, cause he might be with us a little bit longer than we expected," stated Jeremiah, as he stared into the dying flames.

Chapter Eight: Buckskins

"WHEN PAUL WAS SPEAKING to the Corinthians, he said, 'I shew you a mystery; We shall not all sleep, but we shall all be changed.' And he went on to say, 'Death is swallowed up in victory. O death, where is thy sting? O grave, where is thy victory. . . But thanks be to God, which giveth us the victory through our Lord Jesus Christ.'"

The preacher from the Community Church in Marshall had volunteered to conduct the grave side services for Elizabeth Thompsett Robinson, wife of the previously departed Doctor Josiah Robinson. He continued, "We leave our dear sister, Elizabeth, in the arms of her Lord and Savior, knowing she had accepted his precious gift of eternal life and is now assured an eternal home in Heaven. Amen." It was a small group, mostly those that lived nearby. Although the Doctor was well known and respected, many were still afraid of the Typhus and didn't want to come near those that had been exposed.

Maizy had seen to the final preparations and the necessary clean-up of the cabin. Everything that had been used by the doctor or Lizzy had been taken out behind the cabin and burned. The only items left in the cabin were the few furnishings and tableware. Jeremiah had helped Caleb gather

49

his few belongings before Maizy hit the cabin like a whirlwind in her efforts to make the cabin livable and usable.

She was surprised to find that Lizzy had made arrangements to leave the cabin and property to her. Knowing Jeremiah was taking Caleb, Lizzy had committed the cash money she had on hand and in the bank to Jeremiah for the care of her step-son. Maizy would probably sell her little cabin and have enough funds to take care of herself until the few crops on the property could be harvested.

Lizzy and the doctor didn't have a lot of money, as the doctor was usually paid in farm goods like a smoked ham, a slab of bacon, a few eggs, or most often a wave of the hat and an empty promise... But the money she did have would be ample enough to get Caleb outfitted and maybe a little more. *Boys don't require much more than a bit of attention now and then.* Thought Jeremiah, hopefully, as he walked with the boy to the barn.

"I gots me a real fine pony, you'll see. My daddy said he's a strawberry roan and comes from Tennessee Walker breeding, whatever that means. But he suits me real fine," rattled on Caleb as he nervously focused his thoughts on anything but his mom and dad. When they stepped into the small barn, the horse stretched his neck over the stall gate to greet his little master with a high pitched whiney.

Caleb ran to the gate, undid the latch and reached for the O-ring at the bottom of the halter to lead his pony out to display him for Jeremiah. Caleb was every bit of four feet tall and the gelding was right at 14 hands high, together they made quite a pair. "He's only 5 years old and he's real gentle. I can handle him fine, and I got me a saddle and everything. He was my Christmas present this last Christmas. Ain't he a beaut?"

"Yeah, he is. What do ya call him?" inquired Jeremiah.

"Rastus!" replied Caleb as he reached up to stroke the neck of the roan as the gelding dropped his head to nuzzle at the boy.

"Well, why don't ya saddle him up, and we'll go into town ta' git ya some travelin' duds."

"Travelin' duds! Are we goin' somewhere?" came the excited question from the lad.

Jeremiah dropped down to one knee to be eye to eye with the boy and placing his hand on his shoulder said, "Your momma told me you always wanted to be a mountain man, but I said, 'Why, he's too skinny!'"

"Skinny? I ain't skinny! I's still growin' anyway. Why, I'm probly gonna be bigger'n you!"

Jeremiah stood up and keeping his hand on the boy's shoulder, stepped back as if eyeing the boy critically, then responded, "Ya know, ya just might. Mebbe we can make a mountain man outta you. But, ya gotta pay 'tention and do whatchur told. Can ya do that?"

"You betcha!" and he immediately set about saddling his pony.

Jeremiah watched as the boy held the saddle on the top of his head, then tiptoed up to drop it on the gelding's back. He reached under the horse's belly and grabbed the cinch to pull it to the latigo, then laced the latigo through the cinch ring, back up through the d-ring, again through the cinch ring then putting his shoulder under the leather strap, stretched to his full height on his tip toes to tighten the cinch.

Holding the latigo tight, he hopped a bit to bring his knee to the horse's stomach and the gelding exhaled allowing the cinch to be tightened a bit more. Jeremiah was impressed with the ability of the boy and the knowledge shown. *This boy is really something, he's gonna do all right.*

Scratch joined them for the short ride into town and all three tied off in front of the mercantile. They were greeted by the same matronly clerk from the week before, but this time she held a sympathetic expression as she looked at the tow-headed boy between the two buckskin-attired mountain men. "And what can I do for you gents today?" she asked.

Jeremiah looked at the woman, paused as he turned his head to look around the store, then replied, "Well m'am, we need a few travelin' supplies and some duds for the boy here."

51

He handed the clerk a short list of supplies and continued to survey the store.

"Were you looking for something in particular?" she asked.

"Uh, I don't suppose you could help m'am. What I'd really like to get is a set of buckskins for the boy but that usually takes some Indian makin's. So, I reckon we'll just get some ready-mades for the lad."

"I'll be happy to fit the boy for some proper clothes, but if you're determined, I did hear that Mr. Abernathy, down at the livery, his woman is a Shawnee, I think, and she might be able to fix you up with some buckskins," she said with a hint of disapproval.

"Thank you very much, mam. If you would be so kind as to fill that list and throw in a couple of sets of clothes and long-johns for the boy, and some socks and anything else you think he might need, we'll be back in just a little bit to pick it all up. I think we'll go down and see Mr. Abernathy."

Mr. Abernathy was not the typical liveryman/blacksmith usually expected in small towns. He was not big, muscular and burly, but more the opposite. Average height and lean, the most impressive thing about him was a bushy handlebar mustache and a couple days' growth on the rest of his face. His full head of red hair framed a friendly face that now surveyed his newest visitors. "What can I do ya fer, fellers?" was the only greeting he felt necessary for the trio that graced his doorway. "Step on in hyar outta the sun so I can see what I'm talkin' to."

Jeremiah began speaking as they walked into the large livery barn, "The lady in the mercantile said you might be able to help us. We were gatherin' up some supplies and needed some duds for the young'un here and I said I'd sure like ta get some buckskins for the boy and she said that mebbe yore woman might be able to work us up a set."

Mr. Abernathy leaned back against the anvil he had been working on and crossed his arms over his chest as he looked over the two and a half men standing before him. "And just why would she say that?" asked the smithy.

"Probably because I mentioned that buckskins were usually a craft only done well by the women of different Indian tribes. She said she thought your woman was Shawnee or something like that."

"Oh," was his only reply but his expression betrayed that some deeper thought had surfaced and was troubling him. "She might be able to help. She is Shawnee and she's real good with just about anything made of hide. You got any hides?"

Jeremiah looked at Scratch and Scratch spoke up, "We got four or five hides, but they ain't been cured yet."

"Go 'head and sit a spell and I'll go fetch her and see if she can help," he tossed over his shoulder as he exited the back door of the livery.

They didn't have time to sit, and there wasn't anything to sit on anyway, when the smithy returned with a lithe and long-haired attractive woman of obvious Indian heritage in her mid-thirties. A slight scowl furrowed her brow as she scanned the visitors and her eyes rested on Caleb. She looked at Jeremiah and asked, "Is he your boy?"

"No mam. He's my nephew. His momma was my sister, Elizabeth Robinson, Doc Robinson's widow. But now that his momma has joined his daddy, young Caleb here has decided to come along with me and Scratch and become a genuine mountain man. That's why we're here, we need to fix him up with some better travelin' clothes, some good buckskins."

Her eyes dropped to the boy and she stepped closer to him stretching out her hand to his shoulder. She knelt before Caleb with a piece of cord and began measuring him, the length of his leg, his waist, his arm length, the size of his feet, everything necessary for her leather work. She stood and turned to look at her husband, a slight nod of her head to him, and left the building without looking back. The two mountain men exchanged glances, and Jeremiah looked at Mr. Abernathy with raised eyebrows in a question and arms outstretched, palms up. The smithy said, "Just hang on a minute. She'll be right back."

When she returned she walked straight to Caleb, dropped to one knee and held some buckskins up to the boy to measure the fit. They were beautiful golden tanned buckskins with fringe running down the outside edge of the legs and the outside edge of the arms. A simple pattern of quills and beads made a straight-line yoke across the front of the shirt top. She then asked him to give her his foot and she took off his brogans and slipped on a pair of moccasins with beaded work across the toe piece. The cuff around the ankles had a short row of fringe and more beadwork that matched the rest of the outfit. Over her arm hung a pair of knee high winter mocs that also matched. The entire outfit looked to fit him well, with plenty of "growin' room" but not so much as to be uncomfortable or awkward. She motioned for Caleb to go into one of the stalls to dress himself in the buckskins. Caleb carefully fingered the smooth leather as he walked to the stall and could be heard continuously repeating, "Wow, wow, wow."

It was a "goin' on" ten-year-old boy that walked into the stall, but a young man walked out. He stood tall and proud as he looked at Jeremiah and Scratch, then dropped his head as he again stroked the smoothness of the leather and admired the quill and bead work. "I shore wish my momma could see me now."

Jeremiah looked at Mrs. Abernathy and said, "I don't understand mam, how'd you come up with that outfit, which by the way, is a mighty fine-lookin' set."

"They were made for my son, but he never wore them," she answered with a slight sob.

Mr. Abernathy said, "We lost our son last year. He drowned in the Spring flood that came through here when the river overflowed. There were also two others that died."

Caleb spoke up, "That was Levi, wasn't it? We were in school together."

The woman, dabbing at the tears in her eyes, looked at the boy and said, "Yes Caleb, our boy was Levi and he was just your size."

Jeremiah asked, "I'm sure Caleb'll be mighty proud to wear them. So, what do we owe you for them?" as he reached into his pocket in anticipation of gathering the coin for payment and at a loss for words to the still grieving parents.

She turned to Jeremiah and said, "Doc Robinson has been very good to us and everyone here owes him a lot. Those are a gift." Looking again at Caleb, she said, "Just remember our Levi."

"I'll never forget him m'am," earnestly promised the boy.

Jeremiah proudly put an arm around his shoulders as the three walked from the livery to the mercantile. Caleb had his city duds under one arm as he proudly strutted between the two mountain man and couldn't help but think, *I'm gonna be a mountain man, just like Uncle Jeremiah and Uncle Scratch. Boy, I can't wait to see the mountains with all those buffalo and grizzly bears and such.*

The familiar surroundings of the village of Marshall brought Caleb out of his reverie and reminded him of his momma and dad. He leaned against Jeremiah and tried to match him stride for stride but his legs just weren't long enough so he had to occasionally skip a step to stay up with the long-legged mountain man. *I'm gonna have to do some growin' so my legs will be long 'nuff to keep up. I hope Rastus can keep up!.*

Scratch gathered up the stack of supplies and the wrapped package of extra clothes for Caleb and the extra-long johns for the men. As Jeremiah was settling the bill, he spoke a thought and asked, "Have you got any long guns back there that might be suitable for the young'un?"

The matronly clerk looked over the top of her skinny glasses and said, "You mean you want a rifle for the boy?" with a startled look on her face.

Realizing her disapproval, Jeremiah decided to dig himself a little deeper into her file of unsavory behaviors and said, "Yes m'am. Where we're goin' there's lots of wild animals and quite a few wild injuns. I want him to be able to bag his share of both. It'll take a pretty good weapon for that and he ain't all that big yet but he's got some killin' to do."

With a gasp and a quick hand to her mouth, she looked at what she perceived as wild men and trotted from behind the counter to the back room calling out for "Rufus, Rufus, you come here this minute!"

When a bespectacled, balding red-cheeked man appeared behind the counter, Jeremiah rightly assumed he answered to the name of Rufus, Rufus. With a smile tugging at the corners of his mouth, Jeremiah restated his need for a rifle for the boy. Rufus Rufus also looked over his spectacles at his customer but simply said, "Follow me."

Caleb was soon outfitted with a fine New Bedford .36 caliber cap and ball rifle with burled walnut stock and brass fittings "fore and aft" that made for a weapon the boy would be proud of and its compact size, which the clerk said was because it had been custom made for a small woman that never picked it up, was just right for Caleb. Now properly outfitted, the two and a half mountain men returned to the cabin to gather the rest of their gear and pack horses and get ready for their journey to the mountains.

Chapter Nine: Directions

DURING THE PREVIOUS WEEK, while Jeremiah had been focused on his sister's failing health, Scratch met an old-timer making his way upstream in an effort to fill his home made creel with enough fish for his supper. He had about 15 years on Scratch but the two had common experiences in the Western mountains.

Ezra had traveled with the American Fur Company after a few years as a free trapper on the upper reaches of the Missouri and Milk rivers. It was that experience on the edge of the Blackfoot country that prompted Colonel McKenzie to recruit Ezra to join forces with the American Fur Company. Now a little long in the tooth, he had returned to his home near the settlement of Marshall to enjoy his sunset years and the company of his sister's family with the many nieces and nephews that thought the world of "Uncle Ezra."

Scratch had been sunning himself on the grassy bank of the Kalamazoo river just down from their camp behind Lizzy's cabin when his snooze was interrupted by the coughing and hucking of the old-timer sitting on a rock beside the prone form of Scratch.

"If'n I'd a been a injun, you'd be missin' yore topknot bout now," growled the old trapper.

As Scratch sat up and looked at the man in blackened buckskin trousers and a linsey-woolsey shirt he recognized a comrade from the past. Although he couldn't remember his name, he knew he'd seen him in the mountains and his attire revealed a common history.

"Wal, lookin' atchu, it 'pears there was a time you didn't wake up early 'nuff either," replied Scratch, referring to the scar that ran from the old-timer's forehead to just over his left ear, a scar that was undoubtedly the result of a partial scalping.

"Yup. It were them dad-blasted Blackfoot that snuk up on me and tried to lift my hair without botherin' to kill me first. But I showed 'em, when I put my Green River skinning knife 'tween his skinny ribs. I think he was apologizing to me for his lack of manners, course, I'm not too sure, cuz I didn't unnerstan' their lingo then."

"So, what're ya doin' so far from the mountains?" inquired Scratch.

"Fishin'. What's it look like?" he replied as he held up his stringer of fish, with a bit of a mischievous smirk on his face.

"Now, I know ya didn't come a thousand miles just ta fish in this hyar stream. So, what is it, ya got family hereabouts?"

"Yeah. That mountain water was gittin' too darn cold for these ol' bones, so I decided to come back to the ol' home place and spend the rest of my years with my sister and her family of young-uns. They could use an ol' man to help put a few vittles on the table an' I kin still catch a fish and pop a deer ever now an then," surmised the old-timer as much to convince himself as Scratch. "But what 'bout you, youngster? Ain't there no place ta take a nap by a creek bank out West?"

The two men spent the next few days remembering some of the "good ole days" and swapping lies about the life in the mountains. After learning of Scratch and company's plans, Ezra gladly shared his wealth of knowledge about the mountain life, but Scratch mined the treasure trove of travel experience that was housed in the old trapper's memory.

As was the necessity of the time, whenever someone had the experience of traveling the trails and/or roads of the previously unexplored country ahead, that knowledge was gleaned and stored away for future use. The memory maps were the only ones available to the common traveler and most quickly learned to catalog every stream, every trail, and every landmark that might one day save their lives. Again and again, Scratch quizzed the old trapper about the trails to follow to return to the mountains. Of special interest were the roads and trails from their present location and around the southern tip of the great Lake Michigan to the immediate West of them. As they had no interest in the growing metropolis of Chicago, they sought to bypass that as well.

It seemed the only thing Ezra enjoyed more than telling tall tales to his nieces and nephews, was sharing his wealth of knowledge with Scratch. It was good to have someone pay attention to him and believe what he had to say, as more often than not, these "darned Easterners" didn't have time nor interest in his experiences and adventures. But now with someone that had been there and understood, it was just good to relive the past with all its trials and travails that he had managed to survive. And Scratch did understand. He also appreciated what the old man had been through and his depth of understanding of what Scratch, Jeremiah and Caleb were about to undertake.

"Well, Scratch, it's been good visitin' with you. But, I gotta go spend some time with the young-uns. So, I guess this is so long. Keep your top-knot on!" and with a wave over his shoulder, he strolled down the creek-bank as he had done the last three days.

Scratch knew he wouldn't see the old-timer again, and hollered after him, "Enjoy the sunset!" and thought about his own sunset years, hoping as always, that he would see his last sunset with the mountains silhouetted before the brilliant colors of the Western sky.

* * * *

THE FIRST DAY'S TRAVEL was an initiation for the tow-headed boy. He was excited about the coming adventure, but as the day wore on and the excitement waned, soreness from the long day in the saddle and the seemingly endless ride made for a very tired boy. The two stops for water and food were not enough to thoroughly refresh the youngster and it was now all he could do to keep from falling off the horse as he fought the temptation to drop into a deep sleep.

His determination to show his uncle Jeremiah that he was up to the challenge of this adventure, however, kept his eyes open and he learned that if he stretched his legs with his toes in his stirrups, he could relieve the bounce of his butt on the saddle seat. Yet when Scratch tossed the call to "pull 'er up, it's time to camp!" relief painted his face with a smile.

It was a small clearing in a copse of cottonwoods and the giggle of the nearby stream offered a reprieve from the dusty trail they had been following. Caleb thought he had eaten so much dust during their long ride that he would be too full to eat any supper, but later on when the aroma of the frying bacon and fresh turnips and other greens caught his attention, he was quickly focused on his appetite.

Camp had been quickly set up, horses tethered, and bedrolls strung out before Scratch put supper on the fire. Jeremiah had stretched out near the fire with his head and shoulders resting on a small log covered with moss. Caleb joined his uncle and even with his stomach practically yelling for sustenance, he fell asleep only to be stirred awake by Jeremiah rising to get his share of Scratch's offerings.

After the trio had cleaned their plates, the remaining daylight offered an opportunity for Jeremiah to start his mentoring of the boy. "Caleb, step over there and get that fancy new rifle of yours and all its gear, and let's see if you can show me whatcha know."

The boy, now wide awake, was quick to jump and run to fetch his gear. Trotting back with the rifle cradled in his arms like he'd seen the two mountain men carry theirs, his possibles pouch dangled under his left arm and his powder horn was to the front of his right arm. The crisscrossed leather straps that supported them formed an x across his chest. Caleb presented himself in front of his uncle with a smile spreading wide across his eager face.

"All right then, how much shootin' ya done?" Jeremiah inquired of the boy.

"Not much, I did do some with the coach gun of my daddy's when we went after rabbits, but he didn't load it very much so it wouldn't knock me down. But I did get a rabbit with it!"

"Well, let me show you how to do it, and we'll work on it together till you get real good with this hyar rifle and you'll be able to get more'n a rabbit okay?" asked the big man.

Lifting his own rifle to his shoulder and pointing it at the top of a nearby tree, he dropped the hammer and emptied the barrel with a sudden blast and a cloud of white smoke. Caleb wasn't expecting the shot and jumped back with a gasp.

Jeremiah emitted a bit of a chuckle and dropped the butt of his rifle to the ground by his foot. "Now watch me, and we'll take it one step at a time. First, we measure out the powder." He then used the horn-cup stopper on his powder horn and measured the powder into the cup to fill it. With a nod of his head, he encouraged Caleb to do the same. The boy quickly brought his powder horn to the front, uncapped it and copied his uncle.

Jeremiah slid his left hand to the end of the barrel to use it as a funnel, and poured the powder into the barrel. Caleb carefully watched Jeremiah, then duplicated his actions. "Next, we'll seat and ram the ball."

Jeremiah reached into his possibles pouch, sorted out a patch, ball, and starter. "Now watch this part closely." The pillow tick patches had been treated with oil and Jeremiah placed one atop the end of the barrel, then taking the ball from his mouth he sat it on the patch with a bit of pressure with his thumb. Taking the starter tool in his hand, he used the shorter shaft to seat the ball, the larger shaft to push it farther down, then slipping the ram rod from underneath the barrel, he rammed the ball and seated it against the powder deep in the barrel.

Caleb had already retrieved his patch, ball and starter and now started to mimic his uncle's actions. Jeremiah instructed him, "If your patches aren't oiled, then it's best to at least dampen 'em a bit with spit… that's why I keep the ball in my mouth. And as you seat the ball, if your patch is too big, ya oughta trim the excess with your knife. But, sometimes, there just ain't 'nuff time to do all that and ya gotta do whatcha can."

As Jeremiah watched the boy, he noted that Caleb had exactly duplicated the example given. As Caleb withdrew his ramrod and reseated it he grinned as he saw the approving nod of his uncle. Jeremiah picked up his rifle, placing the butt stock under his right arm and holding the fore-stock with his left, he demonstrated how to place the cap on the nipple in front of the hammer, then carefully lowered the hammer over the cap.

Again, Caleb copied his actions with dexterity as Jeremiah said, "Always be careful when dropping that hammer. Usually we don't drop it on the cap if we're traveling. Now, watch me as I show you how to shoot properly." He then dropped to one knee, placed his left elbow on his left upraised knee and rested the fore-stock on his left palm. He watched Caleb as the boy assumed a similar stance to the right of Jeremiah.

"Now," he continued, "we pull back the hammer to full cock and don't release the hammer until you hear that last click. We're shooting at that piece of bare trunk on that cottonwood yonder so line up the front sight between those rear buckhorns slowly," as he demonstrated. "Then take a deep breath, let about half of it out, and with that front blade right on your target, slowly squeeze, not pull, but squeeze the trigger. Like this."

Caleb was watching closely yet was still startled when the Hawken spit its ball in the cloud of white smoke and thunder. "Wow!" exclaimed the boy, then turned his attention to his task. He wiggled his back leg a bit for more comfort then, dropping his cheek to the maple stock he lined up his sights, left eye closed. Jeremiah heard the click of the hammer to full cock, watched the boy draw his breath and let it out, then waited for the discharge. The .36 caliber Bedford did not disappoint as it's white cloud and thunder was minimally less than the Hawken and the resulting recoil rocked the boy back on his back leg but new shooter held his place.

Scratch, the supervising shooting coach, hollered, "Bullseye! Good shootin' squirt!" And Caleb earned his new nickname.

To The Tall Timber

Chapter Ten: Homesick

THE GREY LIGHT of early morning was pushing the shadows to their greatest length before beginning the retraction towards midday. Another early start for the trio of mountain men saw them well on their way with a due West bearing.

Scratch was in the lead and turned around in his saddle to speak to his companions, "Ol Ezra said to head south west from the cabin until we hit the first river, which would be the Elkhart. That's where we spent the night. Now, we need to bear due west to the next river and if'n we don't get lost among all these hyar trees, that next river will be the Kankakee. If we make good 'nuff time today, we should hit it about sundown."

Caleb was already showing himself a trooper and he was determined that his Uncle Jeremiah would never hear him complain. But when Scratch talked about another long day in the saddle, his butt and inner thighs forced him to let out a low groan. Jeremiah looked over at Caleb, now riding side by side with his uncle and said, "Did you say somethin' Squirt?"

"No sir. Not me. I'm just gittin' comfortable in my seat here," as he forced a smile when he turned toward his uncle.

"Well, that's the way it's gonna be for a while, boy. Whenever ya start on a journey like this, it takes a while 'fore ya get yore muscles toughened up. But once ya get used to it, you'll be able ta ride twice as far in a day and it won't hurt a bit. You can do it, you're a tough'un," encouraged Jeremiah.

Caleb wanted to believe his uncle, but he wasn't sure it would be possible to ride twice as far. But he was game to try.

At the noonin' stop the stock had cinches loosened and a good bit of pasture grass to graze and a small stream that allowed for fresh water. The travelers didn't take the time for anything but coffee and jerky, but Jeremiah decided that Caleb could use a bit more instruction with his shooting.

The boy eagerly gathered his gear and rifle and went to stand beside Jeremiah at the edge of the clearing. Jeremiah's brow wrinkled up as he looked to the edge of the meadow and standing still, watched closely. About 150 yards down the tree line, something was cautiously stepping into the clearing. It was unusual for a deer to reveal itself in the brightness of mid-day as the normal feeding would be early morning or dusk.

It was a young buck with velvet covered antlers just pushing up between his ears. When Caleb saw the buck, he whispered to Jeremiah, "Do you want me to shoot it?" His question revealed a slightly apprehensive, yet excited hunter-to-be.

"Well, we could use some fresh meat, but that's a bit far for your first shot. You just watch me and learn," cautioned Jeremiah as he leaned against a nearby tree. "Whenever you have a chance at a firm rest to steady your aim, like a tree or branch or rock, use it. Every shot is important and you never want to waste your powder and lead. Now, can you give me a guess at how far away that shot is?"

"Golly, no sir. I couldn't say."

"Just look at the size of the trees here, then look closely and see how they get smaller and smaller down by where the deer is, just put that in your mind and always pay close attention. That is about 150 yards. So, put that in three equal distances of 50 yards each, and you'll begin to get the idea."

While he spoke, he followed the deer with his sights as it dropped its head to snatch a few bites of green at its feet.

As the animal lifted its head, the Hawken belched his messenger of death amid the cloud of white smoke and with a thunder felt by Caleb. As the smoke cleared, the buck could not be seen. "Let's go get our meat!" directed Jeremiah as he took a trail at the edge of the trees with Caleb following close behind.

Caleb pestered Jeremiah with questions as they walked to the site where they last saw the buck. There were questions about distance, sighting, how to clean and skin the deer, and how much further they were going today. The rapid fire dialogue distracted Jeremiah and as they neared the site of the deer, he suddenly stopped when he saw two Indians standing over the carcass.

Looking down at the buck, he noticed a feathered shaft protruding from the neck of the deer, but the heart shot he took was also evident with the blood draining. Caleb slowly stepped behind his uncle and let him know of his presence with a slight tug on the leg fringe of his buckskins.

As Jeremiah lifted his eyes to the two men, he noticed a third stepping from the tree line. The two men by the buck showed no threatening moves and Jeremiah let his Hawken rest in his hand by his hip. He then looked at the third man as he stepped beside the other two and thought he looked familiar. "Long Walker? I thought we left you a ways East of here," he questioned the newcomer. It was the Pottawatomie brave they met on their journey North to Michigan.

"These are my people. After I left your camp, I found them and we have since traveled West. There are very few of us left in this land. Most have been sent to the Indian Territory in Oklahoma. I see you have a new one traveling with you," he said motioning toward Caleb who was now craning his head around the leg of his uncle. "He is a curious one."

"Yes he is," said Jeremiah as he nudged Caleb from behind him, "he was my sister's son, she is no longer with us and now I have taken the boy under wing."

"It is right. The mother's brother is always supposed to do this," emphatically stated the stoic man as if that was not to be debated. It was the tradition of his people and most Native people that the Mother's brother was to be the protector and provider for any orphaned children.

"I see we had the same idea with that buck," stated Jeremiah as he nodded his head toward the downed deer, ". . . but it looks to me like your arrow made its mark before my slug, so, why don't you and your people enjoy..." Jeremiah knew the presence of Long Walker had prevented what could have been a very difficult confrontation and since they were not short on rations, it was easier to be magnanimous.

"My people will be grateful. Until we meet again, go in peace my friend," shared Long Walker as he brought his arm across his chest and with the palm down moved it in a flat motion to extend his arm straight out toward the mountain man.

"And you too, my friend," answered Jeremiah as he and Caleb turned to return to their camp. He turned back to the men and said, "If you hear some shootin' it'll just be the boy gettin' in some practice," and with a wave turned again toward their camp.

Caleb was silent on the return walk, but when they made camp, he couldn't hold it in any longer and began to spill all the details of their first encounter with Indians to Scratch. He was so excited, Scratch had to tell him, "Slow down Squirt, I cain't hardly keep up with you. Now, what's all this about Indians?" He looked up at Jeremiah and noticing the smile, he knew there was nothing to be alarmed about, so he patiently listened to the excited youngster. "And you didn't git scalped?" he asked as soon as Caleb took a breath.

The boy cocked his head to the side and said, "Do I look like I'm missin' any hair?" with a bit of disgusted tone to his voice. "Sides, if they'd a tried, I'da had to shoot 'em!" This remark brought a broad smile to the men as they both let loose with a good belly laugh. "Speakin' of shootin' Uncle, ya gotta give me another lesson." Jeremiah nodded his head and led the boy to the edge of the clearing facing away from their previous encounter.

"Okay. Now, I'm gonna watch you and see how much you remember. You do it all, load and shoot. See that big branch on the right of that Oak yonder, the crooked one?" he motioned with a nod of his head, "That's your target, right where the branch leaves the trunk."

With the close supervision of both Scratch and Jeremiah, Caleb flawlessly loaded and fired his rifle four times with every shot hitting its mark. "I'm a thinkin' that we got us a natural here. Don't you think so, Jeremiah?" asked Scratch.

"It's sure lookin' that way. I couldn't shoot that good when I was that size, could you?" Jeremiah asked the other mountain man.

"No sir, but it didn't take me long to git ta where I was hittin' the mark most o' the time."

This off-handed praise stretched the smile on Caleb's face so far, he thought he'd never get his mouth shut again. But he thought he better try to take it in stride, because Scratch had told him about a man that never quit smiling and every time his horse took to running, the man was picking bugs out of his teeth and Caleb didn't think he'd like the taste of any bugs.

All three made busy as they pulled latigo on the horses and the mules to get back on the trail. Scratch said they had a good way to go and they were burning daylight. The remainder of the ride that afternoon was spent with Caleb reliving the day's experience with the Indians and mostly reliving the shooting and the praise. He was greatly encouraged by Jeremiah's remarks especially but his mind began to wander back to times with his dad and mom.

He was wishing he could show both parents what he learned and was able to do. He didn't often get that chance when he was at home. His dad was always busy with his doctoring and his mom did what she could, but mostly he just remembered he was too young and too little to do much more than play in the yard and the nearby woods. It was a little different when his dad got his horse for him, but even then, there wasn't much he was allowed to do. Then, when they got sick everything changed.

Jeremiah had been watching Caleb and noticed the change in his countenance. He had been happy and excited after they left camp, but the chatter had subsided and now his head was hanging almost to his chest. The occasional deep breath brought a slight stutter to his shoulders and Jeremiah recognized the signs of sorrow. He had been surprised the boy had held so much of his emotions inside, as most youngsters his age would have been doing their fair share of weeping and blubbering, but he had not seen any of that from the boy. He knew that oftentimes the sorrow sets in some time after the loss and he thought that might be happening now and he understood.

Dusk overtook them and by the fading light, the trio made camp at the edge of the river. It was the Kankakee River, their goal for the day, and it had been a long ride for all of them. They divided the chores with Scratch tethering the animals, Jeremiah starting their supper, and Caleb rolling out the bedrolls. Scratch noticed the long face on the boy and looked askance toward Jeremiah receiving a shrug of the shoulders and outstretched palms in answer.

After their supper was finished and pans and plates cleaned and repacked, Jeremiah sat down beside the boy and put his arm around his shoulder. "I think I know what you're feelin' Squirt," and he began to relate his own experience when his mom had been killed by the drunken Pottawatomie, his sister left with family and he and his dad headed West. He shared about his dad being killed by other Indians in the mountains and how he had been adopted by Ezekiel, the escaped slave, and raised by Ezekiel's family among the Arapaho Indians.

After telling about losing Ezekiel in the fight with the slave catchers, he summarized with, "So, I understand. You're missin' your mom and dad and you're probably missing your home and other friends as well. It's called bein' homesick. And of course it's sorrow over your mom and dad. It's only natural. Whenever we move away from those familiar things, that's homesickness, because we miss those things and those people. That's O.K.

But now, to be able to move on, here's what we need to do. We try not to look back so much, although that's O.K., it's kinda like checkin' your back trail, and we focus on lookin' forward. You know, to that which we haven't seen yet, what tomorrow's gonna bring. What new adventures are waitin' out there for us? When we can look forward, keepin' in our hearts what lies behind, then we can enjoy what the good Lord has for us just around the next corner. Think you can do that Squirt?"

Caleb leaned over closer to his big uncle and looked up at him with a bit of a smile and said, "I think so. Just keep lookin' forward. Yup, I can do that."

"O.K. Squirt. But, remember, it's O.K. to look back. Everybody does, Scratch does, I do, everybody does. That's what keeps us on the right path," summarized the fatherly uncle.

To The Tall Timber

Chapter Eleven: Classrooms

ANOTHER DAY and another early start, Caleb was beginning to understand the routine. It was not like at home, summer was a time free from school and a time to run or ride in the woods and explore and have fun. The riding and exploring was certainly a part of his day, but he wasn't too sure about the fun. It seemed like one moment he's having fun and the next it's almost like work or even school, but the excitement level never waned.

The most insignificant moment of the day was still robed in discovery. Whether the noisy cricket that sang its lullaby each night or the croaking of the frogs that greeted the mornings, noises, smells, sights, creatures great and small, and the amazing new vistas that filled his eyesight each new day was indeed a new discovery.

"So Squirt, me'n Scratch been talkin' bout yore education. Your momma made me promise to teach you everything I know . . . " started Jeremiah, but he was interrupted by Scratch.

"Yeah, and after he's told you everthin' he knows, which'll only take a day or so, then I'll fill ya in on everthin' else!" wryly stated Scratch as he turned and leaned back toward the boy.

Caleb laughed at the two mountain men and responded, "But my momma said I already knew everything there was ta know!"

"Well, you mighta done all right with that book larnin' but there's a couple things lackin' in your education. Scratch and me will teach you most everything ya need ta know about the outdoors, ya know, animals and plants and such, but there's some things that even we don't know much about," stated Jeremiah.

"Now hold yore horses there boyo. Just what is there that I don't know about, anyhows? asked a frustrated Scratch as he leaned on the rump of his dawdling horse.

"Women," stated Jeremiah flatly.

"Oh, yeah, them."

After Caleb quit giggling at the two confounded would-be teachers, he said, "I don't think I need to know anything about women. I ain't never gonna be interested in them!"

"Um hummm," replied Jeremiah, then began the instruction in the classroom before them. "First thing ya need to know shortstuff, is the trees and such that grow hereabouts, don't always grow in the other places you'll find yourself. Ya see, where we are now is what we call the flat lands, cuz there ain't no mountains and everything is kinda flat," he observed as he waved his arm about to emphasize his point. "Now, when we get up in the mountains, a lot of these here trees and plants don't grow there cause there ain't 'nuff water or it's too cold. And likewise, some of the plants up there, don't grow down here. Unnerstand?"

"I think so. I guess I'll just have to wait and see, huh?" replied the boy.

Scratch was leading the caravan and now drew his horse up beside a sizable leafy tree and stopped. Then turning to the eager student said, "Now looky here Squirt, do ya know what kinda tree this'n is?" without waiting for a response he continued, "It's a Sycamore. Look at that ugly lookin' bark, all those different colors, and those big pointy and curled leaves.

That's how you can tell it's a Sycamore." He nodded his head to the boy and gigged his horse to continue on the trail.

The men did not make it a continuous teaching time, but took advantage of any new opportunity when presented. They would take turns dropping a tidbit of wisdom to the boy and then occasionally quiz him when the same kind of tree would appear beside the trail later in the day. He learned about Sycamore, White Oak, Red Cedar, White Pine, and Black Walnut. On each quiz, he successfully recalled each one.

There were a few he knew from the walks in the woods with his mom, like the Cottonwood, Black Cherry and Dogwood, but he was surprised to learn about the Sugar Maple from Scratch as his mom used to get the maple syrup from the neighbor and serve it on her pancakes, which was Caleb's favorite breakfast. He never knew something so sweet and good could come from a tree.

The lessons were more than just how to identify the trees, but to learn the uses of certain ones. He learned about the use of the Cottonwood buds for treating wounds and sores, and the willow for a tea and pain remedy. Some woods were good for gun stocks, some for bows, and others used for making furniture or building houses and barns. It seemed everything had a purpose if a man just knew how to use it.

Each day had a different topic that was at the fore. The first day of the outdoor classroom was focused on trees, the second day was the flowers. He learned about those that were common to the mountains and the plains like the columbine, the phlox, and the sunflower. He also learned about some of the edible plants like the cattail roots, rose hips, and wild turnips.

The third day was kind of a review of both trees and flowers with a few new ones added but Caleb's attention was often taken by the passing of an animal or the flight of a bird. His interest was more in the animals and birds than the plants and trees and his excitement grew when the mountain men began to share their wealth of knowledge about what Caleb thought of as the real living things of the forest and plains.

Their westward route had kept them on the South side of the Kankakee River and late the third day after their contact with the Pottawattamie they came to the confluence of the Kankakee and the Iroquois Rivers. They had only crossed one river so far and it wasn't deep or swift enough to cause concern, but now facing the Iroquois, Jeremiah had to carefully consider the crossing and Caleb's inexperience.

"All right Squirt, here's whatcha gotta do. Scratch's gonna lead out and his mule will follow, then you'll be behind him, but not too close. Then I'll be right behind you. Now, if your horse stumbles or somethin' and you come unseated, just make sure you hold onto the saddle horn, even if you ain't in the saddle, you can just let your horse pull you on across. But, I'll be right behind you and ya ain't got nuthin' to concern yore little head about, okay?"

"I, uh, I guess so. I think I can do it. But you'll be right behind me, right?"

"Yup, and I ain't gonna let nuthin' happen. You can count on that," then looking forward to Scratch, he signaled him to start out. The river was deep and muddy, the current wasn't too fast because the land was mostly level but the water was about chest high on a man.

As Scratch started out, it took a few steps until his horse sagged into the water and started swimming across the current. The strength of the river was evident but not overwhelming as the horse and mule were able to keep a good line across the river without being swept downstream.

With a quick look at his uncle, now beside him, and receiving a nod to go, Caleb dug his heels into the Roan's ribs and started for the water. His first reaction was to lift his feet up, then realized he wouldn't be able to stay dry and let his moccasins and buckskin trouser legs drop into the water. Letting the horse have his head, he took a death grip on the saddle horn with both hands.

76

As the gelding sagged into the water and started his swim, Caleb's eyes widened and Scratch, now turning in his saddle to watch the boy, could see the whites of his eyes from his considerable distance ahead. Jeremiah quickly followed the boy and led his mule closely behind his horse.

Without more than an arm's length behind the Squirt, Jeremiah spoke words of encouragement, "You're doin' great youngun', just let your horse have his head and he'll take you safely to dry ground. That's it, keep goin', we're almost there," he calmly said as he watched Scratch ride his horse up the grassy bank and turn to watch the water-borne parade of his companions.

After all were on the opposite shore, each one dropped out of his saddle and stretched their legs, pulling their tight buckskins off and wringing out the excess water. Caleb followed suit and quickly replaced his trousers over goose pimpled skin and shaking legs. He was shaking all over as much from the cool breeze on wet bodies as from the drop of adrenaline and relief from his fearful first crossing. But it was another lesson learned.

Scratch proclaimed, "Well, youngun' now thatcha been baptized in the muddy waters, you're gittin' pretty close ta bein' a real frontiersman!" and patted the boy on the back. "Now, let's git mounted up cuz we still got some daylight and mebbe we can find us a good campsite and have us some hot coffee and a warm supper, whatcha say?"

Before they started out, following the example of his uncles, (he now thought of Scratch as his uncle just like Jeremiah) Caleb used his ramrod to empty his rifle of ball, wad and powder that had been ruined by the water. Then, wiping it dry with the rod and a bigger wad, he reloaded with fresh powder, patch and ball. Once all weapons were cleaned and loaded, the trio hit the trail again in search of their night's camp. All three were looking forward to the night's repast and the anticipated rest, it had been a tiring day.

To The Tall Timber

Chapter Twelve: Mimic

THEY WERE ON THE TRAIL before the grey light of early morning began to sneak a few tendrils of light through the scattered trees, bathing the travelers with the warmth of the Eastern sun. Jeremiah was the first to roll his shoulders back to feel the warmth against the buckskin shirt and the boy soon followed with a similar reaction that chased the chills of the night away.

Scratch led the cavalcade north and west according to the directions gleaned from the old trapper, Ezra. To the southwest the land fell away in open plains and grassland that was occasionally broken by the appearance of a settler's attempt at farming with a few ramshackle buildings and a small farmhouse of logs or sod.

The rolling terrain was monotonous to the eyes of the mountain man that sought to pull the images of the snow-capped peaks from his memory to remind him of the promise held by God's country. The travelers followed a game trail that stayed to the edge of the timber, occasionally dropping into the long shadows of the morning to disappear among the green.

Scratch was startled out of his reverie by the "bark, bark, scraaaww!" of a grey squirrel that protested their intrusion. As he looked at the tree's landlord that was raising such a fuss, he heard an echoing chatter from behind him. He turned in his saddle to see if he could spot the probable mate of the squirrel but was unable to locate the fellow fur-ball. He returned his gaze to the squirrel on the high limb now almost overhead, only to see him scamper to a higher perch when the call again came from behind Scratch. Another quick swivel and a scan of the treetops yielded nothing but frustration for the mountain man. Then with a simple, "Humph" he focused again on the Northerly trail.

The two instructors of the wild continued the quizzing of their sole student regarding the identities of the various forms of vegetation and the boy was repeatedly distracted by the sighting of wildlife. With the trail now getting deeper into the woods the glimpse of an occasional deer or small game was common, but when Scratch heard the distant bark of a fox he swiveled his head to identify the location of the culprit, only to be startled to hear an identical yip from behind him.

The bark of a fox can be an alarm of intruders or predators but is also used as a mating call. Their bark is a short high-pitched yip that resembles the cry of a hard bitten dog. Easily identified, the close-by bark caused Scratch to state, "That darned red headed fox ain't only loud, he's quicker'n a lightnin' bolt on a dry day. That bark sounded exactly the same so it musta been a fast travelin' rascal."

He then slipped into his professorial mode and instructed his student, "Ya can allus tell a fox, cuz he sounds like he just had his tail stepped on with that high pitched bark o'his."

Caleb nodded his head and muttered, "Uh hum."

Jeremiah was beginning to suspect his apprentice but acknowledged Scratch's soliloquy with a nod unseen by his protégé. Jeremiah was pondering the task of teaching the boy and realized how inadequate he felt. It would be more than learning about the woods and animals, it was about what most folks called "book-learning" with the knowledge that could only be gained in a classroom or through books and both of those were in short supply... actually downright non-existent.

And then there was the making of a man, a man of integrity and judgment and character, those qualities that Ezekiel had often stressed during those years spent in the outdoor classroom with the Arapaho and the time they enjoyed together as they built their horde of gold with work by the streams with both the rocker and pans.

It wasn't about accumulating gold but about building the man that Ezekiel often told him he could and would become. That's what he wanted for the Squirt. As he thought about the tools needed, he realized the only book used by Ezekiel was the Bible, the same Bible Jeremiah had recovered from beneath Ezekiel's burned body. Everything else he had learned was from Ezekiel, his Indian family and the Arapaho village.

But he was quick to admit that learning in the years of youth was just the beginning, but if a love of learning could be instilled, then the remainder of his years would be spent as an avid student of life. Caleb was a good student of everything around him and Jeremiah had noticed the boy learned as much and more from his own observations as he did from the lessons given by the mountain men.

Each of the three travelers were leaning against their chosen tree to take advantage of the shade while watching the stock lazily graze the nearby grass during their noon rest. The giggle of the nearby stream was just enough to set the mood for a quick nap before taking to the trail for the remainder of the day. As the two men let their eyes droop and their hairy chins rest on their chest, the boy stood and walked to the edge of the trees to take in the view of the wide open grass covered plains before him.

Stooping down he snatched a sprig of the same Indian grass the animals were consuming and put the stem in his mouth, biting down. He surveyed the area around him and caught movement above that brought his focus on a diving red-tailed hawk that screeched his cry as he dove toward the ground.

Caleb watched as the hawk swooped over a small rabbit and sunk his talons into the animal. The rabbit tumbled head over heels but before it was able to scurry away, the hawk returned for a better grip and was soon airborne, and returning with dinner to its nearby nest. Looking toward the nest, Caleb cupped one hand to the side of his mouth and perfectly mimicked the red-tail's cry. The screech prompted the hawk to look up from his nest and search for the source of the cry. Again, Caleb screeched and was echoed by the nest-bound bird.

"So, it was *you* who got Scratch all turned around!" came the voice of Jeremiah from behind him, and Caleb spun around to see his Uncle standing with his arms crossed over his chest but a big smile painting his face.

"Uh, yeah. Are you mad at me?" he asked warily.

"Mad? No. Why should I be mad? I think it's great! How many can you do?"

"How many what?" the boy timidly questioned.

"You know, animal calls, like that hawk you just did."

"Uh, all of 'em, I guess."

"All of 'em?" quizzed Jeremiah, a little more than astounded.

"Yeah. I can do any of 'em, once I hear 'em. It's just always been easy for me. When I used to walk in the woods by myself that's what I'd do. Whenever I heard sumpin', I'd make that sound right back at 'em. At first, it was a little hard, but when I learned to listen closer, I could do any of 'em."

"Can you make 'em without hearin' 'em each time? You know, if you've made 'em before can you do it again?" queried a bewildered Uncle.

"Yeah, pretty much," he replied with a dauntless air about him.

Jeremiah chuckled with amazement at the boy as he gazed down at him with a sidelong stare. Then, shaking his head with a mischievous smile he said, "Let's not tell Scratch, we'll just wait for him to find out on his own. You can have a little fun with him if you want," Jeremiah stated conspiratorially.

Jeremiah placed an arm around the boy's shoulders and turned him back to the camp to awaken Scratch and gather the stock to return to the trail. It had been easy traveling for the last several days and they anticipated making good progress the remainder of this day. Three horses, two mules, two men and one quickly growing boy, each with different personalities, paces and motivation take considerable time to blend together into a harmonious cavalcade.

With over a week together on the trail, despite the fact the men and their mounts and pack animals had traveled much longer together, the addition of the boy and his roan gelding into the mix required all to make adjustments.

Animals have a pecking order that is manifested when grazing together, as well as traveling together, and that order was firmly established with Scratch's bay at the top, followed by Jeremiah's grey and the two mules, (although the mules tested this order quite often with an occasional nip or a loud bray of protest), All that changed with the boy and his roan. The new order revealed itself as the animals were returned to the camp to have rigs and cinches tightened and each made ready for the trail.

Again, Scratch led out along with his mule, but now Caleb followed on his roan with Jeremiah taking up the rear on his grey and leading his mule. It was only Jeremiah's firm hand on his grey that kept the horse from reverting to the old pecking order and trying to take a nip out of the "strawberries" rump to show him he was "out of order!"

Finally, the animals willingly stepped out to reach the goal for the day which was to reach the Illinois River that traveled Westward. True to form, the miles were quickly consumed by the ground eating gait of the now experienced traveling trio and their mounts. Occasionally a nearby bird would trill it's call, only to be copied and answered by the boy who enjoyed "talking" to the various animals on the journey.

Each time, Caleb answered only once and was silent before Scratch could catch him mimicking the creatures of the forest. The action oft repeated by the older mountain man was a spin in his saddle, looking to the tall trees searching for the echoing bird without success, then he would turn around again and invariably scratch his head and mumble something unintelligible. Jeremiah watched the boy's ruse and his shoulders shook with silent mirth at his antics.

The sun was dropping to rest on the distant treetops in the West and the clouds began to blush with soft shades of orange when the travelers made camp on the South bank of the Illinois River. It had been a long day of travel and all three were anxious to roll up in their bedrolls for the night.

The evening meal was quickly prepared and consumed. Caleb took the tin plates, cups and other utensils to the nearby spring-fed stream to do his chores of clean-up while the two men repacked the panniers and tended to the remainder of the gear in preparation for the coming days travel. Soon all three were looking at the star filled sky and searching for the doorway to dreamland.

The men had settled into a restful sleep but the boy was still awake and listening. Nearby the low rumble of hoo-hoo, hoo-hoo drifted over the camp. Then again, the call came. Caleb rolled to his side and faced away from the camp, then with his hands cupped to his mouth he answered the great horned-owl.

Quiet reigned for several minutes as the startled and territorial owl listened to his intruder. Then, with a flutter of wings, he landed closer to the camp. Again, the deep throaty hoo-hoo, hoo-hoo rolled across the night. Caleb waited a few moments, then muffling his sound with a corner of his blanket, he mimicked the owl's call perfectly.

The owl did not move nor answer and soon the beating of outstretched wings on the stillness of the night heralded his exit. Scratch rolled over and mumbled but did not awaken. Jeremiah rolled to his side to muffle his chuckle of laughter and soon drifted off to sleep.

To The Tall Timber

Chapter Thirteen: Muddy

THE SUN HUNG above the Western horizon and shone its brightness through the river haze like an anxious bride smiling through her veil. The golden globe reflected its blaze of glory off the muddy waters of the Mississippi to confound the "night vision" of the travelers.

Astride a mount with a hanging head, Scratch held one hand to shield his eyes and spoke to his companions lined along the bank like pigeons on a branch, and exclaimed, "Thar she is boys, that's the big muddy. Cain't hardly see it fer the goldarned sun shinin' so bright, but that's what we been lookin' fer!"

Like mirror images of their travel guide, Jeremiah and Caleb held their hands with outstretched arms to shield their eyes in a valiant effort to observe this mighty river that held as much mystery and intrigue as all the stories told by a host of frontiersmen. Scratch pushed his heels against his mount's ribs to lead the way across the recently constructed stone and brush dam that led to the fabled Rock Island in the middle of the river.

Their goal was the ferry on the opposite side of the island and the final phase of their river crossing. "Ol Ezra never said nuthin' 'bout no dam bein' here, when he came through this way some years past. The onliest thing he talked about was that Fort Armstrong yonder, thereabouts," he parlayed as he waved his arm toward the large fort structure near the point of the island.

The fort was large by any standard, stretching 300 feet on each side with imposing three-story blockhouses on two opposite corners. The lack of activity and the broken down gates that stood open announced the emptiness of the still impressive, though silent, structure.

Ezra had said it was constructed because the Sauk and Fox Indians refused to peacefully surrender their land to the encroaching settlers. Later, a war named after the chief, called the Black Hawk War ended their resistance and resulted in the abandonment of the fort. The three travelers looked over the structure as they continued their way across the island in search of the ferry landing on the Western side. As the trio passed, each in his own way allowed his imagination to picture what the fort would have been like with all the activity of defending soldiers and attacking Indians.

Waving a greeting to the ferry operator that sat propped against a lone tree, Scratch gigged his horse to the operator's side to ask, "What's it gonna cost a couple o' poor pilgrims ta get across that thar river on yore ferryboat?"

Without moving the poor excuse for a hat that rested over the man's eyes he replied, "Don't make no nevermind to me if yore rich or poor, still gonna cost ya the same. One dollar per animal and fifty cents fer each of you two gents. The boy can go free." Dropping his three-legged chair down and rising to his feet added, "But ya gotta help pull the rope."

Jeremiah had ridden up beside Scratch and said, "That sounds like five dollars to me. That's a lotta money just ta get that little ways across the river."

"Yore welcome ta swim it iffen ya want to, but it'll still cost ya six dollars and some strong pullin' to keep yore feet dry," the old man responded. The two mountain men smiled at the grey whiskers on the black face that grinned at the travelers while he stood with one hand on the single shoulder strap of his bibbers and the other hand sweeping toward the river with his palm up in a "climb aboard" signal.

Dropping from their saddles, the three led the animals aboard the fenced flatboat and secured each one to the railing and spoke softly to reassure the suspicious horses. The mules' only hesitation was at the boarding, but once the decision was made they now stood calmly, watching the passing water.

Caleb was instructed to stand by the horse's heads and talk to them and stroke their necks to keep them calm during the crossing. Jeremiah and Scratch took their stations to assist with the rope pull. This was as calm an area as could be found on the mighty Mississippi but the current was evident even to the high riding flatboat ferry. Upon touching the shore, the animals showed no hesitation to gain the solid ground and made their way up the slight bluff on the well-groomed trail dragging the lead ropes and the men behind.

Anxious to put the "Big Muddy" behind them, the travelers mounted up and stretched out to the West. The terrain was broken by many coulees, sloughs, and intermittent streams outlined by small copses of woods and ground-hugging brush. Seeking a protected, yet dry site with nearby water, Scratch finally called a halt as they approached a cluster of hardwoods perched on a small shoulder of a bluff overlooking a coulee that harbored a sliver of a stream.

As the bluff dropped to the water, a grassy stretch of bank offered graze for the animals and was surrounded with steep banks leading up from the opposite side of a trickle of water. As Caleb did a belly slide off his saddle and stretched his toes to reach the ground, Scratch instructed him to gather what firewood he could while the men stripped the horses of the tack and led them to the graze.

With arms loaded with firewood and emerging from the trees, Caleb walked toward the campsite but was focused down the trail behind them. His forehead wrinkled as he squinted into the distance and said, "Uh, I think we got compny comin' yonder," nodding his head east.

Scratch was squatting before the cool campfire and had flint and steel in hand as he turned and stood to see where Caleb was looking. Jeremiah lifted his head from hands that held the frying pan, coffee pot, and eating utensils and searched the fading light for unexpected visitors.

A long wagon with canvas covered bows, pulled by four matched blacks with a man and a woman in the seat and small faces peering over their shoulders, was rattling in their direction. Each observer had frozen in place with the wonderment and surprise of seeing company. It wasn't unusual to see other travelers, especially in the Midwest of the country, but it was unexpected to see a family with a wagon this late in the day and on the fringe of the frontier.

A petite, pink-cheeked blonde woman attired in a dark gingham sacque with a skirt of matching material covered by a full-length linen apron smiled at the men standing in their camp. She had one hand latched onto the arm of a sizable hulk of a man that sported more red hair above his chest than the new breed of Hereford bulls sported on their entire body.

A floppy felt hat did little to control the windblown locks that obscured most of his facial features excepting the cherry red nose-bulb that forced its way out from the fiery bush perched on his upper lip. A mischievous twinkle sparkled from his eyes while his Lindsey-Woolsey shirt stretched across a massive chest, also sprouting red hair above a straining row of buttons.

The couple waved a greeting as the wagon pulled closer to the campsite. "Evenin'" The red man cried. "We're da MacGregors. Dae ya mind if we jine ye at yer braw fire. We be needin' ta get our bahoochie offn da bench and get some tatties on the fire!"

Turning to Scratch, Jeremiah grinned and said, "I think he's askin' to join our camp and share the fire."

With a smile and a slight chuckle, the woman spoke clearly, "My husband has a thick Scottish brogue and many have difficulty understanding him, although he finds that a little bewildering, but yes, that's what he was asking. May we join you and share your fire? It has been a long and tiring day and we would certainly appreciate the company. I'd be happy to do the cooking if you'd like?"

Without hesitation and thinking only with his stomach, Scratch quickly replied, "Why yes'm, you folks would be welcome to join us. Go ahead and pull up right over there by those trees and you can tether your horses with that bit of grass. Course, ya might wanta water 'em first. There's some water just down in that coulee yonder," he motioned with a nod of his head. "I'll have the fire goin' real quick here and get the coffee started."

Jeremiah's mind was also pondering the possibilities of a meal prepared by a woman and joined in with, "And we got some fresh venison, e... deer meat too. You can use our pans and such too, if ya like," his eagerness betraying his lack of composure.

Caleb walked to Scratch's beginnings of the fire and dropped his armload of firewood. "Guess I better get a bit more wood, ya think?" then started back to the copse of trees to search for more downed branches to replenish their wood supply.

When Scratch selected the campsite, it appeared as an island of shade and vegetation in the midst of an empty plain shrouded with grass and scarred with ravines and gullies and an occasional slough or bog. It was the best site for several miles around, was near fresh water and was close by a confluence of trails and roadways.

It was also evident the site had been used many times by other wayfarers in the near and distant past. What Scratch did not anticipate was the magnetic draw the island campsite had and the attraction caused by the visibility of their blossoming

91

camp fire. But even the best kept secrets don't remain secrets long when announced on the prairie winds.

Carrie MacGregor had seated herself on a stone near the fire to attend to her banquet preparations. Her husband, Ian, tended the stock by taking them to water and returning to the edge of the clearing to tether the four blacks within reach of the new-growth Indian grass. The MacGregor's children, twin girls, Katie and Kristi, were busy exploring their temporary home and followed Caleb into the woods to assist with the wood gathering.

Scratch and Jeremiah stood silently, awaiting instructions from the little bit of woman that had taken over their normal evening chore of preparing supper. Jeremiah turned to speak to his partner and was stopped by the sight of two more canvas topped wagons approaching the camp. "Did somebody put up a sign to direct everybody on the trail to turn in here?" tossing the question to no one in particular, yet it caught the attention of Scratch who turned to follow his gaze.

Held speechless by the burgeoning crowd, he watched as the two wagons pulled within shouting distance and heard a man call, "Hello the camp! May we join you for the night?"

Jeremiah looked askance at Scratch who shrugged his shoulders then turned to answer the newcomers, "Might as well. Everybody else in the country is here!"

He motioned the visitors to pull their wagons to the opposite side of the sheltering trees from the MacGregor wagon. Both wagons were pulled by a pair of sturdy dray horses and easily navigated the bit of rise to the bluff and the campsite. The first wagon ejected a middle-aged man of average size with thinning wavy brown hair and a fair complexion. A floppy felt hat drooped over his ears.

He was accompanied by a youth of about fifteen years that sported a lanky frame, freckled face and curly, reddish brown hair. The youngster assisted his father in unhooking the team from the wagon and led one of the grey, Percheron horses to follow his father as he led the other to the stream for water. As they passed the others near the fire, the man introduced them as "Levi and Gabriel Farmer, from Chicago- most recently," then continued to the stream.

The second wagon yielded a young couple that were obviously newlywed and still showed the courtesies and attentions of the young in love. While the young man tended to his stock, the young lady joined the growing crowd at the fire and said, "We're the McCormick's from Indianapolis. My husband is Michael, and I'm Sally." Looking at Carrie tending to the beginnings of supper she asked, "May I be of some help? Perhaps some biscuits or something?"

Carrie replied with, "That would be nice. Biscuits would go fine with what we're fixin' here," and smiled.

Sally turned to her wagon and tossed, "I'll be right back," over her shoulder. She soon returned with a Dutch oven to set by the fire in preparation for the biscuits. Then, she walked back to the wagon to prepare the biscuits in a large metal bowl with flour and lard. Moments later, she returned and lifted the lid from the oven with a handful of calico skirt, placing the biscuits gently into the large cast-iron container. Using a nearby stick, she drew some hot coals to the side, set the Dutch oven on the coals, and then borrowed a shovel to put more coals on the rimmed lid. "There," she stated and turned to Carrie, "Is there something else I can help with?"

Scratch and Jeremiah had stepped back out of the way of the ladies and turned to one another with smiles that split their faces and eyes that told of their anticipation of a supper they had heretofore only dreamed about so far on this trip.

The return of the Farmer duo turned their attention to the big animals and Scratch said, "Those things look big enough to pull a train all by themselves!" as he admired the broad-chested horses that stood just over sixteen hands at the shoulder. Jeremiah nodded his head in agreement.

When the horses had been tethered to their assigned spot near their wagon, Levi and Gabriel Farmer returned carrying a small satchel and walked to the ladies to offer the contents to them. As Carrie peered into the satchel, she looked back to Mr. Farmer with a surprised smile and said, "Why Mr. Farmer, bless you. What a treat this will be, fresh strawberries!"

The usual number for the evening meal had been four, but now eleven hungry faces lined up before the fire and each, in turn, drew in deep breaths of the delightful and diverse aromas of the pending banquet. But before the tin plates were filled, young Mr. McCormick asked, "Would anyone object if we asked the Lord's blessing on our meal?"

With no remarks to the contrary and most heads nodding in agreement he began, "Dear Lord, we thank you for the meal you've provided for all of us on this fine evening. We thank you for new friends and those so willing to share both comfort and sustenance. Mostly Lord, we just thank you for your many blessings. This we pray in our Savior's name, Amen." A chorus of murmured "Amens" echoed through the campsite and everyone dug in to eat their supper.

Venison steaks, fried potatoes smothered with gravy, seared greens and fluffy biscuits seemed like a meal fit for a king to Scratch. Followed, to his absolute amazement, by fresh strawberries with sugar syrup over another biscuit, he thought he'd died and gone to heaven!

That was the consensus of opinion as the quiet of hungry travelers was slowly replaced with the usual get acquainted questions of strangers that shared a common bond.

Chapter Fourteen: Friends

THE NEXT MORNING, Scratch showed his skill with his razor-sharp Bowie knife as he drew it across the sow belly and dropped thin slices of bacon into the skillet. Carrie MacGregor was busy flipping flapjacks and stacking them in the assorted tin plates. Because of the many words of praise from the previous night about her biscuits, Sally McCormick was again tending a double layer of the fluffy fare in the nearby Dutch oven.

The remainder of the crowd slowly gathered around the fire and the breakfast preparations with Jeremiah standing to the rear with an arm hanging loosely on Caleb's shoulder. As he eyed the many hungry faces that stood speechless, mouths watering in anticipation of another feast, he couldn't help but ponder the differences in the assorted families, but the similarity in their goals.

He looked at the burly bush of red hair and bulk that was the Scotsman, Ian MacGregor and thought of his fine family and their goal of establishing a "foine tattie farm, wi rich sail and fat tatties" (or, in American vernacular, a potato farm with rich soil and fat potatoes).

The newlywed couple, the McCormick's, and the young man's plan to "take the Gospel to those most in need", wherever that may lead. And Mr. Farmer and his boy who simply wanted to make a new home- away from the sorrows they were leaving behind, and were willing to do whatever that might require.

And then there was the . . . *wait a minute, who's that? Where . . . when . . . who?* Jeremiah's eyes got big as he spied a new face standing at the rear of the group. He was a stranger to the mountain man but appeared familiar with the others. He sported a clean shaven face, youthful features, a floppy felt hat and a neckerchief tucked into a Lindsey Woolsey shirt with the tail hanging over canvas britches tucked into high topped boots.

There was something off though and Jeremiah wondered, *Wait... is that a man or a woman? Surely not a woman in britches!* Jeremiah slowly, and as inconspicuous as possible, made his way to the back of the crowd to greet the stranger and noticed the eyes of the visitor following him. "So, who might you be and where'd you come from?"

The stance, manner and attitude said one thing but the voice revealed the character was indeed a woman. "Charlie, Charlie Clark. I rode in late last night and threw my bedroll over yonder. Since I'd met some of these folks before, I didn't think they'd mind if I joined 'em."

"You mean Charlotte, don't you?" Jeremiah answered as he peered down at her from under his bushy eyebrows, trying to look as stern as possible. Scratch had noticed what his partner was doing and had casually stood up to back Jeremiah's play but now, seeing what the ruckus was all about, he strained to keep from letting loose a belly laugh. He couldn't restrain his smile, though.

"Ah come on, Jeremiah, there's plenty here for one more. 'Sides, we had us an odd number, eleven, and with Charlotte there, it makes an even dozen!"

The rest of the group had turned to watch the confrontation and many smiled. Some walked to her and extended a welcoming hand.

With breakfast complete and everyone packing and hitching up, Jeremiah asked everyone to gather around the remains of the cook-fire. The entire group complied and several sat on the larger stones or logs while others remained standing.

Scratch and Jeremiah stood opposite the crowd and Jeremiah began, "Folks, I don't know why we all ended up here together, or if it even means anything. Course that'd be more of a discussion with the Preacher there, but here we are. Now, y'all have different ideas about how to get where you're goin' but after all the talkin' we did last night, it 'pears to me, ain't none of ya ever been this way before and ya ain't too sure of what you're headed into.

Scratch and I were talkin' last night and bein' kinda concerned 'bout y'all, we thought we oughta tell ya just what you're up against. See, where we are now is what is known as Sauk and Fox country. That's the two tribes of Indians that used to inhabit this part of the country. They've been pretty well tamed down and I don't think we have too much to be concerned about with them. Careful? Yes. But concerned, not so much.

How-some-ever, though, once we get further west we'll run into Sioux, Crow and Arikara… and probably a few other brands of Indians that don't appreciate us coming into their country. And they will do everything they can to decorate their lodges with our hair. That's just the Indians!

There'll be plenty of other problems to contend with that'll make you wish you'd a stayed home or make ya wanna turn around and go back. Last night, Mr. MacGregor asked if it'd be all right if they traveled along with us since we know a little bit more about the country and such. At least, I think that's what he said, ain't it?" he asked as he looked toward the big man who was casting a broad smile his way.

With an energetic nod of his head, he motioned for Jeremiah to continue. "So, even though me and Scratch weren't lookin' for company, matter of fact we usually shy away from it, we agreed to have the MacGregor's join up with us, and we figgered it'd only be fair if we made the same allowances for the rest of ya."

The other members of the group looked from one to the other and replaced their looks of concern and anxiety with grins of anticipation and excitement. "That sounds great to us, Jeremiah, and takes a lot off our minds. You and Scratch are certainly an answer to our prayers!" enthusiastically declared Michael McCormick, turning to elicit a nod of approval from his young wife. The others added their comments of appreciation and all quickly busied themselves to start this new portion of their journey.

As Scratch pulled the latigo to tighten the cinch on his saddle, he was mumbling to himself but Caleb heard the grumbling and asked, "What's the matter Uncle Scratch? Ya need some help with somethin'?"

"No young'un, I was just talkin' to myself. Tryin' ta figger out how in the world we grew from three to a dozen just overnight."

"Oh, I can answer that. You got caught in the fryin' pan trap!" stated the Squirt.

"The what?" queried the confused Scratch.

"My momma used to call it the fryin' pan trap. That's when a man thinks more about what the lady's got in the fryin' pan than in what's goin' on around him. She said that's how a lotta women catch themselves a man! That's cuz he's thinkin' with his stomach and not his thinker." Caleb smiled with the expression of a teacher that has just imparted great wisdom.

"Oh Pshaw. Tweren't neither, no-how," emphatically replied the mountain man and busied himself with the rest of the packs and animals.

Jeremiah lined out the wagons with the MacGregor wagon in the lead followed by the McCormick's and the Farmer's. The newcomer, Charlie, as she preferred to be called, rode beside Caleb in the middle of the horse-backers while Scratch led and Jeremiah brought up the rear. While watching Charlie talking with Caleb, Jeremiah was trying to figure out how this woman found herself alone on the edge of the wilderness and now joined up with a group she barely knew.

Jeremiah noted she was well-outfitted; a Hawken rode in a scabbard under the fender leather of her saddle while on her hip she sported a Paterson Colt just like the one he carried. She appeared to have well-stuffed saddle bags and a parfleche as well, as a bedroll behind the cantle. Her mount was a well put together though flashy black and white paint mare.

He thought her attire was both for disguise as well as comfort and convenience. The thought of riding side-saddle with a long dress and carrying a parasol elicited a snicker from the mountain man. Yet there was something worrisome about the woman, disguising herself, traveling alone, and now he noticed she was closely watching their back-trail.

The plan was to head due West until they hit the North Platte after they crossed into what would be called Nebraska Territory, which wouldn't happen for, at least, a couple of weeks. Now it was up to Scratch to find or blaze a trail for the wagons to make it through the obstacle course of ravines, gullies, rivers, rock piles, cliffs and any other manner of complication that came their way.

The day started with a long but easy pull from the low, level river bottom land that had been carved out eons ago by the mighty "Big Muddy" and the much smaller tributaries that fed the thirsty ground-eating beast. Caleb enjoyed the company of Charlie and at every opportunity he switched roles from student to teacher as he shared his growing knowledge of the flora and fauna of the countryside. It was evident that all this wisdom was not totally new to her and that made Jeremiah think that at least she had some knowledge of something besides the fashions and styles of the city.

Jeremiah gigged his mount up alongside Scratch and said, "Scratch, I'm gonna tie my mule to the tail of yours and then I'm gonna take these two out to make meat. We're headin' off a little bit to the North yonder, towards them hardwoods to see what we can find to feed this growin' menagerie." Scratch looked at him, then back at the two following him, and at the mule, and grimaced.

"If'n ya get yourself lost, don't 'spect me ta come gitcha. With all these pilgrims to watch out fer, I don't have time ta be worryin' bout you, too!" he complained.

After tying the lead rope of his mule to the tail of Scratch's pack mule, Jeremiah said to the young'un and the new addition, "You two come on with me, our job for the day is to make meat for this herd," and without waiting he turned his horse away from the trail to make for the trees in the distance.

Charlie asked Caleb as they followed the big man, "Make meat? What's he mean?"

"We're hunting for meat for supper, whatever we find that we can eat. Sometimes it's a deer or maybe some fish or birds, whatever we find. Course, when we get a little further west," he looked at her as he echoed the words of Jeremiah, "we'll probably be shootin' some buffalo. But for now, we just gotta ketch as ketch can."

The hunters walked their mounts slowly through the towering oaks, hickory's and silver Maples that arched their branches together to form an umbrella covering the woods. Jeremiah held up a hand, then slipped off his mount and signaled for the two to follow. They dropped to the ground and each led their mounts until Jeremiah motioned for them to tie off the horses and follow him on foot.

A few steps further, he whispered, "There's a small creek and a little pond through there and we might see just about anything. Are your rifles primed and ready?" He looked from Caleb to Charlie. Caleb nodded excitedly and Charlie copied with a single nod. As they neared the edge of the trees,

Jeremiah motioned for them to drop down and pointed to the small clearing across the creek.

A flock of turkeys were fluffing their feathers and dropping their heads to pick morsels from the ground. "Squirt, I want you to get us a turkey. Your rifle has a smaller ball and won't damage the bird too much. Course," he added, "if you could take a head shot, you wouldn't spoil any meat. But you do what you can, okay? Now, come up here beside me."

Watching the boy, he smiled with pride as Caleb flawlessly brought his rifle up to rest on his left arm, which was propped on his left knee. He pulled the hammer to full cock, then slowly squeezed the trigger, keeping his sights on the bird without wavering. The hammer dropped and the thunder and smoke was echoed by a larger roar from behind them.

Jeremiah quickly turned to see Charlie facing away from the creek and towards the deeper shadows of the woods. She brought her Hawken down from her shoulder and rested the butt on the ground as she began to reload without comment.

"What the blazes were you shootin' at?' Jeremiah asked angrily. "Or were you just tryin' ta scare the daylights outta us?"

Charlie looked at him, then nodded her head in the direction of her shot and said, "You said we were here to make meat. I thought that little buck over there might taste pretty good tonight."

Jeremiah stood and looked in the direction of her nod and through the trees he saw the patch of tan hair that told him of the downed deer. He then looked back to see the result of Caleb's shot and noticed a hump of feathers with some still fluttering to the ground. The remainder of the flock had disappeared.

"Well, if you two ain't a couple of mighty hunters. Caleb, you wade across over there and bring your bird back here. Charlie and I will drag that buck back and then we'll clean up our mess." Turning to Charlie he asked, "Have you ever dressed out a deer?"

"To be honest, no. All I've ever done is small game. I shot deer before, but my brother did the rest of it. So, I've seen it, but never did it," she replied.

After putting Caleb to work plucking his turkey, which he had downed with a clean head shot, Jeremiah turned to the task of dressing the deer. Before dragging it to the clearing, he cut its throat to let it bleed out during the drag. With his Bowie knife, he split the deer from anus to chin, and reaching into the chest cavity tore loose the innards, cutting and dragging them to a pile beside the carcass.

He set aside the heart and liver then turned to show Charlie the method of skinning and began to strip the skin from the carcass, both carefully slicing through the membrane and pulling the skin away.

He demonstrated how to debone the quarters and directed her to cut out the back straps. After the meat was piled on the skin, Jeremiah had Caleb place the turkey carcass on top of the stack of meat, then folded the four corners of the hide over the pile. "Now we need the rest of our supper. Leave that right there and follow me."

Jeremiah pointed out the cattail sprouts near the edge of the water and instructed them to pull the sprouts and even dig a few of the smaller roots up. In short order, they had a good stack and he turned and walked back towards the edge of the clearing. Stooping down he pulled a couple of hands full of onions and the two students followed suit.

"One more thing…" he murmured. "don't touch this with your bare hands," He pulled the neckerchief from around his neck he began to harvest a collection of green and purple nettles. Plucking just the leaves and being very careful not to touch them, he soon had a pile of about a half bushel. The assortment of wild vegetables was impressive and Jeremiah took a spare cloth shirt from his bedroll and gathered them together.

When they caught up with the caravan, Jeremiah went to the rear of the MacGregor wagon and dropped the hide full of meat and the shirt with the vegetables in the back. Moving his mount alongside the wagon and speaking to Carrie MacGregor he said, "M'am, we put some meat and vegetables in the back of your wagon. If you've never cooked the cattails or the nettles they're just like any other vegetable. But the nettles, don't touch them with your bare hands, okay? You cook 'em like any other greens, they're plumb good, but be careful of 'em 'fore ya cook 'em."

"Well thank you, Jeremiah. That's real nice of you. Are you sure there's enough for everybody?"

"Yes'm, there's a whole deer and about a bushel of vegetables, so if you can get that McCormick woman to make some more biscuits, it oughta make a purty good meal," he smiled and gigged his horse to catch up with Scratch and the two mighty hunters, all the while thinking about what wonders that little lady would do with the vittles he provided. *Gravy! I plumb forgot to mention gravy. I hope she makes some, cuz her gravy was deelishus!*

To The Tall Timber

B.N. Rundell

Chapter Fifteen: Flood

IT DIDN'T TAKE LONG for the cavalcade to fall into a comfortable routine. Each day's travel had an early start with the wagons stretched out on the trail by first light. The three wagons rotated position with a different team taking the lead one day and dropping to the rear on the next. Jeremiah and Scratch quickly realized that one or the other of them would have to scout farther ahead to find a trail suitable for wagon travel which was quite an adjustment from letting the horses have their heads and taking a suitable trail for single file horses.

It was necessary to find an easy and wide trail that avoided the usual obstacles of deep ravines and steep climbs and also provided good sources of water for the stock. Often the one with the scout duty also took advantage of any opportunity to provide game for the crowd. Occasionally, Charlie and Caleb would swing wide of the trail and search out any game that could be easily taken, and the small wagon train seldom went without fresh meat.

Jeremiah usually enjoyed the scouting duty as it afforded him a time of solitude. Those times without company also gave him opportunity for contemplation. The years ahead of him offered much promise and challenge. He was anxious to get back to his home in the mountains and especially to be with Laughing Waters once again.

He often thought of her and their future together and every thought of Waters as his wife brought a wide smile to his face and warmth to his soul. But he knew that future had taken on a different picture with the addition of Caleb. Although he was certain that Laughing Waters would be pleased with him and of his bringing Caleb to live with them, but he had some reservation about the rest of the Arapaho people and how the entire village would accept the boy.

Jeremiah often pictured the Squirt enjoying the same kind of life and adventure of growing up that he had enjoyed in his youthful years with Ezekiel and his family and the joys of learning the way of The People. He was determined that Caleb would have the best life possible and that he would learn to be a man of character and integrity in the same way that Ezekiel had instilled in him.

But today wasn't to be a day of solitude. Caleb had begged his Uncle Jeremiah to take him along on the day's scout so he could learn to find the necessary route like his Uncles did so maybe he could one day do the scouting. The broad and optimistic smile that painted his face challenged any resistance that Jeremiah had tried to conjure up and the two headed out before first light to scout out the trail.

As dusty shades of pink stretched across the sky overhead to herald the beginning of the new day, the lazy sun clawed its way over the horizon behind the two scouts. When the pink was replaced with the cobalt blue of a cloudless sky, Jeremiah stood tall in his stirrups and surveyed the countryside before them. Motioning the boy to follow, he kneed his horse to a small knoll that would provide a better view of the land ahead.

Sparsely covered with tall old-growth hardwood trees, it still had a bare shoulder on the Western side that offered a view of the plain that stretched westward. Traveling the last several days had been relatively easy with few detours for ravines and gulches and the path before them appeared no different. Again standing tall in his stirrups and shading his eyes to enhance his distant view, he was copied by the boy who often sought to mimic his favorite uncle. When he dropped back into the saddle, he turned to Caleb and asked, "Whatcha think, boy?"

"Just looks like more of the same to me… lotsa trees and tall grass."

"Well you're right about that, but didja notice, way in the distance yonder, how the color of green is just a little bit brighter and the trees a bit taller?" asked Jeremiah.

Turning and looking in that direction, standing in his stirrups and shading his eyes again, Caleb dropped into his saddle, turned to his uncle and responded, "Uh, no. It looks the same to me."

"Well that's alright Squirt. But notice that when it *does* look like that, it usually means there's water there, probably a river or maybe a small lake or something. We'll just have to scout it out a little bit so we'll know what we have to plan on for the wagons to get across."

He clucked his horse to drop off the knoll and the boy and his roan followed closely behind. Jeremiah naturally fell into his habit of sharing his knowledge with the boy and pointed out different plants, trees, birds and animals as they continued on their scout.

"See those kinda pink flowers over yonder, the ones with the bushy tops? Those are milkweeds and where ever ya see a bunch of them, there's usually some swampy ground and it's a good sign ta stay away unless ya wanna get bogged down," advised his uncle.

"What's all those yeller ones over there?" inquired the boy as he pointed to the middle of the meadow they were passing through.

"I don't rightly know all of 'em, but those yeller and pink ones over yonder and kinda bunched together, I think they're called coneflowers," replied Jeremiah, "But far's I know, they ain't good fer nuthin' ya can't eat 'em or anything."

As the two were discussing the plants, the movement of the horses through the tall grass kicked out couple of rabbits that ran into the flat in their attempt to escape. Before they reached the sanctuary of the next patch of tall grass, a swift moving and silent shadow dropped with razor sharp talons and snatched the leader from the ground. Lifting its prey that squirmed its last bit of life away, the broad winged golden eagle caught a slight breeze to carry it high above and to its nest in the top of a large snag of a dead tree arching above a slight knoll.

The two scouts watched wordlessly and respectfully as the magnificent bird of prey began to feed the hungry beaks reaching upwards. The big eagle hopped to more solid footing, looked below at the distant spectators and let loose a high pitched kee-kee-kee that sounded like a warning to the intruders. When an answering call came from below, the eagle cocked its head to the side in curious wonder. That movement was copied by the big mountain man as he looked in wonder at his youthful charge.

Approaching the water, Jeremiah noted it was what was often referred to as a mature river by the old-timers. That simply meant it was a wide and often shallow river that had a lot of horseshoe bends that formed as it meandered through the flat land of the area.

With a considerable clearing between thick forested banks, the two scouts walked their mounts down a slight drop that bordered a wide stretch of sand. A deposit of high water, the sand was firmly packed and the horse's hooves did not sink in the sandy soil as they approached the riverside.

Jeremiah dropped from his saddle and walked to the edge of the water as he surveyed the slow moving and murky river. It was easily forty yards wide and he could see a similar sandy bank on the opposite shore. It was hard to determine the depth, but it appeared to be somewhat shallow, Jeremiah speculated it was no more than chest high on his horse.

B.N. Rundell

"Well younker, we best be gittin' back to the rest of 'em so we can git 'crost this water before nightfall. It'd be best to be on the other side, come mornin'," observed Jeremiah. Mounting up, he turned his mount Eastward to retrace their trail and direct the remainder of their group back to the river. The clear blue sky that the two enjoyed on their scout was quickly getting covered with grey skirted and towering clouds. Jeremiah continued to look back at the gathering clouds and didn't like what he thought was happening.

The wagons were just stretching out after their early noonin' stop with Scratch and Charlie leading the way with the pack mules trailing. Greeting their scouting duo with a "Well, howdy boys. Where ya been keepin' yoreselves? Ya just missed gittin' some vittles, but ya don't look none the worse for wear," Scratch lived up to his nickname as he scratched at his growing bush of whiskers. He noticed a look of concern on the face of his partner and said, "So, what's up that's got you so long-faced?"

"See those clouds over my shoulder? I think they might be packin' a considerable punch of water and maybe sumpin' else," replied Jeremiah while he tugged at his floppy felt hat that was starting to flap in the growing wind.

"Well, a little bit a rain ain't never hurt nobody, fact is, most everbody here could use a bath after that dusty trail we been on," observed Scratch.

"Yeah, but there's a sizable river up yonder that if we don't git across 'fore floodwaters come, we'll be stuck for quite a spell and be goin' nowhere," informed the younger mountain man. "I suggest we git these pilgrims movin' a bit faster and see if'n we can't git acrosst that river before it gits too big."

"Suits me. You go on back and let 'em know what we're up against. Me'n Charlie here'll follow yore trail and see if'n we can set things up a mite." Scratch nodded at the woman and they gigged their horses and pulled on the mules' lead ropes to pick up the pace. Caleb waited while Jeremiah worked his way back down the three wagons and informed each of the

109

families of the plan. When he returned, the two rode side by side and led the cavalcade toward the river crossing, all the while eyeing the gathering clouds.

Within the hour, the dark clouds had obscured the last remnants of blue sky and brought a foreboding to each of the travelers. They too, were now watching the gathering clouds and sought to quicken the pace of their teams in a futile effort to escape the coming storm.

Then, without further warning, the deluge was loosed and within minutes the entire group was baptized with nature's fury. The canvas coverings of the wagons were flapping in the rising wind as the rain began to pelt the members of the train without mercy. Each splatter of water felt like the slap of an angry parent that sought to discipline a wayward child and there was no escape. The horses bowed their necks and dipped their heads to escape the wind-driven onslaught.

Arriving at the river's edge, Scratch had to yell to be heard as he directed Jeremiah, "You all wait here. I'm gonna cross to check it out and make sure it's O.K. When I get across't, I'll signal ya if there's anything ya need ta know. Then you send the wagons, and don't let 'em get too far apart, but not too close neither."

With a wave that acknowledged Jeremiah's nod of understanding, Scratch gigged his horse to the water and wrapped the mule's lead rope around the saddle horn. The wagons were now side by side at the edge of the sand enabling everyone to watch the mountain man make his way across the river. The bobbing action of the horse and mule revealed the depth of the water, but it was evident it wasn't too deep to prevent crossing. Gaining the far bank, Scratch could barely be seen through the downpour but he waved his arms to signal the remainder to start out.

The Farmer wagon led the way with the big Percheron mares plodding into the water without hesitation. The tall and muscular horses kept their footing and were able to keep their heads high above water as they made their way across the growing river. The current was not too strong but threatened to increase with the rising level of water. Without difficulty, the big horses walked up out of the water and pulled the wagon high above to a grassy knoll.

Scratch motioned them to the nearby grove of Maple and Oak and turned to watch the MacGregor wagon working across the river with the four blacks doing their job. With the smaller horses, the current was pushing the wagon farther downstream, but they struggled valiantly to pull the wagon and keep their footing in the sandy bed beneath them. Finally, the wagon with the bushy red beard and his family made their way to join the first by the trees.

Jeremiah, Caleb and Charlie followed the McCormick wagon into the water and immediately noticed the rising current. Although the wagon was pulled by two large dray horses, they were not as big, nor as strong as the Percherons of the Farmer wagon. They were struggling against the current but continued to make way.

Just over half way, one of the team stumbled as it lost its footing and his head went under water. Fighting and struggling with fear in his eyes, the horse sought to get upright and gain footing. As the horse struggled, the current caught the wagon that now teetered to the downriver side. The young bride was tossed from her seat as she emitted a scream that pierced the wind-driven storm.

Jeremiah tried to kick his horse to the wagon but his mount was too busy fighting the current and the pull of the mule's lead rope added to the struggle. The tight rope across his leg prevented Jeremiah from leaving his saddle and he threw a glance to Caleb who was now out of his saddle and holding to the saddle horn as his little roan fought the raging stream. Charlie was behind the two, but was still astride her mount with her head ducked and hat down to shield her face from the onslaught.

Jeremiah watched helplessly as the young bride bobbed over the growing waves and continued to scream whenever her mouth wasn't full of water. Although she wasn't too far from the West bank, the current continued to hinder her from reaching the shore. Jeremiah noticed what appeared to be a man in blue treading water towards the woman, but the rain obscured his vision and she disappeared from view. Finally, the dray horses gained their footing and dug in with their big hooves to pull the wagon to the shore.

Preacher McCormick halted the horses on the sandy bank and jumped from his seat to search the water and the downstream shore for some sign of his beloved wife but he could barely see the approach of Jeremiah and the others. Dropping to his knees he turned his face heavenward and pleaded, "Please God, please," and began to sob to add his tears to the deluge.

Chapter Sixteen: Blue

CAPTAIN JAMES ALLEN, the commanding officer of Fort Sanford and of Company I of the 1st U.S. Dragoons stationed there, led the contingent of 18 men on their expedition following the West bank of the Des Moines river toward the confluence with the Raccoon River to find a suitable site to establish a more Northern location for the Sauk and Fox Indian agency and a new Fort to be named Fort Des Moines #2.

With a late start mid-day, the troops bivouacked near a copse of trees on the outside of a horse shoe bend of the Des Moines. They made camp early as they anticipated making this a base of operations to reconnoiter the area for the possible site of what would be their new home and the site for the new agency. The men successfully pitched their tents and gathered their firewood in preparation of putting together their evening meal when the first drops of rain warned of the coming inclement weather.

They quickly finished their early meal so they could seek shelter in their small tents and the usual selection of guards was posted even though no threat was imminent, but regulations required it and their commander, being a West Point graduate, was a stickler for regulations.

Sergeant of the Guard, Sergeant, First Class O'Reilly selected two of the newer recruits, Private Smith and Private Jones, who shared the same name with half the other recruits in the army, to stand the first watch. One was stationed on the bank of the river while the other walked his post to the West of the camp. As the drizzle turned into a downpour, both guards sought the protection of the trees.

Private Smith was more fortunate as a thick foliaged towering oak tree stretched its branches to the edge of the river and offered a wide umbrella of protection from the rain. As he leaned against the rough trunk of the broad tree, he dug into his trousers pocket searching for a bit of tobacco to wedge into his lower lip. Then, something caught his eye across the river and he watched a man on horseback leading a pack mule wade into the unfriendly water. That movement drew his attention to the wagons that waited on the opposite shore. The private quickly returned to the bivouac area and sought out his Sergeant.

The Sergeant called for the other guard, Private Jones, to follow him and the trio returned to the riverside to watch the promised parade of pilgrims. The seasoned Sergeant sent Private Jones back to camp to secure as much rope as he could find and to also notify Captain Allen of the approaching wagons. The Private, with a rope dangling from one shoulder, followed the Captain to return to the riverside. The four men stood in the downpour with only the brims of hats and bills of caps to keep the rain from obscuring their view of the unfolding drama. Soon a few other curious troops joined the spectators.

They watched the hardy souls fight the swelling floodwaters with occasional comments on the wisdom or lack of same exhibited by the pilgrims and a few even placed bets as to the outcome of certain wagons. With the advance scout on horseback and his mule leading the way, they watched as the next two wagons struggled ashore when their attention was drawn to the last wagon. By this time, they noticed that the water had actually approached their observation point and it was quickly rising with the added downpour filling the upstream tributaries.

A scream riveted their attention on the teetering wagon and they witnessed a woman plummeting into the water, watching as she fought for air. The troopers were over fifty yards downstream from the crossing and the woman was quickly being swept in their direction.

Without hesitation, Private Smith pulled off his boots and jumped into the raging river. He treaded water as fast as he could as he sought to intercept the maiden in distress. Sergeant O'Reilly ordered Private Jones to give the rope to him and then ordered Jones and two other troopers now standing and watching to "Wrap the end of that rope around your butts and hold on!"

Sergeant O'Reilly took the coils of the rope and with a quick looping swing over his head he let fly in an attempt to drop the loop in front of the still treading Private Smith. Unsuccessful, he quickly retrieved the rope in a coil to try again. With another swing over his head he stretched to the tip of his toes trying to make it go further and successfully dropped the end of the rope across the back of the swimmer.

Smithy, as he was often called by his peers, rolled to his side with a wide sweep of his arm and grabbed the rope, and with another spurt of energy and a valiant kick he snatched at the waterlogged dress of the now floating, still form of the woman. Pulling her to him to gain a better grip, he motioned to the men on shore to pull away. The current took the duo further downstream but the anchored men continued to pull the pair and successfully brought them to the water's edge.

The Captain and two other troopers pulled Smithy and Sally McCormick from the water and laid them on the sandy shore. Sally showed no signs of life and the Captain quickly grabbed both her arms, rolled her over on her stomach and pulled upwards on her arms to try to force air into her lungs. With repeated effort, he was finally rewarded by a cough from the woman and a pull-back on her arms. She put her hands on the sand and sought to push herself up as she continued coughing and trying to catch her breath. Wiping the sand from her face, she sat up and looked around at the crowd in blue that now stood staring at the waterlogged woman that vaguely resembled a drowned rat.

"Who . . . who . . . are you? Where am I? Where's my husband?" she stammered with fear filling her eyes.

"M'am, it's all right. We're soldiers with the 1st Dragoons and lucky for you we're camped right over there by those trees. Fortunately, Private Smith here saw your party as they started crossing and he notified us, but when you went in for your swim, it was Private Smith here that fetched you outta that river. By the way, I'm Captain James Allen and I'm proud to place the entire company of the 1st Dragoons at your service," stated the dripping Captain as he joined his company of equally wet Dragoons.

"But . . . but . . . where's my husband, and the others?" she stammered.

"I believe they all made it safely ashore M'am. I'll have one of my men ride up there and let your company know that you are safe as well. Now, if you'd be so kind, I believe we have a warm blanket and a dry tent that might be of comfort to you."

She was assisted to her feet by the Captain and Sergeant O'Reilly and both men offered their arms to accompany her to the much anticipated warmth. The splashing of hooves told of the trooper's departure on his mission to tell the others of the fortunate rescue of their missing member.

Chapter Seventeen: Waiting

LAUGHING WATERS was seated cross-legged in front of her buffalo skin lodge and was working with both quills and beads as she wove a blend of colors and textures into an exceptionally colorful and beautiful display of art and craftsmanship. The white, soft-tanned buckskin that was her canvas was held taut between her knees as she focused her attention on the intricate pattern she had chosen for the beaded yoke of the dress.

Artwork covered the entire yoke area from the shoulder seam to what would be the rise of her breasts and stopped at the row of fringe that accented the cut of the yoke. Each piece of fringe had been knotted with a tuft of a yellow feather at the end to accent the movement of the wearer.

This had been a long-term project of Laughing Waters that had started upon her return from the vengeance quest of White Wolf, or Jeremiah Thompsett. Although White Wolf had sought to go on the quest alone, the tribal council gave the charge to Broken Shield and Laughing Waters to accompany him.

The quest was in response to the slave hunters' brutal murder of Buffalo Thunder, an adopted and respected member of their tribe. Buffalo Thunder had been White Wolf's mentor and adopted father and had raised the young man to become a bold and fearless warrior.

Broken Shield and Laughing Waters had been friends and companions with White Wolf since they were all youngsters and whenever one was found, the other two would not be far away, so it was only natural that the lifelong companions were determined to accompany Jeremiah on this quest. The responsibility for the quest was rightfully his, but because of the standing of Buffalo Thunder among the tribe, the council determined all three should take the responsibility.

When the three departed on their journey, they were in pursuit of a group of seven renegades. After just over a month, they had been successful in downing four of the seven. After finding another and engaging in a hand-to-hand battle with the renegade Arapaho, Broken Shield was victorious but was severely wounded.

Laughing Waters aided Broken Shield as they returned to the village and White Wolf continued with his new companion, a seasoned trapper named Scratch. Before they parted, Waters had told Jeremiah to return to her, for she would be waiting. Although he didn't answer her, he held her and did his best to express his equally strong love for her in the only way he knew. She was used to the way Jeremiah spoke with his eyes rather than his lips and she often went to sleep with that image on her heart.

She hoped the dress she now crafted would be her attire at her mating ritual with White Wolf. Whenever she labored on the traditional costume for the ceremony, her mind would conjure the image of the two of them together and taking the vow of union. The picture of her in Jeremiah's arms always brought a smile to her face as she now bore.

"You are thinking of him again, aren't you," asked Walking Dove, her voice startling Waters.

Looking up at the woman of Buffalo Thunder who still mourned her husband, she smiled at the thought that this woman knew her Jeremiah as well as anyone for her man had been his adopted father and White Wolf spent many years under her care and guidance as well.

"Yes, as I work on my dress I can't help but picture us together and it brings me joy to think of us as one," she mused as she looked for approval from Dove, and continued, "Am I wrong to think such thoughts? Should I wait for his return before planning such things?"

"You are not wrong," she reassured, "I remember when I first saw my man and how I longed for his return even if he was gone for less than a day. It is only natural for you to feel this way about the man you have always loved."

Waters was surprised at her remark. She didn't think anyone knew she felt that way about Jeremiah even when they were youngsters involved in the games of training and competed against each other. Yet, from the first time she met Jeremiah when he was brought into their village by Buffalo Thunder, she was fascinated with him and that interest never waned but instead blossomed into the love she now felt.

"Black Kettle, your father, tells me that other young men have expressed interest in you for a mate. He said Walks-with-a-Limp is worse than a new born fawn after his mother when he looks at you and has asked for a bride price and so too, has Standing Elk." Walking Dove had a mischievous glint in her eyes as she looked for Waters reaction.

"Waaww, he better not speak to them about me. I would never be with either of them! They are like boys compared to White Wolf. I have already given my heart to him," she declared emphatically. As she looked up at Dove with fire in her eyes, Waters could see she had been tricked by the wise older woman who stood smiling down at her.

"How long do you plan to wait for him?" Dove asked.

"I have asked the Great Spirit to let him return by the Moon of Colors and before the snow paints the mountains again."

"And if he has not returned? Will you take another?"

"No! I have earned warrior status, and if I must, I will go in search of him." She had earned her warrior status and was considered to be better than any man in the village with her skill with the bow and with her experience on the recent quest with Broken Shield and White Wolf, none questioned her rank. The expression on her face showed her determination and commitment that went unquestioned by Walking Dove.

Although she had stated what she considered a very real possibility, she had resisted those thoughts, fearful that allowing them to take up residence in her mind would make it more likely to become a reality. Dispelling them from her mind, she again focused on her crafting of the marital costume still in her lap. The beauty of the colors and the imagination of the future were more pleasant thoughts that would continually bring the warm feeling to her spirit and a smile to her face. She would dwell on these.

Chapter Eighteen: Grateful

THE MASSIVE TREES nearby drooped with the weight of the continual deluge. Although the wagons were near the sagging boughs, they were not sheltered by the tree line. The white canvas that had been stretched tight over the wooden bows, now sagged between the bows giving the appearance of a boney sway-backed plow horse that stood in the rain with drooping head.

The animals had been freed of their harness but were hobbled as they sought shelter under the few trees with trunks that held branches of sufficient height. No effort had been made for any semblance of camp or fire and the entire group huddled in the different wagons. The MacGregor family had Caleb join them so the children would have company.

Charlie had been welcomed into the Farmer wagon with Levi and Gabriel, and Jeremiah and Scratch joined Preacher McCormick in his wagon to help him in his time of loss. Although as a student of the Scriptures, Michael knew he should be "strong in the Lord," all he felt now was loss and emptiness at the thought of continuing without his beloved Sally. While he should be giving words of comfort and reassurance to others, he now stood in need and all he knew was hopelessness.

The sound of splashing mud increased as Jeremiah listened. He knew that rhythmic splashing could only be from a four-legged animal and his first thought was that one of the animals had freed itself from the hobbles, but the faint call from outside made him quickly rise and look from the rear of the wagon. He was confronted with the sight of a blue-clad man with a stubble of a beard that was shouting for attention. "Hello the camp! Hello the camp!"

"Over here, come on over here," called Jeremiah. The man on horseback reined his horse to the rear of the McCormick wagon. Jeremiah asked, "What can we do ya for young man? Ya need help with somethin'?"

"No sir. It's more what I can do for you. Would you folks be missin' one of yore number?" he asked with a wet smile forcing its way through the rain streaming down his face.

"Why yes, what can you tell us?" Jeremiah replied as he was shoved aside by an anxious Michael. The others had craned their heads around from the front of the wagon while the rest of the party from the other wagons were also staring in interest.

"Quickly man, what can you tell us about my wife?" asked Michael.

"Why, she's finer'n frog hair, mister. We fished her outta the river and she's in the captain's tent all covered up with blankets and waitin' fer her husband to come git her!"

"Oh praise God! Praise God. And thank you sir. Uh, do you wanna get down and step in outta the rain. We have some coffee here," offered the Preacher with a smile that split his face.

"Nah, I'm gonna git back to my own blankets. We're camped just about a hunnert yards South of here, right next to them trees yonder. If ya wanna wait till the storm lets up, she'll be nice and dry when ya come. Is there anything ya want me to tell her?"

"Wait just a minute, I'm comin' with you!" declared Michael, then turning to Jeremiah asked, "Can I use your horse to fetch my wife back here? I can't wait any longer."

Jeremiah understood and replied, "Sure. Git yourself some blankets to wrap her in and I'll get the horse ready for you. It'll only take a couple minutes."

Within the hour the Preacher had returned with a soggy bundle that he lovingly placed in the back of the wagon. Jeremiah and Scratch had vacated the wagon in favor of the Farmer's to leave the couple alone in their reunion. The entire group was greatly relieved when they heard the good news about Sally and all were determined to give the young couple any help they could to replace the few belongings lost with the mid-stream tipping of the wagon.

It was after midnight before the storm began to slacken and just before daylight the storm clouds skittered on their way to the East leaving behind an ample supply of mud and bogs. Scratch was the first to roust out to take care of his ablutions and to search out some semblance of dry ground and some wood to make a fire. He was hankering for some coffee and wasn't about to start a cool, wet morning without it.

About twenty yards into the trees, the ground had enough rise to it that the water had quickly retreated to the river and left behind a sizeable area for a good campfire sufficient for fixing coffee and breakfast. Gathering some wood and assembling the stack over the handful of dry leaves and twigs he piled for starter, he dug in his pocket for the flint and steel. After several attempts, the sparks finally flared and with an encouraging puff of air from Scratch, smoke began to rise and flames began to hungrily consume the dried wood.

Ian MacGregor joined Scratch with a coffee pot in hand and a draw string canvas bag marked coffee. "Whit's fur ye'll no go past ye, but we be needin' a bit o' da brew," said the big Scot.

"I understood 'a bit o' da brew' and I'm certain sure ya mean the coffee, and I'm agreein' with ya on that," replied Scratch.

The large stone near the now budding fire served to smash the beans sufficiently to make the coffee with and a good handful was dropped into the warming water. Dusting his hands of the remnants, Scratch looked to the sky and said, "If the sun comes out nice and bright, we might be able to make a few miles this afternoon. But if not, we'll have to wait till tomorrow. It's a waste of effort to move a wagon in this kinda mud," he stated shaking his head for emphasis.

"Aye, more'n a wee scunner, it was," came from the red bush of a beard.

"He means, the rain is more than a little nuisance," clarified Carrie MacGregor as she joined the men by the fire. "Are you fellas ready for me to get breakfast started?" she asked as she simultaneously used hand gestures to be certain both men understood.

"Well then, fetch me some pans and somethin' to put in 'em and I'll get it started."

Both men understood and started for the wagons to do her bidding which they knew would result in a satisfying reward for their labors. They met Jeremiah and Charlie on the short path and enlisted their help in the preparations. Caleb and the girls had already made their way to the fire and stood with hands outstretched to absorb the heat and dispel the moisture, but were quickly sent after more firewood. Levi and Gabriel followed the children to supervise the gathering to ensure that only dry or mostly dry wood was gathered. All agreed to let the McCormicks sleep in and each went about their assigned task as surreptitiously as possible.

Chapter Nineteen: Visitors

IT WAS EARLY AFTERNOON when the cry, "Hello the camp!" rang out from the approaching squad of blue-clad soldiers. Quickly answered by the group just breaking from the campfire and clean-up duties following the noon meal, it was Jeremiah's voice that echoed from the edge of the trees, "Come ahead on, and welcome." As the soldiers approached, the group of travelers, now with the McCormick's in their midst, spread out from the trail to give everyone a look-see. The troopers were met by a gaggle of smiling faces with several holding hands to their brows to shade their eyes against the high noon sun.

With a bright shining sun unhindered by any clouds and aided by a gentle breeze out of the West, the water had dissipated and the mud was drying up. They had considered trying to make a few miles on their journey but the overwhelming opinion was that the stock, and people alike, needed a rest day.

When the troopers dismounted, they were invited to join the group back by the campfire site where several logs and stones and been assembled to provide everyone a resting place. After the greetings, the captain started the introductions, "I'm

Captain James Allen and the shave-tail here is Lieutenant Charles Ruff. The rest of the men are Sergeant O'Reilly and Privates Smith and Jones and Jones. It was Private Smith there that dove in after the mermaid," he stated with a smile in the direction of Sally McCormick, who dropped her head with a blush.

The Preacher stood and stretched a hand to Private Smith and said, "We're forever in your debt, Private. What you did was very noble and very brave and we both greatly appreciate your efforts." Turning to the Captain, he said, "And I'm sure he had considerable help from the rest of you, from what my wife tells me. We are eternally grateful to all of you."

The sentiments of the couple were echoed by the remainder of the extended family of vagabonds with nodding heads and many other comments of appreciation. Caleb and the girls remained behind the seated group of adults and all three were mesmerized by the burly looking soldiers in their impressive blue uniforms. The two officers had black billed forage caps with gold braid at the top edge of the bill, while the other men had similar headgear but without any of the decorative braid.

Their trousers were a lighter shade of blue with gold stripes running the length of the seam on the outside of the leg. A white leather saber belt accented the short waistcoat worn by all. Caleb had noticed that each of the saddles held holsters that contained a dragoon saddle pistol, and some had one on each side. Everyone was totally at ease and the conversation continued with the usual comments and questions about destinations, goals, and families left behind.

"So, Mr. McCormick, your wife told us that you are a minister of the gospel and you are in search of your new ministry. Have you decided on any particular location yet?" inquired the Captain.

"No sir, not yet. We've enjoyed the company of these fine folks and we're not sure exactly where the Lord will lead us. We've thought there might be a new settlement in need of a church that would be our favored landing spot somewhere in the West," replied the preacher, with a bit of uncertainly.

"After your wife spoke about that, my men and I were trying to place any settlement west of here that would be sizable enough to support a church and pastor. There's Sante Fe, down in the Mexico territory, but besides that, the only thing west of here is Caldwell's Camp near the location of Council Bluffs on the Missouri, but that's nothing more than an Indian village of Potawatomie.

Moses Merrill had a Baptist Mission there to the Otoe but he recently passed with consumption and Mrs. Merrill returned to the East.   The Otoe have moved North so there's nothing left. There's a few trading posts or what they're calling forts that have been put in by the American Fur Company, but for the life of me, I couldn't think of any place that had more'n a few White folks," stated the Captain resolutely.

A very somber Michael McCormick responded, "That's not very encouraging, Captain. Why the way folks were talking about the West when we were back in Indianapolis, it was like we better hurry up and get out here before all the good spots were taken. I don't know what we'll do now," he drawled as he turned and placed his hand on his wife's, looking at her sad eyes.

"Well, like I said, Preacher, we were talking about it last night while that storm was flapping our tents and we couldn't sleep, and I might have an idea that would suit you."

With a hopeful expression, Michael looked to the Captain and said, "Go ahead Captain, we're listening."

"We have a post just South of here that used to be an American Fur Company post and there are several good cabins. In the coming months we might be moving that post North of here a- ways, up by the confluence of the DesMoines River and the Raccoon River.

Right now, our post is just referred to as the Sauk and Fox Indian Agency and wherever we go, it will still be the headquarters for the agency as well as an army outpost. Now,

I did a little engineering when I was stationed up at Chicago and as I looked over the available maps, and there's very few of them, this area here is right smack dab in the middle of where folks will be traveling to settle the West.

Right now, there are about fifty ornery soldiers and two tribes of Indians in need of the Gospel, but in the coming days, years maybe, I think this area is gonna be one of the first areas to be settled. There's prime farm country, plenty of water, and lots of wide open spaces. If you and your missus were to start out here, I think you'd kinda have the market cornered concerning churches. What do you think?"

"My, the way you tell it, it does sound promising!" replied the Preacher.

"Yeah, the Captain here is a pretty good salesman. But the rest of us are in agreement with the Captain. We could certainly use a good influence among us, and we would make sure you never lacked for provisions, too," enthusiastically exclaimed the Lieutenant as he nodded his head hopefully.

While this conversation continued, Jeremiah noticed Charlie had slipped away from the group. Looking for her he noticed she was standing near the edge of the trees looking out on their back trail. He also noticed she kept herself obscured from view of anyone beyond the trees as she stood half in the shadow of the big tree.

With shaded eyes she was scanning the horizon to the East across the river when Jeremiah approached behind her. He spoke softly to warn her of his approach and she quickly dropped her hand and turned toward him. "What are you doin' sneakin' up on me? Ya practicing your Indian stalking or something?" she gasped querulously.

He noticed she was somewhat jittery as she turned and tucked her hands in her pockets but Jeremiah noticed a little shake of her hand before it disappeared into her trousers. "No, I was just checkin' on everybody. Don't want to go swimmin' again for no reason. One bath ever so often is enough. You okay or are you expectin' some company?"

She dropped her head and started to move past him as she said, "No, just lookin' that's all." Then she walked to the grassy knoll where the animals had been tethered. With so many animals, they had to be moved often to ensure plenty of graze. Jeremiah returned to the gathering at the fire ring.

"Well, Captain, you've certainly given us some food for thought. First, my wife and I will need to make it a matter of prayer, and then we'll have to talk it out. Since we're going to be camped here another night, would it be all right if we let you know in the morning?" asked the Preacher with an expectant look.

"Of course, you don't owe us anything. And we'd completely understand if you want to continue on with these fine folks. So whatever you say will be fine with us."

"I'm sure it would be all right with the rest of these fine folks if you and your men would join us for supper, Captain. And I'll fix some of my famous biscuits for you," shared Sally. Her invitation was met with smiles all around, especially from the men in blue.

"Why yes, Captain, it would be our pleasure to have you join us. We still have a good portion of that venison left and I think you'd probably enjoy what we have to offer," added Carrie MacGregor.

"Well, ladies, that's asking quite a lot to add six hungry men to the tally for a meal. But I'm sure I will get no argument from the men as to their willingness to partake," answered the Captain.

Jeremiah motioned to Scratch to join him on the trail that led deeper into the small copse of woods. As he was joined by his partner, he said, "I noticed Charlie has been watchin' our back trail pretty often and I think she might be afraid of something or someone followin', so I think we need to keep an eye on both her and the trail."

Scratch replied, "Yup. I noticed it too. Mebbe she left sumpin' behind she shouldn't had oughta or could be some varmint's after her. It'll take bof of us ta keep an eye on that'n."

"I wanted you to know. I figured you had noticed but just in case, it's best we both keep an eye on the situation. Can't be too careful. Also, I'm gonna take the young'un and see if we can't add to the larder with some more meat. We won't go far, just headin' out to that patch of woods over yonder. I figure if we don't get somethin' now, them women'll feed everything we got left to those soldier boys. You know women and uniforms."

Scratch nodded his wooly head in agreement as Jeremiah turned to fetch Caleb. The two started out afoot with their goal the line of trees about two hundred yards distant. As they entered the darker grove of trees, Jeremiah asked Caleb, "Are you all loaded and primed?"

"Yes sir. I cleaned and reloaded after the rain last night. And it's all set," he whispered his response.

"All right, you walk out ahead of me, watch your step as I showed you cause ya don't wanna snap a twig and warn anything we're here, and if you see somethin', freeze and prepare your shot."

Caleb nodded in agreement and started his stealthy walk, always putting the ball of his foot down first then the heel and making certain there was nothing to give them away. After about twenty minutes of walking into the woods, he thought he heard a slight sound and froze. He scanned the forest before him looking for any movement. A squirrel chattered and scampered up the tree and turned to watch the intruders.

Without moving anything but his eyes, Caleb continued his survey. The squirrel lost interest and sought refuge in another tree with a noiseless flight from limb to limb. Then Caleb noticed another movement. He still had not moved even a finger and slowly examined the area for more activity, then he saw the flick of an ear. Almost in slow motion, a grey tan patch of fur revealed a young buck stepping into a slight clearing between trees. When the buck dropped his head to mouth a snack of grass, Caleb leaned against a nearby tree and cocked the hammer of his rifle as quietly as possible.

Up came the buck's head at the sound of the cock. He searched the trees for an intruder and turned his head around away from the hunters and tensed to flee, but a high pitched squeal followed by a slight grunt caused the buck to freeze. It was the sound of a doe deer on the hunt. He searched the trees to find the source of the call, but with no movement to give them away, the buck took another step further for another bite of grass. The crack of the rifle and the belch of white smoke startled even Jeremiah, but the messenger of death sent by the young hunter hit its mark in the deer's neck and the buck dropped without another step.

Jeremiah stood amazed. The maturity shown by the boy to remain motionless and then to call the buck to stand still had astounded Jeremiah. And the shot the boy made was exceptional. He could not be more proud of the boy. "You did fine, boy! That was . . . well, that was great. I never heard anything like that, except of course from a deer itself, and then to do it at the right time to stop that buck. Wow, I know a lot of men that couldn't do that and couldn't make that shot either!"

Caleb didn't know if he was happier with the praise or happier with his first deer. It made him feel like a real mountain man, and he was thrilled.

To The Tall Timber

Chapter Twenty: Company

RESUMING THEIR ROUTINE of an early start, the nomadic group broke camp before full light. The order of travel had the Farmer wagon taking the lead followed closely by the MacGregor's but today saw the caravan shortened by one wagon. Before the excursion began the entire group assembled beside the McCormick wagon to bid their good-byes. Though the acquaintance had been brief, the connection was strong, especially between the ladies as tears streamed down their cheeks.

With a tight hug between the two, an arm-length embrace shared assurances of a hopeful future. Michael McCormick shared with the group, "When we first planned our mission trip, we hoped we would be able to join the Merrills at Fontenelle's post, as we had corresponded with them. However, with Mr. Merrill's passing, the Lord closed that door, but it seems He has opened a new door for us here with the Sauk and Fox tribes.

I would ask that you folks keep us in your prayers and write us, in care of the Agency, and let us know how everyone fared. We will also remember to pray for your safe journey."

The parting of the men was less emotional as they shared handshakes, waves or a nod of the head.

With another wave over their shoulders the remainder of the number of adventurers lessened by two. Scratch had said his good bye the night before and had already departed for the day's scout into the distant territory. His preliminary short scouts had given direction based on the counsel of Captain Allen. He had advised them to follow the valley that stretched somewhat south and west, continuing between the bluffs toward the far hills. The route would be the easiest but it would also be a steady though gradual climb. The head of the valley would lift them towards a wide plateau that extended upwards to the sage covered hills and eventually down the other side to drop into the watershed of the great Missouri river.

It started out as one of those lazy days when the sun shines bright, the light breeze lifts the spirits, and the ride is easy. Scratch stayed in the middle of the valley as the terrain allowed and his horse parted the tall Indian grass that reached to the cantle of his saddle. When he walked his mount away from the grass to the edge of the valley seeking an occasional patch of shade, the mountain man's ever observing eyes continued to survey the countryside, never missing a movement or flash of color.

He watched as a scrawny coyote pursued a cottontail with a determined pace and a mouth with a tongue lolling to the side as he anticipated a tasty dinner. In the distance, he heard the gobble of the flock of turkeys taking their morning stroll to the small stream in the bottom of the valley. As he worked his way along the tree-line at the edge of the flats he watched the sky for hawks and occasional smaller birds like woodcocks and camp robbers.

It was a land of plenty. Game was abundant, edible plants were prolific and the soil was good. Scratch pondered the view and imagined the many settlers that would soon find this country and in his thinking, spoil a perfectly good part of God's creation with their houses and barns and plows that would tear up the ground.

The growling from just above the drawstring that held his britches in place reminded him it was time to take a break and feed his face. Selecting a broad, spreading old oak that sat back from the small spring-fed stream and bordered a good patch of grass, he dismounted, loosened the cinch on his mount and ground-tied sorrel where he could reach his lunch of grass and the fresh sprouting buds of other spring growth.

Scratch dug a handful of jerky from his saddlebags, his leather covered water bottle and made it to the shade under the tall oak. He dozed for a while and was stirred by a change in the breeze, or was it the smell? Peering from slightly opened eyes, nothing seemed amiss. His horse was peacefully grazing with no sign of alarm, no unusual sound was evident, but a mild musky odor drifted on the west to east breeze.

His Hawken by his side, Scratch slowly rose to his feet and stepped from the shade of the oak to survey the valley. To the west of him about two hundred yards, a small herd of buffalo had walked into the tall grass to make their way to a small pond formed by the low contour of land and fed by the creek. *Buffalo! No wonder my belly was growlin'. It musta knowd there was Buffler around. Won't the folks be surprised to have some fresh Buffler steaks for supper!*

Scratch started his stealth approach within the shadows of the tree line. He made his way to a tree at the edge, within a hundred yards of the buffalo. He watched the herd and looked for a cow without a calf. Of the dozen in the herd, he finally spotted a sizable cow that grazed by itself and without a calf. He watched carefully to be certain the other cows and calves matched up as pairs and satisfied, raised his rifle to take his shot.

With careful aim, lining up the front blade between the buckhorn sight at the rear, he squeezed off the kill shot. When the white smoke cloud dissipated, the cow was down and the rest of the herd hadn't moved more than a few yards away.

Returning to retrieve his mount, he climbed aboard and made his way to the downed cow. Charging directly at the herd and waving his arms and yelling his loudest, the herd finally dispersed and left the downed animal to Scratch. He dismounted and started the butchering by opening the gullet and reaching in for a slice of fresh bloody liver to satiate his hunger.

* * * * *

JEREMIAH RODE SIDE by side with Charlie as each held a lead-rope for the pack mules. Caleb was doing a "scout" by leading the way about thirty yards ahead and staying within sight of his uncle. The two wagons trailed a short distance behind with Carrie and the kids walking alongside the larger of the two wagons. The Farmer wagon had Gabriel on the seat and handling the team while his father walked with one hand resting on the sideboard.

Jeremiah occasionally looked back to ensure everything was in order. He caught Charlie turning around in her saddle to again survey the back trail. He considered asking her directly about her apparent fear, but hesitated and thought *Maybe a better time or opportunity will come along.*

A slight rise in the trail enabled a better view of the eastern horizon and Charlie made the excuse of stretching her legs and pulled to the side and the higher point of the hill. Jeremiah waved her off and continued along the trail knowing she could easily overtake them. Within a quarter hour, he heard the trotting pace of horse and mule as she pulled alongside him without comment.

Travel continued with little more than small talk and observations of the trail until the approach of dusk that was signaled by the diminishing light and lengthening shadows. With a cough and a "Harummph" Jeremiah turned sideways in the saddle to face Charlie and started, "Charlie, I don't know what's bothering you, but anybody can see you're jumpier than a kid sittin' on an anthill. Now, normally, I wouldn't be askin' but there's too many folks here that could be caught in the middle of whatever it is that's ailin' you. So, I think it's only right that you let me in on the secret and maybe I can help you with it. My momma used to always say, a burden shared is easier on both. So, what's up?"

She dropped her head and stared at her hands resting on the saddle horn. The horses continued thier easy rocking gait following the trail of Scratch through the parted grasses. The silence stretched then she raised her head skyward and turned to Jeremiah. "Look, you seem like a nice guy. Everybody on this trip has been great, but this is my problem. There's nothing you can do, really!"

"Charlie, we haven't known each other very long, but out here . . ." he motioned with a broad sweep of his arm, ". . .we get acquainted a little quicker than most folks. And it doesn't make any difference what the problem is, we are all part of this "sorta" family and we help each other, no matter what. Now, if the MacGregors back there had a problem like getting' stuck or losin' one of them kids, you'd help 'em out, wouldn't ya?"

"Yes, of course, but that's different."

"No it ain't. You've got a problem, so we help you out. Next time, you help us out. That's the way it works out here. That's the only way anybody's gonna make it," he explained. He watched her expressions and waited for her response.

She sighed deeply and turned to Jeremiah, "There's this man . . ."

Jeremiah interrupted with, "I kinda had that much figgered out." Then smiling at her to help her relax, he motioned with his hand for her to continue.

"He's been chasin' after me since St. Louis. I thought I'd escaped him when I took the riverboat up the Mississippi, but then I saw him and his henchmen on the shoreline before we made the stop at Rock Island. When I got off there and switched to horseback, I was pretty sure I made it away, but I've got this nagging feeling he's still on my trail."

"Why's he chasin' you?"

"He took a shinin' to me when I was singin' in the dance hall in St. Louis. He thought I should be his girl and I wasn't havin' any of it. But he wouldn't give up. He followed me to my room one night and tried to force his way in but the bouncer had spotted him and threw him out. Jacques killed him for that. That's the kind of man he is- if he doesn't get his way he'll kill anybody that interferes. So you see, it's not the kind of problem you want to get involved in."

"How many does he have with him," inquired Jeremiah.

"Usually, just two, but they're just as bad as he is. That's all I saw him with before Rock Island."

The two wagons formed a sort of circle with the tree-line as the third side of the protective arrangement. The center of the triangle or circle held the cook fire used for the evening meal of Scratch's buffalo steaks. With the camp chores completed, several were seated on the stones and logs arranged around the fire. The bedrolls of Scratch, Jeremiah, Caleb and Charlie had been arranged on the tree-line side while the others had placed their sleeping rolls near or in the wagons.

Jeremiah had wasted little time informing the remaining members of the troupe of the problem facing Charlie and subsequently the entire crowd. Preliminary plans had been made and now, as they pondered the future travels and potential challenges, discussion centered on the next day's plans. Although all were aware of the possibility of visitors, most were startled when out of the black a loud voice sounded with the familiar greeting of "Hello the camp. We're friendly, may we approach?"

With a quick glance around, Jeremiah responded with, "Keep your hands high and come in real slow."

Two men approached, the first of average height and well-attired for the frontier. He wore a black flat-brimmed hat over black slightly curly hair that framed a light complexioned face sporting a pencil thin black mustache. High cheek bones and a sharp angled jaw accented his well-dressed outfit including a black, long-tailed jacket over a silver brocade waistcoat topping a tailored pair of black trousers.

His appearance was as foreign to the country setting as an elegant lady in a pigsty, yet he reminded Jeremiah of a weasel. His companion was larger in every aspect but as impeccably attired as the first man was, he was slovenly in both attitude and attire. Emitting the stench of a dead carcass, the expressions of those gathered around the fire reflected their revulsion.

"Pardon me messieurs and madam, we regret the intrusion, but we have traveled far to find the one we seek," stated the weasel.

"There ain't nobody here that you want," responded Jeremiah, noting the absence of the third member of their group.

"Ah, but my friend, we have followed her all the way from St. Louis, and we know she is among you, although I do not see her at present. Her name is Charlotte, but perhaps you know her as Charlie," he said with a widening grin on his face. He began to drop his arms.

"Just keep your hands high," warned Jeremiah, "and stand where you are. Even if we had the person you speak of, there's not one chance in a hundred that we would let the likes of you take her. My momma always said don't trust snakes, no matter what they look like or what they sound like. Just 'cause they don't sound with a rattle, don't mean their bite ain't just as poisonous."

"Surely you are not comparing me to a snake, monsieur?

"I don't know you well enough to think anything pleasant about you, now do I?" commented Jeremiah as he noticed the bigger man side-stepping closer to the Farmer wagon. "And you, big boy, nobody invited you to move either!" he raised his voice.

Ian MacGregor was standing by the seat of his wagon and now began to move closer to the larger intruder, watching him closely but trying to appear nonchalant. While all the attention was focused on the two visitors, no one seemed to notice the third man that circled the camp and approached from behind the MacGregor wagon.

When Ian moved away, the intruder stepped from behind the wagon holding Carrie MacGregor in front of him with one arm around her waist and the other holding a knife to her throat. The slight scuffle drew everyone's attention and Ian started to run to his wife's aid but was stopped mid-stride with a warning from the Frenchman, "No, no! That would be foolish wouldn't it? You cannot reach him before he would slit her throat," then turning to the rest of those gathered around the fire said, "Everybody stand up and step apart." Everyone did as commanded, carefully watching the three invaders.

"Now, if you would be so kind as to summon Charlotte, we will take our prize and leave you fine people."

Jeremiah watched as the one holding Carrie slowly stepped closer and stood in front of the MacGregor wagon. Then, looking at the other two opposite the fire that had dropped their hands and now held pistols on their captives, he called out, "Charlie, your friends have invited you to join them. Come on out."

The simultaneous explosions from the edge of the trees made almost identical blossoms of red on the chests of the two men opposite the fire and filled the edge of the circle with clouds of white smoke. The unexpected roar temporarily froze the third interloper giving Jeremiah enough time to launch his blood-letting Bowie knife into the neck of the man standing slightly beside and behind Carrie MacGregor.

The razor sharp broad blade almost decapitated the man and severed his spine at the back of his throat rendering him unable to do anything but drop to the ground as his blood began to pool around him. Carrie had gasped in alarm but realizing she had been freed, she ran to her husband who was standing over the corpse of the bigger of the three interlopers and spat in his face. He turned to catch his beloved bride and wrapped her in his protective bear hug.

The entire affair was over in minutes, and as Scratch and Charlie stepped through the remnants of the smoke cloud, his smile of confidence was overshadowed by the look of relief that painted her face.

"Wow, Uncle Jeremiah, that was sumpin'! Course, I wasn't scared or nuthin' cuz I knew you and Scratch would take care of everything, and I was protecting the girls here, but that was sumpin'!" said an exuberant Caleb as he joined the circle of friends.

"And here I thought we was gonna get to sleep early tonite," grumbled Scratch, "but now we gotta git these varmints planted fore they attract ever wolf and coyote in the country. "

"It's gaein be awricht ance the pain has gane awa," said Ian, "Ah dinnae ken bout othern, but Ah be doin the task."

Carrie smiled and said, "He said it's going to be all right once they're buried and gone, and he'll be doing the digging. So Scratch, he's said you've done your bit and now it's his turn."

"Well, he'll sure get no argument from me 'bout that. But, I can't turn in yet cuz one of them varmints is layin' on my bedroll."

All the men joined in the gruesome task and the three graves well apart from the campsite were soon occupied by the would-be kidnappers. No remarks were made over the three as no one felt anything but relief, most of all, Charlie.

She spoke to the group as she said, "Folks, I am so grateful to all of you and I ask your forgiveness for having brought this upon you. I am so thankful no one was hurt and I promise I will spend the rest of the journey trying to make it up to you." With many hugs and smiles, the group expressed their appreciation for her and all were ready to call it a night.

To The Tall Timber

Chapter Twenty-One: Progress

WITHOUT A GIVEN TRAIL to follow, the progress often seemed furtive and challenging. The previous two days had been a continuous, though gradual climb to their distant goal of the hills that were on the Western horizon.

Although Scratch and Jeremiah scouted out the trail beforehand, the route necessary for the wagons required somewhat circuitous travel from clearing to meadow between the fingers of the forests that continually sought to detour the vagabonds. Once the plateau had been crested, the group chose to rest the remaining day to give the horses and travelers a rest break.

Axels were greased, harnesses mended, and every possible weak point on the wagons was inspected and often oiled or cleaned or repaired. All the animals were inspected for sores or wounds and treated accordingly. It was even necessary for the travelers to inspect their own paraphernalia and mend clothing and footgear. The respite was necessary and appreciated by each one, animal and man alike. The women spent their time mending clothes and preparing meals that would last more than one feeding.

143

Once they left the plateau at the foot of the rolling hills, their chosen trail was a slow downgrade but held considerable challenges with the many south-westerly bound streams. Often it seemed the travel was up a hill, down a hill, cross a stream and repeat. Yet the progress was evident with the changing scenery and an occasional glimpse of the distant Missouri River valley encouraged the travelers.

They looked forward to replenishing their supplies from the trading post Scratch told them was by the riverside. However, what Scratch remembered was the small post Jeremiah and he had visited when they traveled from Fort Union to St. Louis. What Scratch didn't know was there were additional posts established since their last visit.

As the group of travelers dropped from the last rolling hill there was one more river to cross before they would reach the shores of the mighty Missouri. By now they were old hands at crossing streams with the two wagons. The four-up hitch of the MacGregor's led the way and easily crossed the rather shallow stream. The opposing riverbank was an easy pull from the water and the team rested in the tall green grass.

The two draft horses of the Farmer's easily navigated the slow- moving muddy water and soon joined the MacGregor's for a short rest as they awaited the two buck-skinners and their accompanying duo of Charlie and Caleb. Jeremiah led the way to a squat log cabin nestled under the towering maple trees near the riverbank. A rough-hewn board sign announced the "Farris Farry, saf river crosin"

Jeremiah mumbled to himself, *I hope his ferry is better than his sign.* He negotiated passage for the group and paid the ferryman to make the necessary two trips to accommodate all the travelers. Once unloaded from the ferry, they located a campsite near the tree line of the many leafy hardwoods that lined the shore and spread out toward the open plain.

Upstream from the ferry landing, a side -heeler river boat was tied off and the crew was busy unloading several crates and boxes of cargo. Three other men were busy loading the cargo onto a waiting wagon and made several trips to the two log structures that contained the Fontenelle trading post. With other cabins nearby, the post had originally been a fur company trading post with the Missouri Fur Company then sold to the American Fur Company and operated by Lucien Fontenelle.

Fontenelle later sold it to the U.S. Government and it was now used as a base for the Missouri River Indian Agency as well as a trading post. It was not uncommon to see members of the Otoe, Pawnee, Omaha and Pottawatomie all trading with the post. This was the post that was used by the Merrill's, Baptist missionaries that had communicated with the McCormick's.

With a few hours of daylight left, Jeremiah suggested to the group that if any supplies were to be obtained, now would be an opportune time. He and Scratch also headed to the post to resupply and for Jeremiah to fill his list of trade goods for the Arapaho. Carrie MacGregor stayed with the wagons and her girls begged Caleb to stay with them. He begrudgingly conceded to their request and watched as the rest of the group made for the post.

Entering the dimly lit building, Jeremiah and Scratch noted most of the product stacked around the post were goods that appealed to the many Indians that traded there, but behind the counter and on the shelves were many goods sought by travelers that frequented the post.

Jeremiah began a stack of items he sought for Laughing Waters and her people. Bolts of cloth, beads and buttons, trade knives and metal tomahawks, blankets, and assorted gee-gaws of bright colors and sounds that appealed to the women for their festive attire built the stack to considerable proportions.

He stepped to the counter to look over the rifles and pistols on display and gaining the clerk's attention, he selected two Kentucky style flint-lock rifles.

"Now, what in tarnation are ye gittin' them fer? Ya already got a pair o' Hawkens," asked Scratch.

145

"They're gonna be part of the price for Laughing Waters. I'm gonna give 'em to Black Kettle to convince him to let me 'n Waters to get hitched," replied Jeremiah.

Scratch was momentarily speechless. He knew that Jeremiah and Waters were sweet on each other and he thought the two would eventually get together, but he had not expected Jeremiah to be so determined and settled on the idea. "Well, I'll be hornswaggled! I shore didn't know you was so set on the idea."

"Yup. Been thinkin' 'bout it ever since you 'n me joined up back at Fort Union. Done decided that as soon as I get back to the Wind River I'm gonna get hitched up proper."

Ian MacGregor had assembled a considerable stack of his own with a large bag of beans, another bag of flour, salt, some salt pork and other sundry items. Joining Scratch and Jeremiah by the counter he asked Scratch, "Ah dinnae ken whit's fur gud gear, kin ye hep?" and he pointed to the rifles in the rack on the wall.

Scratch followed his gaze and knew he wanted help in choosing a proper rifle. Scratch leaned on the counter and looked over the weapons, noted a new Hawken at the end of the rack and pointed it out to Ian. Both men motioned the clerk over and with a little dickering, the rifle and necessary accouterments were secured for the big Scotsman. As the men were settling their accounts with the clerk, the man behind the counter asked, "Are you fellas with that wagon train over in the flat, yonder?"

Jeremiah looked at Scratch and Scratch turned to answer the clerk's question, "No, didn't know there was a wagon train over yonder. How long's it been there?"

"They come in a couple days ago from down St. Louis way. At least some of 'em are from there, don't know 'bout the others. They're headin' West. Way I hear it, they's some o' the first. 'fore long, it's gonna git plumb populated out there."

Without further conversation but plenty of thought, the men gathered up their supplies and started out the door.

146

Jeremiah made several trips and stacked his purchases at the side of the building intending to go to camp and bring back a pack animal for the gear. On his last trip out of the post he almost ran over a man approaching the doorway. With both men stepping aside and offering their "Scuse me friend..." Jeremiah dropped his last load atop the stack. The man he bumped into had turned to watch the buckskin clad mountain man deliver his goods to the mountain of plunder by the building.

"Say, are you with those two wagons camped over there by those trees yonder?" asked the stranger. He was attired in canvas trousers and a Lindsey Woolsey shirt with a floppy felt hat holding down dark tousled hair streaked with grey. A sun darkened complexion did little to hide the wrinkles that betrayed hard days in the sun, probably behind a plow. His britches hung from broad suspenders under which he had hooked his thumbs as he looked over the remaining pair of men. Ian and the Farmers were already on their way to their wagons to bring their horses back to haul their plunder. As Jeremiah straightened up and turned to look over the stranger, he responded, "Yes, we are, and who might you be?"

"I'm Bart Barham, I'm with the wagon train that's camped down in the draw yonder. Are you folks headed West?"

"Pleased to make your acquaintance, Mr. Barham. Yes, we are headed West. I'm guessing that's where you folks are going as well?" he questioned.

"Well, that's the idea. But, the guide we had took ill and didn't make it. Now we're tryin' to figger out what to do next. Ain't none of us been out West, but we're all anxious to get movin' as time is not on our side."

"So, this 'Out West' that you're headin' for, just what are you lookin' for and would you know it if you found it?" asked Scratch.

With a deep throated chuckle, the flatlander responded, "Yessir, and what we're lookin' for is good land to settle in and make our homes. We heard there's lots of good land out there just for the claimin' and most of us have been dreamin' and hopin' for somethin' like that just about all our lives. Would you folks have a guide or somebody that knows where they're goin' or could help us find somebody?"

Scratch looked at Jeremiah and Jeremiah looked at the ground. Scratch shook his head and muttered something about pilgrims and turned away from the men to scuff his moccasins in the dirt and stomp around muttering and scratching his beard. Jeremiah stood watching his partner and chuckled as he knew what was coming.

Scratch didn't want anybody else cluttering up his beloved mountains, but he also didn't know how to say no to someone in need. If they didn't help the stranded train, they would probably start off on their own and the whole train would end up decorating the plains with their bones and broken wagons and scattered furniture.

He turned back to the inquiring farmer and said, "We'll think 'bout it. Let me 'n my partner talk to the rest 'o them folks and we'll let you know." Without any additional comment, he turned and stomped off toward the wagons and with a turn of his head toward Jeremiah said, "I'll bring the mules back. You jest wait right there, young'un."

B.N. Rundell

Chapter Twenty-Two: Train

IT WAS NOT THE REACTION Scratch expected or even wanted. Secretly he hoped the group of familiar travelers that had shared their lives for the past couple of weeks would not want any company and would be happy to continue their travels as before. However, the thought of company and the greater number of travelers that would afford better protection in Indian territory was met with positive responses from the entire group. Again Scratch walked away from the group scuffing the toes of his moccasins in the dirt and mumbling in his beard. Jeremiah closely followed him into the trees for a partner-to-partner palaver.

"Didn't you say that you had scouted for a wagon train across this country before?" asked Jeremiah.

"Yeah, I did," curtly responded Scratch.

"So, what's the problem? We're going that way anyway, and it's obvious these folks need the help, and I know you can't say no, so, what's the hold-up?"

"It's just . . . I don't know. I ain't real fond of the idée of all these pilgrims civilizin' the country. They shoulda stayed home and leave well 'nuff alone."

149

"Everybody else is in favor of the joinin' up, so maybe we oughta at least go talk to those folks, whatcha think?" probed Jeremiah looking at his partner as he leaned against the trunk of a large Maple with one leg crossed over the other and his hand on his hip. He was looking into the deeper part of the woods but had a glazed look in his eyes.

"Yeah, probly, but I'm just not real shore I wanna see a bunch of graves scattered all over the prairie."

As the two mountain men strolled into the camp of the larger wagon train, they were warmly greeted by the man they met earlier in the trading post. He walked up to them with his hand outstretched and a broad smile spreading across his weathered face. "Welcome, welcome friends," and turning to the other travelers he said, "These are the men I was telling you about."

Looking back to the two he motioned them toward the larger fire in the middle of the scattered group of wagons and said, "Take a seat, men. Would you like some coffee?" Both men nodded in the affirmative and took a seat on a large log lying back from the fire.

As he poured the coffee, several of the families drifted towards the fire to meet the newcomers. Bart turned to a short, buxom woman standing behind him and introduced her, "This is my wife, Kimberly, and my son Douglas," and looking up at the semi-circle of folks that were now eyeing the strangers, he began to introduce those nearest to the duo.

"I know you won't remember all the names so I'll just shorten it for you, for now." Motioning to the nearest couple he said, "This here's Slim and his wife Maggie, next is Mac and Mabel, then there is Benjamin and Eleanor, Johnathan and Gertie, and that there's Roscoe and his man Freddie, and the rest we'll get to later. These folks have been with the train since we started out. We've got a total of ten families, eleven wagons. Mr. Boggs, Roscoe, has two wagons as he's gonna be settin' up a tradin' post."

As the crowd searched the faces of the visitors, Jeremiah and Scratch had been looking over each couple as they were introduced. All seemed to be of hardy stock, with certain exceptions, but first impressions were not always accurate. Those that seemed to be able to face the hardships and challenges would quite often be the first to buckle under and others that didn't appear to be able to wade across a creek without drowning would become the cornerstones of the group. With a quick glance at Jeremiah and a deep sigh, Scratch stood to his feet.

"Now folks, I'll be honest widcha. When Bart there first told us of yore predickyment, I weren't too happy to hear 'bout it. I've often said, pilgrims should stay where pilgrims belong and stay the blazes outta my mountains. How-som-ever, I know you folks is bound an' determined to make yoursefs a new life out yonder and I cain't be arguin' with that. But the trip ahead ain't gonna be easy. I've been 'crost this way afore and there's plenty of things that will fight you all the way.

Injins, buffler, grizz, heat, storms, wind like you ain't never felt afore, and countless other things. You'll be lucky if more'n half of ya make it, some of you will be buried out there without yore hair cuz some injun will be usin' it to decorate his lodge. Others will wanna turn around or stop where they is, but who knows what's gonna happen?

I've talked it over with those we been travelin' with, and we didn't start out with them neither, but they's willin' to join up, if'n you want to, and me'n Jeremiah here will do our best to git as many of you 'crost this hyar prairie and to the Shinin' mountains or someplace tween here an' there, if'n you want." Drawing a deep breath, he dropped to the log and looked back at the faces that appeared to be full of questions.

Jeremiah looked at his partner and said, "That's more talkin' than I've heard you say all the time I've known you," and stretched his arm around his partner's shoulder. As they looked back at the crowd, one man spoke up and said, "Wal, he said what I wanted to hear. He's been there and knows the way. That's good 'nough for me."

Several nodded their heads and spoke softly to one another, then the one named Mac spoke out with a rather high voice. Addressing himself to Scratch he asked, "How do we know we can trust you, that you won't just take off and leave us stranded or something?"

Jeremiah stood and with a hand toward Scratch bid him stay seated, then turning to the belligerent-looking inquirer said, "Your man asked us, we didn't go looking for you. We are willing to help and we're not asking anything of you, but I *will* educate you on the manners of the wilderness. You *never* ask a question or make a comment like that unless you're ready to die. Those kind of remarks are never acceptable out here. There is no law, no government, no one to appeal to except those with you and who have proven their character. What a man was or believes is his own business. Out here in the wilderness, we can only depend on one another and anyone that undermines that trust will eventually pay the ultimate price."

The crowd had grown silent and still. It was obvious that most did not agree with the man that asked the question and all were moved by the education provided to the belligerent bully. Farmer Bart stepped forward and told the folks to talk it over and let him know what their decision was when they returned.

Turning to Jeremiah and Scratch he invited them to join him as they did a walking inspection of the wagons and their camp. As the trio walked about camp, the two mountain men noted the condition of the wagons, harness, and livestock. Like most personal possessions, the condition of the equipment and the animals revealed much about the owner's character.

Returning to the campfire, the crowd remained and their faces appeared hopeful and happy as they greeted the men again. The tall skinny man appropriately called Slim stepped from the group and told Bart, "We all agreed, Bart. We would like Mr. Scratch and Mr. Jeremiah to take over guidin' for us, if'n it's still all right with them, of course."

Bart looked back at Scratch with a questioning look and sought his answer. Scratch nodded his head and reached up to scratch the whiskers in front of his ear, then said, "Folks, we'll head out first thing in the mornin' and first thing means when ol sol (referring to the sun) peeks over the eastern horizon, it'll be shinin' on our backsides on the trail.

Also, there'll be things we'll be tellin' you as we go along that'll be fer yore own good an' we'll 'spect ya to abide by 'em. Now, one thing ya need ta do before ya start out in the mornin' and that is ta sling some canvas or material of some sort under yore wagon like a hammock. That'll be fore buffler chips. You'll be pickin' 'em up as we go, cuz there won't be a whole heap of firewood out there. So, till tomorry, me'n Jeremiah here's gonna go git ready to leave our ownselves."

As the group dispersed, the chatter was full of excitement and expectation as the train now resumed the journey to fulfill their dreams.

To The Tall Timber

Chapter Twenty- Three: Platte

BECAUSE OF HIS EXPERIENCE in the area, his knowledge of the territory and the trails, Scratch naturally gravitated into the leadership role as wagon-master. But he was reluctant to give up his role as scout and chose to lead the first day from his position in the distant front. Jeremiah called for the wagons to line up with the MacGregor wagon in the lead followed by the Farmers. He explained to the rest the order of wagons and the daily rotation giving each an opportunity to be in the lead. As Scratch had foretold, the wagons stretched out on the riverside trail as the sun threw its first brilliant rays of the day over the Eastern horizon.

Remembering the large Northern loop of the Platte river, Scratch had determined to save a couple of day's travel by heading due west from the confluence of the Platte and the Missouri Rivers. This plan was hindered by the north to south bearing taken by the river as soon as they were inland from the Missouri basin.

Scratch was scouting the river for the first possible crossing. Knowing the reputation of the Platte as "too thin to plow and too thick to drink" and that it was wider than it had to be and shallower than it should be, the first crossing would be a challenge to the wagons. He realized the river would be deeper at the confluence than anywhere upstream, he also knew there was a greater chance of a more solid bottom to the river with the silt washing on into the Missouri.

Just over two miles from the start, Scratch saw what he was looking for and moved down the riverbank to survey the possible crossing. Consistent with the proliferation of shale stone in the area, the crossing revealed a considerable portion of hard sandstone shale covering the bottom. Though the water was far from clear, he could make out that the crossing was mostly rock with a stretch of sandy silt near the far bank. He decided to make the crossing himself to ensure it would be possible for the wagons to make it safely over. His efforts were rewarded with an easy ride where the only challenge was the silt near the far bank, but it was not difficult for his horse to wade through. Returning to the northeastern shore, he waited for the wagons to arrive.

Scratch instructed Ian MacGregor and Jeremiah as to the chosen path and order for the wagons. He cautioned Jeremiah to be certain the last of the wagons continued to edge upstream as they crossed, so the silt on the far side would not bog them down after so many others would tear it up. Then mounting up, Scratch led the way and encouraged Ian to follow directly in his path. Ian's wagon was the only four-up hitch as the others were rigged similar to the Farmer's with only two draft horses to do the work.

None of the teams were as large as those used by the McCormicks with the matched Percherons, but all came from sturdy farm stock and appeared strong enough for the task ahead. The crossing went off without a hitch much to the relief of the two mountain men, especially Jeremiah. The younger buck-skinner didn't know what to expect as his book of experience with wagon crossings was being written on the fly.

With the crossing made, Scratch switched off with Jeremiah to let the trio of Jeremiah, Caleb and Charlie take the lead on the scout and hunting expedition. They were happy to take on the assigned task and resume that portion of the journey more suited to their interests. Scratch had explained this would be the most challenging part of the trail with the rolling hills, many ravines, and thick forested areas. There was a trail in the direction they were going, but it was more suited for pack trains than wagons. Although they were not the first to travel this way with wagons, the trail ahead would still be a challenge.

The scouts followed the trail as it wound around the shoulder outcroppings of the hills and traversed the easier paths of travel between the forested areas and the steeper hillsides. Always vigilant for game, Charlie was the first to spot a group of deer watering in the shallow ravine below the trail. They stopped the horses and Charlie led the way to a small group of boulders that shielded them from view of the animals.

Jeremiah let Caleb line up his shot and allowed Charlie and the boy to bag the day's initial take of game. They quickly field-dressed the two deer, dragged the carcasses to the edge of the trees and hoisted them high off the ground- yet in an area of shade. Returning to the trail they made a small cairn of stones beside the trail with a green sprig pointing to the hoisted game.

Mid-afternoon found the scouts searching the area for a campsite for the wagons. With the larger group, the task was more difficult what with the rolling hills and thicker wooded areas but finally, a reasonably level area along the tree-line was deemed suitable. There was no source of water nearby, but every wagon carried a barrel of water and one night without fresh water would not be a hardship. Making their separate camp just inside the trees, each one set about their assigned duties from unpacking the pack animals to setting up the camp fire with freshly gathered wood and rolling out the bedrolls.

"We're gonna need to teach these pilgrims about smoking some meat, so you two see if you can gather up a bunch of those skinny green sprigs over yonder so we can make up a smokin' rack," directed Jeremiah.

He was busy checking the many panniers and packs that now held his newly purchased goods marked for the Arapaho. After the first day's travel, much is revealed as to the sturdiness of the packs and the necessity to adjust the gear in the panniers of each of the pack animals. When Charlie and Caleb returned with arms loaded with the long sprigs of the young saplings, they set about cutting and assembling a smoking rack for the curing of the fresh meat and making jerky.

Still waiting for the wagons, Jeremiah had the two join him for a trek through the woods to search for berries for pemmican. A short walk yielded choke cherries, currants, and rose hips. Jeremiah explained to Caleb and Charlie how the pemmican was made, "So ya see, we'll have to dry these berries out before we can use 'em for the pemmican. But we'll keep our eyes open for more berries every chance we get." Caleb was interested and excited about making food like the Indians, but Charlie had a pessimistic look that showed her inherent skepticism.

With the arrival of the wagons, Scratch directed them to form a circle with the tongue of the following wagon to be placed beneath the preceding wagon, with the exception of the next day's lead wagon which was directed to point the tongue in the expected direction of the morrow's travel. He instructed each family to either tether their horses to the nearby trees or to hobble them on the uphill side of the circle.

He made sure there was ample grass for the large number of livestock and also told them to be certain their animals were well watered. With relief on his face, the mountain man joined his companions at their camp within the trees and dropping to the ground, asked Caleb to take care of his horse for him as he stretched his frame with feet to the campfire.

"I'll tell you what, Jeremiah, them pilgrims seem to be plumb stupid! I don't think that other guide they had told them nothin' 'bout nothin'! I'm surprised they made it this fer, they was askin' questions about questions. Durn flatlanders are gonna ruin this country, I swear!" exclaimed Scratch, finally able to vent his frustrations with someone that would understand.

Jeremiah just laughed at his partner and said, "You said the same thing about me, Scratch, and you know that wasn't true. You just gotta give folks a chance. They ain't had the experience like us, it's all new and a big adventure to them. Patience, my friend, patience." It was Charlie's turn at the cooking and she had some fresh venison steaks sizzling in the frying pan along with some sliced potatoes they traded for at Fontenelle's. A separate pan held cornbread that was slowly rising and adding the aroma that tickled the taste buds of the four friends. Scratch took a deep sniff and expressed his hunger and appreciation for the anticipated meal.

When the wagons had circled up, Jeremiah took the smoking rack to the center of the circle and the larger of the fires to give the people their wilderness education for the evening. He asked Carrie MacGregor to help him slice some of the fresh deer meat into real thin strips for the rack. He carefully demonstrated to everyone that was interested how to assemble a rack and place it on the smoky side of the fire.

Then, carefully placing the many thin strips on the rack, he explained, "Folks, we won't always have the time to take a long noon break and we'll still need to eat and there'll be times we won't have fresh meat and this is what will keep you alive. Once the meat is dried, as you know, it's called jerky and can be kept for a long time without spoiling. So, be sure to do this, every time you have fresh meat, set aside some to dry and keep your larder full of jerky. You'll be glad you did."

After thanking Carrie, he returned to their camp and joined the others for their evening meal. It wasn't long after they completed their supper that several of the men from the wagon train came to their fire with more questions. Levi Farmer was with them and greeted his friends in his usual friendly manner, then spoke up for the group with him.

"Scratch, several of the folks were hopin' to get an idea of what's ahead and what they can do to help. Some are willing to join in the huntin' and anything else that needs doin' and we were all wonderin' what we're in store for the next few days."

"Well, go 'head on and sit, fellas. I'll see if I can fill ya in. As I think about it, tomorrow will be 'bout like today with these rollin' hills and such, but we should reach fresh water by the end of the day. We'll follow that crick around and probly hit the Platte agin' as it turns back to the South, mebbe by the end of the next day we'll be thar.

After that we'll cross over the Platte and head on west. After we're on the North side of the Platte, we'll probably run into some buffler and we gotta keep watch fer Injuns. As fer as any o' ya doin' some huntin' those of you that are any good at it, well you can join the scouts on occasion and help out thataway. As fer as anythin' else, we'll just have to take it one day at a time."

"How many miles a day do you 'spect we'll make, Scratch?" asked one of the visitors.

"Don't make no nevermind how many does it? We'll go as fer as we can ever' day, and stop when we have to. Ya see, pilgrim, outchere this country is so big, we don't measure it by miles, we measure it by days. Now, it takes a good pack train about four weeks to get from the Missouri to Fort William, so it'll probly take the wagons nearer to five or even six weeks. That is of course, if we don't get into any big trouble."

With most of the men satisfied with the answers given, the group turned to the wagons to join their families and prepare for the night. As they departed, Scratch said, "Don't ferget to check yore animals 'fore ya turn in. Make sure they ain't wandered too fer away." The camp of companions had fallen silent as they pondered the long journey ahead. It was one thing to take it one day at a time, but when Scratch had put a number to the long days ahead, it made it seem even longer.

Chapter Twenty-Four: Snakes

STANDING TALL IN HIS STIRRUPS, Jeremiah surveyed as much of the river as the trees would allow. The riverbanks on both sides were cluttered with cottonwoods and willows clinging tenaciously to the only moist soil in the valley. Jeremiah and Bart Barham's son, Douglas were on scout duty and the youth was anxious to learn as much as he could from the seasoned mountain man.

"Are we gonna cross here, Mr. Jeremiah? It looks okay to me, whatdaya think?" eagerly questioned the young man. Doug was a tall but lean young man that served as a poor rack for the oversized farmer's duds his mother had hung on him. Almost as tall as his father, he had a growth spurt that stretched his frame taller than it did wide, making him resemble a scarecrow in the farmer's field. His blonde hair matched his straw hat for color and texture and it was difficult to determine where one began and the other ended. But he was a quick learner, handled horses well, and was a tolerable marksman. Today was his first day on scout duty and the two had an early start. But within the first hour they approached the east bank of the Platte River.

"Well, boy," although it seemed strange to refer to someone almost as tall as he was as boy, "we gotta look it over. Scratch warned me to be careful for quicksand as this river is well known for swallerin' up dumb pilgrims. He said there's probly as many under the sand as has crossed o'er it," stated Jeremiah struggling to keep a straight face. Scratch didn't miss any opportunity to belittle pilgrims, even if it was by telling tall tales.

"How can we tell? Whatsit look like? Huh, Mr. Jeremiah?"

"I don't rightly know, boy. But Scratch did say sometimes ya can tell cuz the current ain't fast o'er it and sometimes it collects a bit of debris, ya know, like leaves an' such."

Both riders dismounted and walked closer to the bank to further examine the potential crossing but found nothing alarming. The shallow muddy water revealed little current and nothing that answered Scratch's description of a quicksand peril.

"All right, boy. I'm gonna cross over first, an' you stay here in case I get in trouble. If I go under, then you can tell the rest o' em to cross somewhere else, okay?" He turned to mount his steel dust gelding.

The boy watched wide-eyed and looked up at Jeremiah, "Uh, okay, I guess," with a nervous move toward his horse. Drawing his mount away from the river's edge, he sought the shade of the nearby cottonwood and turned to watch Jeremiah enter the water.

Jeremiah had never experienced quicksand before and was a little apprehensive after Scratch tried to explain how the death trap was so easily obscured. He gigged his horse to start across the water and the gelding easily stepped out and walked readily through the knee deep muddy water. The silt was deeper on the West side but not enough to hinder the quick-stepping gelding.

Jeremiah dismounted and turned to give the west bank a cursory examination for any tell-tale sign of quicksand or other unforeseen peril. Returning to the east bank, he waved for Doug to join and as they crested the bank to look over the tall prairie grass, they could see the approaching wagons no more than a half mile distant.

The wagons were lined out in order with the Whipple wagon in the lead. Young Benjamin and his wife Eleanor had been a continual source of enthusiasm and eagerness with their willingness to do more than their share of any task set before them. Now with the opportunity to lead the train across the Platte, his anxious slap on the rumps of his team with his leads caused Scratch to holler, "Hold up there! Hold yore horses there young'un. Ya don't even know whatcha gotta do or where ta go!"

"Uh, sorry, Scratch, I just thought . . ." stammered Benjamin with a flush rising from his collar to show red from his chin up.

"Ya cain't go gittin' in no hurry pilgrim, it'll gitcha kilt!" scolded the mountain man. "Now, you just foller Jeremiah there. Stick close and don't go right 'er left of 'im. Unnerstan'?"

Jeremiah led off and was closely followed by the Whipple's. Scratch remained on shore and gave instructions to each of the following wagons to follow closely but no more than a wagon tongue's length behind and to stay directly behind the lead wagon. Each driver was careful to follow his instructions as the wagons continued to stir up the latent silt on the riverbed.

The last three wagons had more of a struggle, with Roscoe Boggs driving his first supply wagon followed by his man Freddie driving his second wagon. Boggs and Freddie had traveled from South Western Illinois to St. Louis where Boggs had outfitted although he wasn't well received by the abolitionist owner of the store where he purchased his goods because of the way the nigra Freddie was being ordered about.

Jeremiah and Scratch had paid close attention to the pair and chose not to intervene in their business unless absolutely necessary, after all, no reason to cause trouble when they already had more than they could handle.

The two supply wagons were followed by Ian MacGregor and his family behind his four- up hitch of blacks. Scratch, Charlie and Caleb followed the MacGregor's. Approaching the western bank the Boggs team was rising out of the water's edge, when a cry from his second wagon was followed by the panicked splashing of the team. Freddie was frantically grabbing at the lead lines as the two draft horses were partially rearing and tossing their heads in a futile attempt to escape something in the water that spooked them.

The horses were screaming a high pitched whinny and snorting as they crashed against one another and struggled with the harness and the hindering weight of the wagon. Scratch kicked his horse to the side of the MacGregor's and urged him to the side of the supply wagon. With Freddie standing in the front of the wagon box and pulling on the leads with all the strength in his lean but muscled body, he was trying to calm the horses with "whoa there, boys, whoa now, come on, whoa up there."

But the panic was still on the horses as they arched their necks to spot the threat in the water. Now bouncing with the waves of the current, a twisted mass of snakes that appeared to be a nest of at least three, were squirming as if they could not untangle themselves and were striking at the panicked horses. Scratch had approached the side of the horses and reaching over the shoulder of his own horse that was now starting to spook and wanting to rear, Scratch grabbed a handful of snake and flipped it toward the bank and away from the horses.

The draft horse on the side away from Scratch was now stumbling and dropping to the level of the water. Scratch immediately knew what was happening and turned to signal the MacGregor wagon to pull alongside. The panicked horses of Freddie's wagon had pulled the wagon out of line and somewhat downstream from the chosen crossing, enabling the MacGregor wagon to easily pull alongside.

164

Scratch hollered at Ian, "Throw me that heavy rope ya got there and pull up with the back of yore wagon even with the front of his horses, an' hurry!"

Carrie fetched the rope and threw it out the back of the bonnet as they passed. Scratch grabbed the rope, dropped off his horse and slapped it on the rump to get it out of the way, then with a hand stroking the neck of the draft horse and talking softly to the still trembling animal, he stepped around the front of the near horse, ran the rope through the neck yoke loop on the end of the wagon's tongue. Then returning to the MacGregor wagon, he took a deep breath and dropped under the tailgate to secure the rope to the back axle of the running gear.

Satisfied with his rigging, he waved to Ian and said, "Put their backs into it and pull away. That other horse yonder is sinkin' in quicksand so it'll be a hard pull, but yore boys can do it!"

The four blacks responded to Ian and bowed their necks and leaned into their yokes and collars digging their hooves into the loose silt to grab footing, with the encouraging "Yah, pull ye little scunners," from Ian, the rope tautened and snapped out the water to tense the stretch between the wagons. The draft team of Freddie's wagon recognized the help and struggled for footing of their own and leaned into their collars as the quicksand and silt fought to keep its grip.

With the sucking sounds and splashing of many hooves, the wheels turned and gave way. As the horses and wagons were freed, Scratch grabbed the tailgate of the supply wagon and let them drag him from the water. Feeling firm ground beneath his wet moccasins, Scratch stood and walked to his waiting Sorrel and watched it shake with a roll of his body back and forth trying to rid the water from his hair. When his horse quit shaking, Scratch's saddle and gear hung a bit to the side and Scratch said, "It's a good thing I weren't on top o' you, cuz I'd probly be on the ground now. Course I guess I am on the ground ain't I?" Mounting up and moving to take the lead once again, he heard Roscoe Boggs yelling at Freddie, "You dumb nigra, why can't you do whatchur tolt?"

Scratch spoke to him as he passed and said simply, "It weren't his fault, it was snakes that spooked them horses. Coulda been you just as easy."

"I'll tend to him when we stop to camp. Ya can't let 'em get away wid nuthin'!" spat the pot-bellied would be trader.

Scratch looked over his shoulder at the man but continued to the head of the train. With a "Head 'em out!" the caravan continued on its way.

Chapter Twenty- Five: Buffalo

AS THE DARKNESS of night surrendered its grip to the dusky early light of morning, the brooding clouds were pushed aside, yielding to the penetrating red of the slow rising sun, the few clouds remaining in the eastern sky were soon painted in pastel shades of crimson.

The scouting duty for the day was on the shoulders of the older mountain man and his two apprentice companions. Their early start put them on the grassy plain at prime feeding time for many of the game animals and Charlie was the first to spot the small tan and white herd on the slight rise of the sand hill North of the trail. "What are those things, Scratch?" she asked and extended her arm to point toward the herd.

Turning to see where she was pointing, Scratch said, "Why those be antelope, missy. That's some of my favorite jerky cuz it's a bit sweeter than most. But they ain't easy to git cuz they kin see ya from a long way off, an' iffn' they gets skeered, they can take off an' outrun just 'bout anything on this hyar prairie."

"Can we make a try for 'em? I ain't never had any antelope before."

"It might make fer a good change up, I reckon. Now, here's whatcha gotta do . . ." and he began to lay out the plan for the two and the antelope hunt. After getting their instructions, Caleb and Charlie tethered their horses to the trees near the river allowing plenty of room for graze, then started their stalk on foot.

As instructed, they assumed a crouch to drop beneath the tall Indian grass that covered the valley floor. They slowly made their way to the slight shoulder of the sand hill and circling around out of sight, they spotted a good sized sandstone formation high enough above the level of the grass to afford a good view of the valley.

Charlie took the lead and upon arriving at the sandstone, she slowly climbed to the top and took a seat facing the herd of antelope, now about 150 yards distant, with her rifle across her lap. Caleb slowly joined her, but lay prone on his belly beside her with his rifle extended to a firing position so that he was obscured from the view of the antelope. Charlie had taken off her hat and fluffed her long hair to allow it to blow in the Southerly breeze. Then remaining completely still, they waited.

The movement on the sandstone was spotted by the antelope, but because of the slowness and distance, they were not alarmed. Now as the girl sat still with only her hair blowing in the slight breeze, a few of the curious animals casually watched this addition to their horizon. At first, they would stretch their necks upward to look, and drop their heads for additional graze. Randomly the three would take a few steps in the direction of the sandstone outcropping, look, and drop their heads to graze. This behavior continued for almost twenty minutes, with no movement from the duo, but slow progress from the antelope. The entire herd of fourteen animals followed the lead of the first three and slowly moved toward the curious creature on the sandstone.

Caleb now had a clear sight of the approaching animals and judging the distance at about sixty yards, whispered to Charlie, "I'm goin' to take a shot. Are you ready?"

She whispered, "Yes," and Caleb squeezed off his shot as Charlie quickly swung her rifle to her shoulder and pulled the trigger on her animal. The shots resounded almost as one and the two rifles belched simultaneous clouds of white smoke obscuring the vision of the two hunters. Standing erect, they spotted two animals down and the rest of the herd flashing white rear ends in the distance.

"Wow! Scratch wasn't kidding when he said those things are fast. Look at 'em go!" observed Charlie.

"You start on the guttin' an' I'll go get the horses so we can pack 'em back to the trail," suggested Caleb. With an affirmative nod from Charlie he trotted off thru the high grass to retrieve their horses. By the time Caleb returned, she had completed the field dressing of the animals and the two worked together to drape the animals, one on the back of the saddle of each of their horses. The mounts were a bit skittish with their loads, but the return trip to the trail took only a few moments and as they were relieved of their load, both soon calmed to their usual mild mannered demeanor. Another cairn of rocks, a stick to point to the suspended meat, and the two hunters were on the way to catch their mentor.

It was unusual for the duo to be left on their own, but they reveled in the liberty. Charlie had spent but a few days on her own before joining the wagons west of Rock Island and every day since she was in the presence of either Jeremiah or Scratch. She preferred the company of the older mountain man because he was totally unattached while Jeremiah would spend most of his time talking about Laughing Waters, his Arapaho sweetheart.

Now with Caleb, she felt her motherly instincts come out as the two talked about his life before Jeremiah. The days of his childhood with his parents back in Michigan sounded wonderful to Charlie for she had not enjoyed a childhood with her father having all the responsibility after her mother left. When she heard about the losses suffered by Caleb, her heart was tendered with reflections on her own youth without a mother. She was brought out of her cloud of reminiscences by Caleb's question, "So, where'd ya learn ta shoot like that, Charlie?"

"When I was younger'n you Caleb, I would have to go to the woods and make meat or we wouldn't have anything for supper. Like you, I lost my ma when I was young. My pa tried hard, but liquor took him under all too soon. So, out of necessity and hunger, I had to sharpen my skills on my own. Didn't have much money for lead and powder, so I learned to take my time, squeeze off my shots, and get game or go hungry. And there were too many times it was hungry. How 'bout you, Caleb, you're pretty darn good with that rifle of your'n."

"I don't know. I didn't do much shootin' before Jeremiah. But when he got me this here rifle, he gave me some pointers, and he said I was a natural. It just seems to be easy for me, I guess."

They finished their noon snacks of jerky and water, let the horses have an extended break with graze on the richer grass at the riverbank, then mounted up to continue their pursuit of Scratch. Early afternoon they were whistled to the shade of a grove of tall cottonwoods with thick willows nearer the river. Scratch waved them over to join him as he enjoyed the shady respite from the bright sunny afternoon. He had already unsaddled his mount, dropped the packs from his pack mule, and made a camp at the edge of the grove.

"Didja get ya some antelope?"

As the two unsaddled their mounts, Charlie responded, "Yeah, it worked just like you said. Their curiosity done 'em in and it only took about a half hour and we bagged two of 'em. We hung 'em in the trees and left a sign for the wagons."

"Well, good fer you. You two keep at it, and ya might make it as hunters yet. Course, ya still got a lot ta learn from us old timers, ya know," he said grinning as the woman and boy finished with their mounts.

"Ain't we stoppin' a little early? I figgered we'd make a few more miles today, seein' as how the weather's so nice an' all," inquired Charlie.

"Take a look over yonder," motioned Scratch turning to the northwest and looking at the distant rolling hills in the faraway haze. She squinted her eyes and said, "Is that a cloud of dust, or what?"

"Ya might say that. That there cloud is gonna be down chere 'bout the same time the wagons get here, and they won't be able to go any further. If'n we kept on, we'd get separated from 'em and that wouldn't be good."

"So, what is it, a storm or sumpin'?" asked Caleb.

"No young'un. That there's a big ol' herd o' buffler. They's so many of 'em, they be raisin' one giant swirl o'dust and tramplin' everythin' in their way. An' they ain't even in a hurry. They's just so many of 'em, that's what happens. They're probly travelin' south to what they think will be greener pastures. We just need to hope this ain't the pasture they be wantin'," stated Scratch. "I'm purty certain, they'll just keep right on a goin' straight on acrosst the river here and hol' up South of the water there. It's a little more open and plenty of graze fer 'em, so lookin' at the lay of the land, I'm purty shore it'll be over yonder they'll cross over and we'll be outta their way here. We might drop a couple of 'em as they go by to give us some meat fer a while."

"I kept us a backstrap from one of those antelope, so we should have some good meat for our evenin' meal," stated Charlie as she pulled it from her parfleche. She laid it aside on the large boulder by the fire ring and went in search of some green willows to hang the slices over the fire to broil the tasty and tender meat for the four of them. As Scratch looked down their back trail for the wagons, he noted the gathering clouds in the East that were filling the late afternoon sky. It had been a good day for traveling but the wind was beginning to pick up and Scratch was certain he smelled rain coming. He pondered the possibility of a coming storm and the approaching herd of buffalo and thought if the storm and the buffalo arrived at the same time, they might have to choose between shelter and meat.

The wagons reached the rendezvous point in advance of the approaching herd. The travelers had been watching the dust cloud and were filled with apprehension as to what was approaching. Some thought a wind storm, some thought Indians, and others speculated on the possibility of Buffalo. Although Jeremiah was the only one to ever witness a herd of buffalo on the move, others had heard the many stories of the moving mass of brown fur and hooked horns and how it would often take days for a large herd to pass.

As they followed Scratch's directions to circle the wagons near the cluster of cottonwoods and the riverbank, the mountain man answered their questions and confirmed the suspicions of the few that thought buffalo. The approaching herd had already caused the ground to vibrate beneath them, the rumble and the approaching dust cloud caused alarm in the eyes of the draft horses.

The men quietly unharnessed the horses and led them off the slight bank to a grassy cutaway between the bank and the river to tether them in an area of safety. As the horses were herded together, the men took them to drink and continued to talk and stroke the big horses to reassure them. Within a few moments, they began to calm down and the men returned to the circle of wagons.

Chapter Twenty- Six: Pawnee

ALTHOUGH THE HERD was almost a half mile distant, the rumble began to shake the ground under the crowd of travelers. With the wind at their backs, the cloud failed to obscure the view enjoyed by members of the train. Standing almost in a straight line at the edge of the circled wagons, they chattered among themselves at the amazing sight while the brown beasts thundered their way into the broad valley of tall grasses.

The grunts and bellows of the animals blended with the clatter of horns and hooves and accentuated the rumble of the moving earth. Mesmerized by the sight before them, every eye was totally focused on the magnificent spectacle. The exhibition of power held their attention to what could be, for many of them, a once in a lifetime event.

Scratch stepped back from the front of the crowd to survey the surrounding countryside. He knew that, where there were buffalo, Indians were likely to follow.

Jeremiah watched his friend as he shielded his eyes to the late afternoon sun and examined the valley to the west in front of the thundering herd, and slowly turning he carefully scrutinized any abnormality of terrain that would be a possible observation point for other hunters.

The slow circuitous move told Jeremiah all he needed to know about the visual search of the mountain man. Occasional pauses in his movement for more thorough searches revealed a very real concern for the scout. With a visible drop of his shoulders signaling relief, Scratch noticed Jeremiah watching him and mouthed one word, "Injuns." But a shrug of the shoulders also told him the younger man there was no immediate concern. A call from the group grabbed his attention when Bart said, "Hey Scratch, are we gonna go shoot us some buffalo for supper tonite?"

He casually strolled back to the group before answering, "Not right now. If we shoot in amongst 'em now, we could spook 'em to change directions and them woolies are plumb unpredictable. I don't want that bunch a runnin' oer me now, would you?" Then putting a hand on the big farmer's shoulder, he continued, "But later on when the tail end of the herd gits a bit closer, we'll probly pick off a few to add to our larder."

"Will the rest of us get ta take a shot at them monsters?" asked Homer Schrade, the blacksmith. He was a big man that looked like he could wrestle a bull buffalo to the ground bare-handed and not break a sweat doing it.

"Those of you that have rifles big enough to bring one of them down, at least a .54 caliber, might get a chance at one," replied Scratch.

Three of the men turned to their wagons to retrieve their rifles and gear in anticipation of the hunt. Scratch called after them, "It'll be a while yet, ya got lots a time."

Scratch turned to Jeremiah and confided, "We don't need a bunch a trigger happy pilgrims tryin' ta slaughter a whole herd o' buffler just for the sport of it. All we'll need is a couple, maybe three to last this whole durned train fer a couple o' weeks. By that time, we'll probly run into another herd o' 'em. Crazy pilgrims!"

"We'll just keep track of 'em and only let 'em kill what's necessary. Lookin' at the bunch of 'em they probly couldn't hit one if they aimed in the middle of the herd," responded Jeremiah.

"Yeah, yore probly right. We'll just have to watch 'em."

Turning to Charlie, Scratch asked, "Could you go tell the wimmen to go 'head on an' fix their supper. By the time we get any buffler and git 'em skinned and such, it'll be way past time to eat. The buffler meat'll have to wait till tomorry."

"Well, one o' you better watch the meat we got hangin' over our own fire or you're gonna go hungry! Caleb can watch it if you two can't," she replied as she turned to her errand.

The buffalo were moving faster than Scratch had first thought. The herd paced at a good trot since the animals anticipated the graze they were bound for, motivating the entire movement. Three men, Homer Schrade, Bart Barham and Slim Gentry had returned to the point of observation with an anxious look about them. Scratch and Jeremiah hefted their Hawkens and stepped out to move closer to the mass of brown.

As they walked, keeping close to the shrubbery of the river bank, Scratch cautioned them, "Now, don't go tryin' no head shots. Aim for the heart or lung just behind the front leg and low on the rib cage. Make sure of yore shot, cuz ya shore don't wanna make 'em mad. It'll take a bit 'fore they drop, if'n ya git a good hit, but if they don't drop purty quick, be shore ta reload and shoot 'em agin. And make certain sure it's the same one. Unnerstand?"

With nods and grunts, the three followers agreed.

Scratch continued, "Now if'n either Jeremiah or me says don't shoot, you better git yore finger off'n that trigger, or we'll rip it off yore hand. Now that's important, it's too durn easy ta git all 'xcited and wanna keep shootin' but don't ya do it or you'll cause problems fer all o' us."

While Scratch was instructing the men, Jeremiah led the way to the point where the hunters could take their stand. The herd was beginning to thin out and the mass was now scattered. Scratch stood in front of the men watching the animals and with a sudden stiffening, he leaned forward catching himself with his left hand on a nearby birch and without taking his eyes off the herd, motioned Jeremiah to his side. Motioning with his right hand he said, "Look yonder, young'un."

In the middle of the remainder of the herd and walking leisurely by himself, a yearling bull with a totally white coat of gnarly fur cantered nonchalantly. Jeremiah said, "That's a medicine bull, Scratch."

"Yup, shore is. Ya probly won't ever see one like that again. To the Injuns, all of 'em, that's powerful medicine."

The other men noticed the confab and asked, "What is it?"

Scratch pointed out the bull and cautioned them, "We gotta wait till he's totally outta the way before we do any shootin'."

"Why? That would make a great trophy! Wow, a white buffalo, I would like that for a rug or a robe," said Slim.

"If you were to shoot that buff and any injun anywhere find out about it, you'd be pushin' up posies quicker'n you can say 'What's fer supper?'"

The men observed the unusual sight and waited until it had crossed the river, leaving several stragglers for the hungry hunters. Scratch stepped behind the three men and reminded them of his instructions, then watched as they took a position to shoot. The big blacksmith chose to lean against the birch, while Bart dropped to one knee and used the other knee to support his rifle. Slim just stretched out on his belly and used the ground to support his elbows for a steady shot.

With Scratch's okay, the three men fired and lifted their heads above the smoke to see the results of their marksmanship. Scratch had responded to a tickling at the back of his neck and turned to see what was behind him. He quickly turned back around to survey the results of the shoot, saw two animals down and another staggering and told Jeremiah to "drop another'n. That'll make it four, an' no more. I'll be back."

Jeremiah took a quick aim and with a standing shot, dropped a big cow just past the two downed animals. He then turned to see Scratch trotting back to the camp. Thinking Scratch was getting horses to assist with the packing, he told the men to wait until the rest of the stragglers passed before going to start work on the carcasses. With a concerned look and troubling thoughts, Jeremiah turned back to see Scratch heading out of camp and away from where the hunters were. He looked beyond where the mounted buck-skinner was walking his horse and saw the reason for his concern.

At the edge of the meadow and on a slightly elevated sand hill, several mounted Indians were slowly moving toward the area where the herd of buffalo had crossed. When they spotted the lone rider approaching, they stopped and waited.

From a distance, Jeremiah could tell was they were Pawnee, the cut of their hair with the tall roach down the middle in what was called a Mohawk cut, was evident from where he stood. He could not tell if they were wearing any paint, but he did see there were women and travois with them which was not usual for a war party. This was a village on the hunt for buffalo.

As Scratch approached the party of Pawnee, he thought *That shore is a hungry lookin' bunch, I hope that's just hunger and not that they're mad 'nuff to want my hair.* He did not hesitate in his approach and held his hand up with the palm open in the recognized sign for peace.

Receiving the same sign from the apparent leader of the group, he walked his horse near the imposing figure that had the traditional Mohawk with an eagle feather trailing down his back. With only a breechclout and moccasins he sat astraddle a solid black horse that reflected his strength with a muscular chest and rippling muscles through the shoulders and hind quarters. The horse had the same calm confidence his rider radiated. With a feathered lance in his right hand with the point straight overhead, he spoke to the visitor in his native tongue.

"Nowa!"

Scratch replied, "Nowa."

The conversation continued with introductions as Scratch introduced himself to the evident amusement and laughter of the Pawnee. He smiled and laughed with them, then listened

177

as their names came. The leader was Spotted Horse, the man to his right was Walks with Clouds and another behind him was Little Sun. With the introductions it was apparent that, at least, Spotted Horse could understand English so Scratch asked, "Are you looking for *ta'raha'?"*

With a quick nod in the affirmative as the answer, Scratch continued. "We've just killed some. There are two just now killed that are for you as our gift of thanks."

Again, nods and a few grunts of appreciation. "As you can see, the herd has passed just over yonder, and you can probly catch up to 'em tomorry, but those two'll feed ya tonite."

The leader turned and relayed the news to the rest of the Pawnee. Scratch added, "By the way. There's sumpin' ya need ta know. There's a medicine bull in that bunch." Spotted Horse gave him a look of question and Scratch repeated, "There's a medicine bull in that herd, a great white buffalo." As he spoke he used sign language to ensure he was understood. Many of the others saw the sign and began to talk excitedly among themselves and motioned to Scratch and the distant herd.

Spotted Horse calmly asked again, "Are you certain, *Taaka Pii'ta?"*

"Absolutely. We waited until it passed over the river before we took any of the stragglers, but there was no mistake. Both my partner and me saw it and it was a beautiful animal. I think it means good medicine for your people since he is on your land."

Spotted Horse lay his lance across his legs and lifted both hands up and looking up to the sky, began to chant what Scratch thought was some prayer of thanks. He was soon joined by Walks with Clouds and the others. Finishing his prayer, he turned to Scratch and said, "You have told us of the Great Spirit's gift and we are thankful. We will celebrate at the fire tonight and roast the buffalo that is your gift. You will join us."

"Uh, I've got a pretty big bunch with our wagon train."

B.N. Rundell

"All are welcome. Join us after the sun sets. Now we must hurry to prepare the *Ta'raha'.*"

The glow of the large central fire of the Indian camp illuminated the visitors as the wagon pulled to the campsite. Not all the families chose to join but a good number were excited about meeting their Indian neighbors. Scratch was reminded of the church picnics he enjoyed with his adopted parents in Kentucky with all the ladies bringing pots or baskets of food to be a part of the feast.

It didn't take long for the women to get acquainted around the setting of the food, although the conversation was much more quiet than a typical get together of women due to the language barrier, but improvised sign language soon bridged the gap and smiles were seen on most faces. Following the example of their hosts, the women served the men and waited for their portions.

The white women were surprised at this but condescended. After the meal was completed, the men passed the pipe and some began to dance their thanks to the Great Spirit. Scratch tried to explain everything the best he could but many of the wagon families just enjoyed the festivities and did not seek to understand. When they finally did comprehend that it was a dance of thanks for the gift of meat, the new friends, and the medicine bull they were amazed and grateful themselves.

Johnathan and Gertie Fitzsimmons smiled at one another and bowed their heads in prayer. As Scratch noticed, he turned to Bart and was told, "They're kinda like missionaries. They're not sure what they're gonna be doin' but they're good folks. He'd make a good pastor for a church somewhere. What I like 'bout him is he ain't pushy like some o' them preachers. They're always pitchin' in and helpin' ever chance they get."

Scratch just let a "Um Hmm" escape his lips and turned back to enjoy the festivities. He was already thinking about the gathering clouds and flashes of lightning in the east and was worried how the storm would affect the next day's travel.

To The Tall Timber

The stretch of trail ahead of them would take them into Sioux country, and he wasn't eager to "greet them devils."

Chapter Twenty- Seven: Storm

THE DISTANT GROWL of the approaching storm prompted the men to fashion a lean-to shelter for protection against the wailing weather.

Jeremiah's favorite time was the early part of descending darkness when he walked among the many stars on the clear nights in the mountains. Often were the times he felt he could just reach up and rearrange the stars to suit his fancy. He knew there were constellations that many different cultures had named and that familiarity had attached great significance to most.

His favorite was Orion in the white man's world, the Great Hunter in the red man's tales. He could easily find the form of the mighty hunter with his upraised sword or full drawn bow standing ready for whatever came before him. Some cultures saw him doing battle with a dragon, while others thought a lion or a bear. Jeremiah never gave much thought to the adversary, just the figure of the hunter and the differing tales associated with him.

But tonight would not afford him the opportunity to star gaze with the heavy cloud cover bringing a thick blanket of darkness to the camp. A scattering of sprinkles convinced the travelers to make for cover. Those in the wagon train chose to huddle in their wagons with the canvas bonnet or covering providing protection from both wind and water. Some were crowded with the entire family like the MacGregor's with their two children and a mountain of a man for their father. While wagons like Roscoe Boggs' provided comfort for the sole occupant.

The circle of wagons was more loosely gathered than on other nights what with the earlier supper with their Indian neighbors allaying any fears of hostile attack, yet the small number allowed for verbal contact between the wagons. After the celebration, many were more talkative than usual but the weather separated the families resulting in hollered "good-nights" between the wagons.

The increasing rain also prompted Jeremiah, Scratch, Charlie and Caleb to seek the shelter of their lean-to among the trees. Most of the animals were tethered below the riverbank on the grass covered wash-up next to a pile of driftwood accumulated from other spring floods. With the supporting inter-woven leafy branches from the nearby cottonwoods and willows, the lean-to also had several hides and blankets to ensure a reasonably weather-resistant covering. With Scratch on one side, Charlie on the other, and Jeremiah and Caleb sandwiched between the two, the only conversation centered on the weather with Charlie expressing her concern, "Boy, I sure hope this lean-to holds up 'cause I think it's gonna get kinda wet tonight."

"Probly will, but this lean-to will do just fine. We've weathered worse storms than this and slept under the stars doin' it!" proclaimed Scratch.

"Mebbe so, Uncle Scratch, but there ain't no stars out tonight!" answered the squirt.

"Okay, you smart lil' pup, ya better be closin' yore eyes and gitcha some sleep 'fore the thunder an' lightning get too close and too loud to do any sleepin'!" directed Scratch who then rolled to his side with his back to the rest as he flounced around in his blankets.

Settling down, Scratch grabbed the near upright of the lean-to and stretched his left leg to the base of the other to give a little extra stability to the structure. He didn't want to tell the others of his gnawing fear about the approaching storm but chose to quietly prepare and pray that he was wrong.

The rising wind and driving rain slapping against the canvas of the wagons prompted the occupants to huddle up and gather their blankets closer. Sleep did not easily come but many were able to enjoy short snoozes between the rocking of the wagons and the insistent scratching of canvas and rope against wood and the splattering of the increasing rain-drops. The rain was also demanding entrance into the scout's lean-to but their hand-made shelter held fast and tight.

Flashing fingers of lightning illuminated the countryside and pierced the darkness of the wagons and lean-to, reminding the huddled numbers of the frailty of their chosen refuge. The expected thunder that followed broke loose with such an explosion and crack, none failed to jerk awake or react with a jolt of fear.

Several let fly an exclamation of alarm that startled those nearby. Scratch knew that was just the first warning and he knew there would be much worse that followed. Another louder clap of rolling thunder startled the mountain man and he let loose with, "Jumpin' Jehoshaphat! How's a fella gonna git any sleep with that goin' on?

Come on Jeremiah, let's take a walk an' check on them pilgrims," he said as he rolled from his blankets. He didn't bother with any covering for shoulder or head, but let the rain wash his hair against his whiskers to give the appearance of a drowned cat. Jeremiah had a heavier war-shirt of buckskin he had grabbed from his possibles and pushed the floppy felt further on his head to resist the water and wind.

As the two men traipsed through the trees separating them from the wagons, Jeremiah followed Scratch and watched as the older man sheltered his eyes from the driving rain to look, instead of at the wagons as expected, but to the dark sky. The skeletal fingers of lightning clawed at the nearby hills and the distant valley. The storm was now close upon them and the rain began driving horizontally as the drops raced away from the wind.

Both men stopped and looked at the horrible monster approaching with its flashes of blinding light backlighting the towering clouds of black that reared above the land and stood ready to release their wrath on the helpless travelers. Scratch stood with his arm outstretched and pointing in a north by east direction, and hollered, "Look!"

Jeremiah followed the direction indicated by his partner and didn't see anything but darkness, then a sudden flash of brilliance by a chain of lightning strikes showed a towering and widespread funnel cloud. The increasing wail of wind pushing the deluge of rain made any discussion almost impossible.

Gaining new footing both physically and mentally, Jeremiah turned to his partner and shouted, "We gotta help 'em!" indicating the circle of wagons that now rocked in rhythm with the wind. The rattle of trace chains and the creaking of side boards accompanied by the slap of canvas drummed out a futile tune of danger.

"Whatrwegonna do? There ain't no place else to go 'cept the wagons. It's gonna be bad everwhere!" yelled Scratch. "We need ta' git the youn'un and Charlie. That lean-to ain't gonna be any good!" and turned to the trees. The two men leaned back against the driving wind and rain and were pelted by a new threat of hailstones, some as big as their fist. Now, hunching over to try to present a smaller target for the frozen projectiles of wrath, they made it to the lean-to. Charlie and Caleb were wrapped together and looked relieved to see the men return. Then Scratch yelled, "Everbody grab a blanket or two, we need ta' git down by the river bank, now!" Without argument Charlie grabbed another blanket, Caleb scratched for his and Jeremiah snatched his big buffalo robe from the

184

ground. With the robe under his arm and his left hand clutching his Hawken, Jeremiah then grabbed Caleb and carried him like a sack of potatoes under his other arm. Turning back to Scratch he said, "Help Charlie, don't let the wind take 'er!"

Jeremiah knew what Scratch meant when he said the riverbank. They had noticed a cutaway just down from their camp and near the tethered animals. It would be barely big enough to put the boy and the woman under and Jeremiah and Scratch could push up against it and gain some protection, at least more than the frail lean-to offered. Gaining their goal, Jeremiah pushed Caleb under the overhang and waited for Scratch to get Charlie under cover. Once in place, he shook the buffalo robe with the wind and settled it over the two. The two mountain men acted in unison as they dug their heels in the sand and pushed their backs against the bank, ducking their head under the slight overhang. Shoulder to shoulder, they looked at each other, turned their faces toward the worst of the storm, dropped chin to chest and prayed.

The pelting hail battered against the wagons with such ferocity the occupants thought the hordes of hell and all its demons were banging on the sideboards. Ice balls struck the canvas relentlessly and began to rip at the weakest points. The wailing of the wind and clatter of hail were soon accompanied by the screams of women and cries of children that were now exposed to the forces of the storm.

Families tried to huddle together in the corners of the wagon-beds for some degree of protection and tears ran with the downpour of rain and hail. The hail decreased and was replaced by greater force of wind and water. The wagons, built with a Yankee bed to be watertight to aid in crossing rivers and streams, now began to fill with water leaving all the contents waterlogged and the occupants no dry retreat.

The lightning increased in frequency and intensity and thunder now accompanied the orchestra of fire and brilliance to add to the fear of every living thing that now endured the onslaught. Every roll of thunder drove through the ground with a vibration that rattled the wagons and even the trees waved in protest occasionally cracking off a heavy branch with a splintering sound that echoed against the thunderous roar around them. The strikes of lightning splintered trees and split rocks and left smoldering ashes blending smoke with the downpour of rain. Then came a continuous roar with a high pitched whistle chasing the sound to penetrate every crevice of resistance.

Scratch stretched to look above the overhanging edge of the bank. Knowing he probably could not see anything, his natural curiosity and concern bade him look. Between him and the wagons and the force of the storm was the copse of trees and willows, but towering over all was the whirling mass of destruction illuminated by lightning and the strange flashes of light within the funnel. The fearful sight elicited a guttural moan, "Here she comes boy, dig deep!"

Chapter Twenty- Eight: Casualties

THE RETREATING STORM left a wide path of destruction in its wake. Quiet descended as the sun peeked over the Eastern horizon to reveal a scene of death and dismay. Slowly, the surviving members of the train began to stir from their shattered shelters. Scratch and Jeremiah pulled away from the muddy refuge and pulled Charlie and Caleb from under the saturated buffalo robe.

No one spoke, but gaining their footing in the sodden soil, began the short return trek to their campsite. Knowing the scene would be nothing for the boy to see, Scratch asked Charlie, "Could you kinda see to the young'un and the two of you try to put our camp back together. If'n yore of a mind to, mebbe see if ya can find some coffee-fixins. Me'n Jeremiah are gonna check on the rest of the folks."

The power of the storm was told by the massive trees uprooted, some snapped off, near the ground. A few, larger than a man could reach around, had been snapped like a piece of kindling for firewood. Most of the cottonwoods and willows had been stripped of all foliage by the blistering assault of hail. Stepping over branches and twisting their way through the downed trees, the duo made their way to the site of the wagons. Clearing the trees, the two stopped and stared at the destruction. Every wagon had the canvas covering ripped to shreds or taken with the wind to places unknown. Some sat a kilter with wheels broken and splintered under the rocking weight from the wind. Strips of canvas mixed with scattered clothing and other cloth were draped on the nearby willows or trampled in the mud, painting a picture of peril amidst the sorrow. People were milling about aimlessly and many were talking to themselves vainly trying to make sense of the destruction around them.

Jeremiah said, "Scratch, there's wagons missin', you don't think . . ."

"Let's just start takin' a tally, Jeremiah. Don't go jumpin' to conclusions, we don't know nuthin' yet. We need to find out who's here and who's missin' and then we can start lookin' and fixin.'"

At Scratch's direction, Jeremiah started around the circle to the right, and Scratch went to the left. Everything was a muddy mess and the walking wasn't without effort, dragging mud laden moccasins through the muck distracted a man on his mission. The first two wagons approached by Jeremiah were the two owned by Roscoe Boggs. Roscoe was chastising his nigra, Freddie, and directing him to "Get busy and unload these wagons. We gotta check everything for water damage. This is gonna cost me a bundle!"

Freddie busied himself with the second wagon and copied Roscoe in the work. Jeremiah did not ask as to their condition as it was evident they were uninjured though upset. He continued to the Fitzsimmons wagon and inquired about the family of missionaries. All were working together to try to get the wagon and its contents back in order. The two boys, Lucas and Matthew were inside the wagon passing the parcels to their parents. Lucas said to Jeremiah, "Boy, that sure was some storm wasn't it, Mr. Jeremiah?"

188

"Sure was boy, it's what we call out here a real gullywasher!" answered the mountain man. "Are you folks gonna be okay... need any help with anything?" he asked.

"Oh, just like everybody else, we're soaked through and through, but we'll be all right. As soon as we get things situated, we'll see if we can help the others. Thanks Jeremiah."

He continued his circuit and stopped at the next wagon to greet Benjamin Whipple, but Benjamin was sitting on the far side of the wagon holding his wife against him and rocking back and forth sobbing. Protruding from Eleanor's back was a broken piece of wagon bow that had apparently broken off and was driven through her torso. It was evident she was dead and what blood had come from the wound to soil her dress had been washed down her side by the rain.

Benjamin appeared to have been sitting with her since it occurred and was oblivious to the presence of Jeremiah. He walked back to the Fitzsimmons wagon, explained to Johnathan and Gertie, and asked if they could help Benjamin. They agreed and followed him on his return. The next wagon was undamaged except for the canvas being destroyed as all the others. Homer Schrade and his wife Nancy greeted Jeremiah with an invitation to some coffee which he gladly accepted. Nancy asked, "How's everybody else doin'?" knowing she wasn't going to like the answer.

"Well, there's some wagon's missin' and, so far the only casualty seems to be Mrs. Whipple, Johnathan's young wife." Nodding toward the Whipple wagon, "She's dead and the Fitzsimmons are helpin' Johnathan."

Scratch arrived just as Jeremiah finished his account and the two conferred about the others. Scratch said, "Well, the Barham's and the Gentry's are O.K. but Ian MacGregor and his two little girls are missin'. Mrs. MacGregor is over by their wagon. She's not hurt, but she's not all right."

"Oh my, I'll go see if I can help her," said Mrs. Schrade and hurried away.

189

Scratch continued, "That's all there was over yonder. Now we need to figger out who's missin'"

As the three men, Scratch, Jeremiah and Homer Schrade conferred, the tally was soon calculated to be four wagons missing with four couples and one baby plus Mr. MacGregor and his two girls. Eleanor Whipple was dead and of the remaining number there were no known injuries. The missing couples were Ashton and Liberty Tilford, a young farmer couple, Marcus and Amy Clare who were hoping to have a second start as storekeepers, Oscar and Ingrid Jensen and their baby. Oscar was a harness maker and they hoped to start a harness and saddle making business. Macklemore McGillacuddy and his wife Mabel had spent their lives as store clerks. Mac was the one that questioned Scratch and seemed to be a belligerent, though cowardly type and was suspected of abusing his wife.

"Well, let's go get the horses, and we'll start a search to see if we can find any of 'em," stated Jeremiah as he stood to take his leave. Scratch stretched and stood to turn toward their camp. As he arched his back and stretched his arms high, he froze, squinted, and said, "Oh Lord, no."

Jeremiah turned back to his partner, and following his line of sight looked to see what had alarmed the mountain man. High above their heads among the split and splintered denuded trees branches, hung the tattered dress wrapped around the frail body of the older MacGregor girl. She appeared to have been dropped in the yoke of branches of the tall and skeletal maple. "That's a durn shame," said the big blacksmith, "how we gonna get her down from there?" he asked.

"Homer, me an' Jeremiah's gonna start our search, why't you find some help and just start cuttin' that there tree down," said Scratch and stepped to the trail and their camp near the horses. All but a few of the animals were still tethered and appeared to be without any injury as they casually grazed on the remaining grass. With the river rising it was necessary to get them to higher ground, but that could easily be done by

190

Charlie and Caleb. Jeremiah and Scratch led their mounts back to the camp to saddle up for the dreaded search. Both men knew they would probably not find a living soul, but the search was necessary with the possibility someone could be found.

The valley was scarred by the path of the storm and littered with the remains of not only the wagon train but with the debris of trees and shrubbery uprooted by the relentless funnel. Riding on the North edge of the swath of rubbish they surveyed the litter for any sign of life or the remains of those missing. A sideboard from a wagon partially obscured the body of Ingrid Jensen and when they moved the board, the flattened body of the Jensen baby was found clutched in her mother's arms.

Wrapping the two tightly together, the men lifted the bodies across the rump of Scratch's horse and he returned to the wagons to leave the bodies for burial. When he returned to Jeremiah's side, he trailed the two pack mules for obvious purposes. Jeremiah just motioned to another body sprawled a short distance away and a second body nearby. Again the men lifted the bodies of Ashton Tilford and Amy Clare to the back of the mule for transport. Jeremiah led the mule with the two bodies to the now busy burial detail.

The bloated body of Mac McGillacuddy was found impaled with a remnant of a tree branch and Marcus Clare's dismembered remains lay amongst a pile of broken branches and clutter from the train closer to the tree line. After helping Scratch load his mule, Jeremiah said, "I'll follow the storm's trail a bit further, then I'm gonna cross over to the side nearer the trees and work my way back."

With a nod of agreement, Scratch returned to the growing gravesite. Scratch was surprised to see a grieving and disheveled Liberty kneeling beside her husband's body and as he turned to Homer Schrade with a questioning look, Homer said, "She just came stragglin' in like she'd been out for a stroll. Had this dazed look on her face and didn't say a word to nobody. When she saw the bodies, she real quick like went to her husband and started talkin' to him like he was wakin' up from a nap, er sumpin', darndest thang I ever did see."

Jeremiah's trail brought him to the previous night's campsite of the Pawnee with little evidence anyone had even traveled this route. Walking to the edge of the river he saw the tracks of their crossing and their trail leading up the opposite bank. *Well, if that don't beat all. I reckon they weren't hit with much of the storm last night so they headed on out after those buffalo. Can't say as I blame 'em. Skinny as they were, they need all the meat they can get.*

Turning back to his task, he noted the absence of sign of the storm's passing. Trees still held tightly to their foliage and there was no debris field nearby. He resumed his trek along the tree line and it was easily seen how the storm had turned North from this point. Now the cottonwoods and scattered maples were once again marred by the storm's passing and the scattered debris into the valley heralded the damage done. A slight swale to his left caught his attention and as he approached, he spotted rubbish and what appeared as a body floating in the shallow water. Face-down in the stagnant muddy water was the body of Mabel McGillacuddy. Wading into the swampy tangle of grasses and broken limbs, Jeremiah lifted her body to his side and slogged his way back to the animals. Dropping with his load to the ground, Jeremiah needed to catch his breath. Scratch, arriving unseen but not unheard, said, "Tirin' work ain't it? Who ya got thar'?"

"The wife of that big-mouthed storekeeper. Don't know her name," Jeremiah responded as he looked to the sky for some sign of relief. With the wide blue canopy showing no resemblance to the death dealing storm clouds and roaring blackness of just a few hours' past, he continued, "it just don't seem real. There we were, mindin' our own bizness, an' along come these wagons and now look at us." Standing and stretching his arms heavenward he yelled, "Get me outta this country and back to my mountains!"

"Amen to that," muttered Scratch. "Let's get her loaded up," pointing to the inert body beside them. "I think the only one we ain't found is that big Scotsman."

Jeremiah trailed his mule with the woman's body draped across the packsaddle and Scratch led the other. With Jeremiah searching the debris field to their left and Scratch surveying the tree line to their right, they slowly worked their way toward the wagons. "Whoa up thar'" ordered Scratch. He dismounted and walking to a cluster of willow he pushed them aside to find Ian MacGregor and his youngest daughter impaled on an upright portion of a wagon tongue. His arms still wrapped around his daughter and her face buried in his shoulder, his lifeless eyes gazed to the heavens past the awkward angle of the up-thrust wagon tongue.

Forever clasped in the familial embrace, the hard oak spear had pierced through the girl's back and through the chest of her father and buried itself deep into the soft soil of the willow's roots. Scratch stood motionless as he surveyed the scene, and joined by his partner, the two men silently sought the grace of God for strength to finish their task.

To The Tall Timber

Chapter Twenty- Nine: Plains

"'LORD, MAKE ME to know mine end, and the measure of my days, what it is; that I may know how frail I am. Behold thou hast made my days as a hand breath; and mine age is as nothing before thee . . .' Friends, as we come together to say our goodbyes to our friends and loved ones, we seek answers for such tragedy. I wish I could tell the why of it, but I cannot. I do know this, those whose bodies lie here, if they knew the Lord as their Savior, they are present with Him in heaven today. Their journey is complete, but ours continues and as we prepare to renew our quest for new homes and a more blessed future, let me admonish each of you, if you have not already done so, then without delay pray and ask Jesus to become your savior so that you might know the promise of an eternity in heaven!

Psalm 39 continues with, 'Hear my prayer, O Lord, and give ear unto my cry; hold not thy peace at my tears: for I am a stranger with thee, and a sojourner, as all my fathers were.' Amen." The reverend Fitzsimmons concluded his message by picking up a clod of newly turned soil, crumbled it over the nearest grave, and said, "Go with God."

The survivors stood by the ten graves that held all but the missing Oscar Jensen. With his Bible in his hand and putting his arm around his wife, the reverend Fitzsimmons turned to make his way back to the wagons. Followed closely by the others with bowed heads and several wiping tears that threatened to escape their reddened eyes, they began to prepare for their journey.

It was a somber crowd that followed the trail of the scouts on this crisp morning. The moisture laden countryside clutched at a slow rising fog hesitant to release the wispy veil of grey that slowly parted for the progression of travelers. The tall dew-drenched grasses shared their wealth of water with the scouts and their mounts that sought to blaze a trail across the plains of the Platte River valley. With the legs of his buckskin trousers dripping with the heavy dew, Caleb looked down to see his moccasins were soaked and resembled the wet leather of his saddle skirts and the drenched hide of his mount. "Wow, I don't think I got this wet when we crossed the river!" exclaimed the boy.

"Course not," replied Charlie, "the river wasn't this deep. But at least if you fall off, you ain't gonna drown in it."

With the wide open valley before them and no obvious sign of problems, Jeremiah had condescended to Caleb's request to let him and Charlie lead the scouting detail. Other members of the group that had previously volunteered for the detail now stayed near their remaining family and rode or walked with the wagons. As tragedy often does, the surviving families and couples were drawn closer to one another and all were made more aware of the frailty of life.

Even Jeremiah spent more time in prayer and contemplation of his future. With fresh images in his mind of his waiting Laughing Waters, he found it difficult not to break loose from his obligations and head straight for the mountains and his beloved. The death of someone near always makes every day of life more precious to those that grieve.

B.N. Rundell

A meadowlark broke loose with his song and Caleb immediately turned to see if he could spot the yellow breasted bird with the lengthy warble. Without success, he duplicated the song to see if he could elicit a return call. Although Charlie had heard him make the sounds of other birds, she was again amazed at the clarity and perfect imitation of the lengthy call of the meadowlark. "Do the men know you can do that?" she asked, referring to his mimic of the sounds.

"Jeremiah does, but he asked me to keep Scratch in the dark about it. He wants to see how long we can keep him confused about it, I guess."

"You kinda like those two, don't you?"

"Course I do, and you do to, I can tell. I been watchin' you and I think you're kinda sweet on Scratch," laughed the boy.

Surprised, she looked at Caleb to see if he was serious or just joking and said, "What do you mean? I ain't done nuthin'" she replied innocently but with a fishing expedition in mind. "What makes you think I'm sweet on him, he's just an old mountain man and I don't need nobody."

Caleb smiled broadly and said, "When my momma would catch me fibbin' she'd usually say that folks that have to deny sumpin' too much it's usually cuz they done did it."

With that rebuke, Charlie replied, "We better keep our eyes on the trail."

Jeremiah and Scratch rocked with the steady rolling rhythm of their mounts. Scratch trailed a pack horse laden with their travel gear and supplies, while Jeremiah had a string of both mules heavily laden with additional supplies and gear but mostly with the trade goods and gifts for his Arapaho friends. Both had retreated into their contemplations as they continued their survey of the countryside.

Jeremiah spoke up with, "So, old man, are you thinkin' 'bout pitchin' yore lodge with Charlie?" he asked with a mischievous grin spreading through his whiskers. Scratch turned in his saddle, putting his weight in the off-side stirrup and resting his leg across the seat, he sassed back at his partner,

"What'd you do, them wasps back there crawl under those whiskers and sting you into some crazy place? Whatchu talkin' like that? This ol' coon ain't climbin' up no tree like that! I swear, boy, you done gone plumb loco!"

Chuckling into his beard, Jeremiah echoed the comments of the boy, though they were separated by a couple of miles, as he said, "You know, my momma used to say that if someone had to deny something as much as you just did, it's cuz they were guilty."

Scratch twisted back in his saddle with a "Humphhh!" in an effort to stop the conversation. It was evident he wasn't interested in discussing that particular topic. Having gained the answer he was seeking, Jeremiah changed the subject, "Did you say we're gettin' into Sioux country hereabouts? Ya ever had any dealins' with them before?"

His shoulders drooped as he relaxed his defenses and replied, "Yeah, we are, it's purty much Sioux country till we get to Fort William. They's the dangest bunch I ever met up with, moody too. They kin be friendly one day and wanna lift yore hair the next. I unnerstand they been doin' some purty good tradin' at the fort and they might be tolerable, but I ain't countin' on it."

Jeremiah was standing in his stirrups as Scratch finished talking and said, "Look yonder, can you make that out. Is that somebody walkin' there?" He was pointing North of the trail less than 100 yards distant. It appeared to be a man stumbling in the same direction on a path that would soon intersect their trail. Scratch handed the lead rope to his pack horse to Jeremiah and said, "Wait here, I'll check it out." Dragging his Hawken from the scabbard beneath his right leg, he gigged his horse in the direction of the walker. The man didn't seem to hear Scratch's approach but when the mountain man hailed him with, "Hey there, stranger!" he turned to look at Scratch. With disheveled hair, a torn Lindsey Woolsey shirt underneath a single suspender, trousers with ripped legs, scratches on most of the exposed skin, the man asked, "Have you seen my wife, my Ingrid, and our baby?"

Scratch recognized Oscar Jensen, the harness maker from the wagon train. The man had been wandering aimlessly seeking to find his wife that had been ripped from his arms as they huddled in their wagon against the storm. Now senseless, he meandered in a daze with no comprehension of where he was or what had happened. Scratch stepped down to stand beside the man and said, "Oscar, you need to come with me. We'll get you back to the wagons and somebody'll be able to help you out."

"Yah, yah, if you say so," he replied nodding.

The first wagon to approach was the Barham wagon and they volunteered to help Mr. Jensen. Kim reached back into their basket behind the seat and brought out some dried buffalo and a water-bag to start their ministrations. "Mr. Jensen, let's get back here on the tailgate and I'll fix up those cuts for you."

"Yah, Yah, haf you seen my Ingrid? I don' know vhere she iss."

"Let's get you fixed up first, okay?" she asked as she escorted him to the back of the wagon, dropped the tailgate and motioned him to seat himself.

Following the Barham wagon was Roscoe Boggs' wagons with Roscoe at the helm of the first wagon. Upon seeing the reason for the hold-up, he hollered, "Hey, let's get movin' we've already lost enough time."

Kim Barham threw a scowl his way and curtly responded, "Why don't you shut up? You've been a constant aggravation this whole journey and everybody's tired of it! Now hush up while I tend to this man!"

Boggs had never had anyone sass him in that manner and never a woman. He opened his mouth to respond but words were not forthcoming. The wagons started to move and he just lifted the lead lines to slap the rumps of his horses to move along. Kim turned to her task and mumbled to herself, *I swear, some people's kids. That man never learned any manners in*

*his entire life. If I was a man I think I'd want to whip him within
an inch of his life, he makes me so mad!*

Scattered hills rose beside the trail with less grass, and
more sagebrush. The rocky ledges of the distant sand hills
became more prominent and the copses of cottonwoods and
willow by the river were more scattered and sparse. Before
them was a line of smaller trees and green that signaled a
tributary stream to the Platte. Standing beside their horses,
Charlie and Caleb waited for the wagons and the planned noon
stop and rest.

There was good graze for the stock and the creek ran with
clear cold water. As the wagons reached the stream, the men
lined them out so the animals would be easily unhitched and
taken to water. Scratch made his way from wagon to wagon
to instruct each one to fill their water barrels and any other
containers they had as fresh water would not be so plentiful for
the next several days. Slim was the first to protest, "But
Scratch, we're followin' the Platte, ain't there water there?"

"Slim, just walk o'er there to that little crick, look at the
water, then mebbe even take a drink. Then if you're still not
sure, walk on down to the Platte and stick yore nose down in
that mud and decide which'n you'd druther drink from,"
advised the whiskered buck-skinner.

Jeremiah heard a ruckus coming from the wagons near the
head of the line and strolled over to inspect. The second wagon
belonging to Roscoe Boggs had dropped a wheel into a prairie
dog hole and was sitting askew. Freddie had unhitched the
team to take them to water and Boggs was hollering after him.
"Git them horses watered and git your rear end back here and
fix this mess, you lazy nigra!"

Jeremiah decided to leave the two to their own problems
and walked back down the line to offer his assistance to the
others. The womenfolk had gathered in the shade of the few
cottonwoods and started a small fire for coffee. The noon meal
was to consist of Johnny cakes and jerky with hot coffee. It

would be enough to satisfy the travelers and not delay the day's travel.

While most of the travelers preferred to prepare their own supper, the noon break was expedited with the joint effort. Jeremiah accepted the proffered coffee and leaned against the smaller cottonwood as he watched the ladies busy themselves. Their conversation, though somewhat subdued, still had the tinge of excitement and anticipation he noticed when they first joined up. These were the hardy breed of settlers that would make this a great nation, people that could face hardship and trial and pick themselves up and continue toward their goal. They were not uncaring, but rather resilient and strong.

It was difficult for all of them to stand beside ten graves of their traveling companions; friends they had known and shared with, but they had to reach down deep and draw on the reserves of strength afforded those willing to risk it all for a better life. Jeremiah was impressed with this group and proud to be a part of what they were doing.

A loud yell and the startled look on the women's faces brought Jeremiah's attention to another disturbance near the head of the line of wagons. He dropped his cup by the fire and started at a trot toward the commotion. Freddie was on his knees with his shirt dropped to his waist and gripping a wagon wheel with both hands as Roscoe Boggs brought a bull whip back in an ark to launch another blistering slap across the nigra's back. When he drew back again to repeat his act, Jeremiah grabbed the end of the whip as it whistled through the air just over his head.

The sudden jerk to the whip caught Boggs off balance and he staggered back a step and whirled to see what his whip had snagged. Jeremiah was walking toward the disgusting pot-bellied bully and could smell the stench of his sweat, dirt and whiskey as he approached, winding the tail of the whip into small loops in his hand. Boggs tried to jerk the whip free, as he snarled, "This ain't none o' yer bizness, let go my whip 'fore I take it to yore back, boy!"

Jeremiah was now an arm's length from the braggart and with a deft move, he jerked the whip from the slave master's hand. Then, slowly stepping back from the man and without a word of response, he made his intentions known as he took the whip handle in hand, and snaked the length of the braided leather to his side. With a flip of the whip's tail to his left, then quickly retrieving it in a smooth motion it coiled overhead and whispered through the air as he brought it down with a crack over the shoulder of Boggs and slapped his back as it ripped his shirt. With a squeal like a fattened pig fleeing a slaughter, the vile man spit out, "What'r ye doin', ye ain't got no right!"

"Whatsamatta Boggs, don't it feel good? And I've got just as much right to do this as you," grinned his assailant.

"He's my property! I've owned him since he was borned, 'sides, he's just a nigra," he enjoined.

Another crack and he squealed again, and the whisper of the whip now became a whistle as it sought out its mark. Boggs had dropped to his knees and begged, "No more, please, no more."

Jeremiah slowly coiled the whip as if considering further punishment, then said, "Boggs, the Missouri Compromise of 1820 outlawed slavery in all the territories. You don't own anybody and you are not this man's master. He is a free as any of us. Now, if he chooses to continue to travel with you, I expect you'll be wantin' to pay him and treat him right. Do you understand what I'm saying?"

"Sure, sure, anything you say, just no more, please," he begged again.

Jeremiah walked over to Freddie and helped him to his feet. Freddie said, "Is that true, Mr. Jeremiah, is I really free?"

"That's right Freddie, and you don't have to continue with that man, if you don't want to, it's up to you." He then handed the whip to Freddie, "Whatever you decide, this is for you." He then walked back to the noon gathering and picked up his cup, pouring himself another cup of coffee. Everyone watched him, but no one spoke either rebuke or praise. Yet their silence was

202

enough for Jeremiah. *I just can't abide that kind of treatment, even if it was an animal, I'd done the same thing.*

To The Tall Timber

Chapter Thirty: Landmarks

THE WEEK OF TRAVEL had proven to be the most challenging the wagon train had encountered. The broad level grassy valley had given way to the rolling sand hills capped by rimrock with each new horizon providing learning experiences no one enjoyed. Dry stream beds with loose sand that sought to trap the steel rimmed narrow wheels of the wagons were mastered by doubling up teams to pull each wagon free.

Sage brush harbored only rattlesnakes and lizards with neither providing any sustenance for the travelers. The occasional jack rabbit didn't go far enough to feed even one family and the occasional white tail deer would be spread so thin that most made soups or stews to stretch their allowance. Although sign was often seen of buffalo, the only benefit the vagabonds enjoyed from the mighty herds were the "chips" used for fuel.

Five days had been endured without fresh, clean water. To provide water for the stock and some additional drinking water, the families would fill containers with the muddy waters of the Platte, put cornmeal in the container and after a couple of hours would have passable water when the silt settled to the bottom of the container to provide for the stock or cooking.

When the cavalcade saw the wilted and dying trees on the banks of what they were certain was a stream, their hopes were dashed to find another dry wash. But Scratch had assured them water was nearby. They were at the foot of a tall bluff they would have to traverse as they looked at the maw of a canyon that swallowed the Platte River. With a casual stroll, Scratch walked down the dry gulch about twenty yards, then turned to motion the others to join him.

When a few curious men approached, he pointed to the moist soil at the bank and then turned to point at a small pool of water surrounded by sprigs of green willows. "This here's cottonwood springs and it'll provide enuff fer everbody, longs ya don't all try ta drink at onct. Git your buckets n such to get water fer yer stock. We'll camp here fer the night, an' that'll be nuff time fer everbody to fill up." He then dropped to his belly and put his face in the water to suck in enough of the fresh cool 'nectar of the gods.'

Leaving the confluence of the North and South Platte rivers, three more days of travel across the dry sandy plains with cactus and sagebrush providing the only semblance of green, their camp was on the narrow flat beneath the ragged rimrock topped hills. The two small rivers crossed in the previous days allowed them to keep their water barrels filled and with the continual grasses, the animals were in good condition after the months of travel endured.

With Slim Gentry, the wheelwright, Homer Schrade, the blacksmith, the group had kept the wagons in good traveling condition, but now with the dry winds of the plains and the hot sandy soil, the axles often complained with loud squeaks and groans that prevented any stealth to their travel. Jeremiah and Scratch agreed that this campsite at the confluence of the smaller Blue River and the North Platte would be a good location for a couple day's rest. It would provide good graze for the animals and fresh water with a greater possibility of the hunters bagging some meat for the train.

Due to the possibility of hostile Sioux, Scratch and Charlie paired up for the first hunt. Riding up through a cut in the ridge above them, they rode the plateau and dropped down into another ravine. The farther they traveled from the camp, the dryer the terrain. It was evident this area had been devoid of rain for some time. Scratch was in the lead and started to crest another ridge when he stopped abruptly and reined his mount back down the side. Motioning Charlie to silence, he dismounted and worked his way slowly to the crest to look over the edge.

About two hundred yards beyond, a caravan of Sioux with lodges and travois trailing, was moving to the West. There appeared to be about fifteen lodges, which would account for at least twenty-five warriors. The remaining number in the caravan would be the others of the village. They were moving but also on a hunt for buffalo. Scratch bellied back to his mount and motioned for Charlie to follow as silently as possible.

Out of earshot, Scratch explained to Charlie what he witnessed. "That was a whole durned village and there's probly scouts out just 'bout everwhere. We need ta' git back and prepare our camp."

"You don't think they'll attack us, do you?" pleaded Charlie.

"Ya cain't never tell 'bout them Sioux. Long as they don't know we're here, we'll be all right, but if'n one o' them scouts stumble on us, we need ta' be ready."

"I sure am glad I'm with you, Scratch," Charlie said with confidence.

Scratch looked back at the woman and smiled. Then he assured her, "Long as yore with me girl, ain't nuthin' gonna happen to ya'. An' you can bet on that!"

Jeremiah watched the return of the two hunters as they came down the ravine from the top of the ridge. Not seeing any game, he walked out to greet the two at the edge of their camp. "What's the matter, couldn't ya find anything?" he asked.

"Oh, we found plenty. But I don't think you'd be wantin' any Sioux for supper!"

"How many?" asked Jeremiah.

"A whole durned village. Prob'ly fifteen lodges or so. Too durned many to tangle with, that's fer sure n' certain!"

"I see ya didn't bring back any meat. What'r we havin' for supper, skeeter ribs and fly steaks?"

"I tell ya what, boy, why'nt you just dig out that there bow an' arree outfit o' yourn and you just crawl up thru them willows over yonder by that little crick, and mebbe you can fetch us some fresh deer liver without makin' too much noise and scarin' our neighbors."

"Guess I'll have ta do that, since I'm powerful hungry. Ya want a big 'un or a little bitty tender one?" asked Jeremiah.

"I ain't particular, just you be bringin' back sumpin' I can chew on. An don't be bringin' back any of them red devils, neither," instructed Scratch.

Caleb joined the two hunters as they tethered their horses with the others and asked Scratch, "Uncle Scratch, I climbed up on the rimrock there and looked out yonder," motioning with his outstretched arm, "and I seen what looked like big rocks stickin' up outta the ground. They were way out there so I couldn't tell what they were, do you know?"

"Was they flat topped or pointed?" asked the mountain man.

"Both. The close one was flat topped, and the other one further on was real pointed like."

"Those were what we call genuine landmarks. The first one is Courthouse and Jail Rock and the other'n is Chimney Rock. I'm surprised you can see 'em this fer away."

"Well, they were a long ways out there. Are we going that way? When will we get there?" asked Caleb excitedly.

"Oh, they be at least a couple days away, mebbe even three, but we'll git there soon 'nuff."

Satisfied with the answer, Caleb returned to their campsite ahead of the hunters and Scratch grumbled, "Long as them durned Sioux don't try ta stop us, that is."

Knowing the nearby bluff protected their fires from sight, Scratch had encouraged the others to prepare for some fresh meat from Jeremiah, confident his partner would return with at least one deer big enough for everyone to have a good meal. Within the hour, Jeremiah returned with a fresh hide bundle with the de-boned meat of a sizable white tail doe. He portioned out a good share to each camp and returned with the liver and heart and a portion of back strap for his own camp. Knowing Scratch's favorite was the fresh liver, he dropped the hide with the liver and heart at his feet, "There ya' go partner. Have at it."

Scratch reached down and brought the raw liver to his mouth, sunk his teeth deep and yanked off a bloody portion to chew and swallow down while the others made faces at his behavior.

To The Tall Timber

Chapter Thirty- One: Thunder

JEREMIAH LAY on his back, hands clasped behind his head, stretched on his buffalo robe with a single blanket over his lower legs and once again walked through the brilliant stars that decorated the black sky. This was his favorite time, free of questions and comments from others, no conversation required, just quiet moments to reflect or contemplate.

Remembering the times he used to sit beside Laughing Waters and share hopes and dreams with her as they looked at the same stars, his heart stirred with longing for his mountains and the woman he wanted for his lifelong companion. As he thought of her, he realized he never considered or imagined a future without her by his side. She was his future, she was his life. With a smile stretching from his mind to his heart, he turned to his side with both hands under his cheek and sought the solitude of sleep.

It was an unusually quiet night. No 'ribits' echoed from mating bullfrogs by the river below, no crickets complained with their crackling rackets, not even an owl on the hunt asking who hid the game. The distant cry of lonesome coyotes was only a memory of previous restless nights and even the nearby tethered horses slept with their hipshot stance and lowered heads.

Surprisingly, even the usual log-sawing snore of Scratch was muffled in his robes. But the early morning hours before the eastern sun dared to show its face, were now filled with the earth shaking thunder from beyond the nearby ridge. Jeremiah was the first to sit up with his Hawken in his hand and searching the deep blackness of the few shrubs and trees surrounding the campsite of the travelers.

Scratch rose to one elbow and said, "Buffler!" then scrambled to his feet spouting instructions to his fellow campers. "Jeremiah, roust out them pilgrims and get 'em hitched up. We gotta move! If them redskins is followin' this herd, they might be paradin' into our camp real soon like. If they ain't, this'll be the best time fer us ta' get away from them without getting' in a scrap!"

Scratch was the first mounted and hollered back to Jeremiah, "I'm gonna see what's goin' on, hold them pilgrims here till I get back. If'n I don't, yore on yore own boy!" and slapping his mount on the rump, the sorrel kicked dirt clods back at the camp. With the black of early morning releasing its grip to the grey light of dawn, Scratch rode to the edge of the bluff behind them.

The many fingers of clay and sand that marked the runoff from the bluff above now appeared as extended roots of a massive stump left in the middle of the plains by some long forgotten monster. Scratch didn't bother to conceal himself as he sat astride his mount to survey the path of the thundering herd before him. The water starved plains protested their passing by raising a massive cloud of dust to obscure most of the herd, as they moved en masse between two larger buttes making their way to the lower valley where the tall waving grass beckoned.

Scratch dropped to the ground and stood by his mount as the brown river of buffalo sought the path of least resistance. He scanned the trail behind and spotted what he was looking for, the Sioux. Scratch led his mount off the butte to a somewhat level shoulder below the crest. He returned to the top of the bluff and stretched out prone to continue his observation of both buffalo and Sioux.

Anticipating the herd would soon slow and even stop when they reached the grassy plains to feed, the mounted Sioux warriors moved ahead of the rest of the village trailing the travois and lodges. The remaining members of the village moved toward a smaller park area with a few cottonwoods that promised a source of water. Scratch surmised they would set up their camp near the water and wait for the hunt to commence. Turning his gaze back to the warriors, he watched as they mounted their hunt for the buffalo by taking a route that would allow a sandstone ridge to shield them from the view of the herd.

Continuing his survey of the land, now made possible by the sun rising behind him, Scratch thought out a strategy for the wagon train to escape a confrontation with the Sioux. He turned and crawled back below the ridge to his mount, then leaning far back in his saddle, allowed the sorrel to choose his own path down the steep sided draw with each step pushing deep into the soft sandy soil to retard its progress to return to the camp below.

Most of the wagons were hitched to the teams as Scratch asked all to join him by the lead wagon. "Folks, here what we're up aginst. Thar's a bunch o' Sioux been follerin' them buffalo that woke us all up, and they ain't too fer yonder. It's a whole village and they got fifteen ta twenty bucks that'd like nothin' more than ta' take yore hair back ta their lodge.

But I'm a thinkin' we might get by 'em if we do things right. Now, here's ma plan." He then related the details of his strategy to avoid the Sioux and continue their journey unhindered. When he paused, Slim spoke up an' said, "Are we gonna get us a chance ta' git us some buffler? I been so hungry lately my stomach done thinks my throat's been cut!"

To The Tall Timber

Chuckling, Scratch dropped his head and used his moccasin to mark out the sketch in the dirt he used to explain his strategy, then looked back at Slim and said, "Well Slim, if yore that hungry an' you cain't pass up a buffler steak, I spose ya could try fer one, but before you can say Jack Spratt your throat will be cut by some young Sioux warrior lookin' fer honors. So, my question to you is, would ya rather be hungry or dead?"

Made even more aware of the impending danger before them, everyone returned to their wagons to prepare to depart. Scratch turned to Jeremiah and said, "You keep Charlie and Caleb close to you and you lead out. I'm gonna scout on ahead an' see if them red devils are busy with their hunt so we can get outta here."

The families were busy with the last preparations as given by Scratch. Several had labored to repair the bonnet or canvas covering for the bows of the wagons. Most had been ripped to shreds by the hailstorm and some were lost entirely, but others had repaired the canvas to provide shade from the relentless sun and to protect their belongings. Now it was necessary to remove the coverings and use it just to protect their belongings with little or none showing above the sideboards, Scratch has said, "Them light colored bonnets are like a big flag wavin' in the wind for anybody to see and them Sioux will shorely be lookin'!"

Anything that could be done to improve their chances of making it through this country without getting involved in an all-out fight with the Sioux was worth whatever task was required. Spurred by the fear that boiled in their bellies, everyone was cooperative in the joint effort.

Within a short while all were ready and poised on the seats of the wagons awaiting Jeremiah's call to "lead out!" It wasn't a cry nor a yell as they expected, but a simple hand signal to start the train on the trail. With the grunts of the teams, the rattle of trace chains, the slap of lead lines on the backs of the

214

horses and the occasional squeal of the axles and wheels, the train stretched out with each wagon closely following the lead.

The usual spacing of the length of a wagon tongue was shortened to half that as they feared the necessity of having to circle up for defense from an attack. The valley of the Platte narrowed to less than one hundred yards with an irregular ridge of rimrock bluffs along the Northern edge. Scattered along these bluffs were scrub juniper and cedar trees with patches of sagebrush and cactus.

The finger-like ravines that trailed from these bluffs reached into the grasses of the river's valley. Jeremiah spotted Scratch returning from the top of one of the bluffs and approaching the wagon train at a canter. As he pulled up next to Jeremiah and matched the pace of his steel dust gelding, he explained, "That herd circled up just where I reckoned, and them Injuns are starting their hunt. I'm purty certain they's gonna be busy fer a while, and if'n we keep a goin' we might just sneak by them devils."

Jeremiah sat easy in his saddle relieved to hear Scratch's report, he turned to look back on the wagons and waved to show it was good news. Scratch said, "I'll ride back along the line ta let them pilgrims know what's goin' on so they won't get too durn excited."

He reined his mount around and walked back to pass each wagon and share what he expected would happen. All were relieved but cautious knowing the danger was not over. At the rear of the train where Jeremiah had asked them to follow, Charlie and Caleb were leading the pack animals and Scratch was greeted with "Howdy Uncle Scratch!" from the boy and a big smile from Charlie which Scratch returned as he reined his mount to walk alongside Charlie's bay gelding.

Less than an hour of small talk with the woman that was dragging Scratch out of his rugged mountain man shell and putting a smile under his whiskers and in his eyes, Scratch thought he better return to the lead with Jeremiah. In that instant, he heard a familiar loud whistle of alarm and he pulled his horse to the side of the train to look to the front where he spotted Jeremiah giving a hand signal to look to the North along the line of bluffs.

Sky-lined on the bluffs were six Sioux warriors. Somber figures astride restless horses, several held lances upright by their sides while others had their weapons across their laps. Too far to identify the type of weapons, the distance also prevented Scratch from determining the presence or absence of paint that would reveal the purpose of their presence.

At a walk and single file, the group came off the bluff in the direction of the train. Scratch gigged his horse to the side of his partner and said, "You start at the front and I'll start at the back and tell these pilgrims to keep movin' but be ready for a signal to circle up. Make shore they have their weapons prepared and handy." Digging his heels into the ribs of his mount, he pulled hard on the reins to turn back to the end of the train. He first warned Charlie, "You an' the boy get alongside this hyar wagon and stay outta sight!"

Without waiting for an answer, he trotted his mount to the front of the wagon and one wagon at a time warned the settlers of the danger. Meeting Jeremiah beside the Whipple wagon, through gritted teeth he said, "Let's go out there an' meet them red devils!"

Stopping about seventy-five yards from the still moving wagons and standing between the approach of the Sioux and the pilgrims, the two mountain men scrutinized the approaching group. "Why, that there's a white man with 'em. He's the only one with a shirt on and that floppy hat, what the devils a white man doin' with them stinkin' Sioux?" growled Scratch.

As they were trying to determine the identity of the white man, one of the young bucks let loose a scream and a howl as he kicked his horse into an all-out run toward the two. Both men held their Hawkens across their legs but Scratch cautioned, "Hold on thar, I think this is just a young buck wantin' ta' count coup."

216

As the screaming buck approached within about twenty-five yards he reined his horse to swing wide and circle around behind the men, without slowing his pace and riding low to his mount, he extended his lance to slap the backs of both men as he passed. Both Scratch and Jeremiah remained unmoving, although Jeremiah whispered, "I wanted to blow that screamin' idjit off that horse and send him back to his momma's lodge with a big hole through his middle. If he tries it again, I ain't gonna resist that urge."

"Well I'm shore glad ya didn't cuz his friends there was just waitin' fer an excuse ta make pincushions of us. Now, lookee thar, here comes the two big uns," observed Scratch as they watched what appeared to be the leader and the white man walk their mounts forward. As they neared, Scratch said, "Well I'll be a cracked open goose egg, if that ain't ol' Willy Sublette! Hey thar, Sublette, you ol' scoundrel. What'r ya doin' playin' hopscotch with them Sioux?"

"Is that you Scratch? I'll swan, we thot you was gone under up on the Yellerstone! What'r you doin' with them pilgrims?"

William Sublette and his partner Robert Campbell had established the primary trading post that dealt with the Sioux named Fort William. With the beaver trade in decline, they bartered mostly for buffalo robes and were doing a thriving business. They built the fort in 1834 near the confluence of the North Platte and Laramie Rivers and had enjoyed a vigorous trade with the Sioux and the increasing number of pioneers and settlers traveling what would become the Oregon Trail. After the initial greeting, Sublette introduced the leader of the party of Indians as Bear Killer and explained he was visiting with the Sioux regarding their trading of buffalo robes and reaching other groups of the Sioux nation. Bear Killer was a war chief with the Brule nation of the Sioux.

"So, are you all headin' toward our post and are ya' stoppin'?" asked Sublette.

"Yeppir, we be doin' just that long as yore friend here doesn't have other plans," replied Scratch. "We'll probably be

217

splittin' up thereabouts, some of them pilgrims wanna go on ta Oregon country and others ain't too sure what they want, but that's as far as we agreed ta' take 'em. Didn't really wanna git mixed up with them pilgrims in the first place, but you know how it is…"

"Well Scratch, I'll probly be gettin' back thar before you do, so we'll see ya' when ya' get there," and he motioned to Bear Killer to leave then said, "Keep yore top knot on!" and waved to the two men now turning back to the wagons. The two men were silent for a short while as they pondered what just happened. Jeremiah was the first to break the silence with, "That's sure not how I expected that to work out. For a while there I thought we were gonna be pushin' up posies right here in the middle of this prairie."

"Just goes to show ya never know how things'r gonna turn out. But that sure makes me feel a whole lot better bout the rest of this hyar trip," replied Scratch as he stretched his hand high to wave at the wagons, "now, let's make fer yonder Chimney Rock." The return wave from the rider at the back of the train did not go unnoticed by Jeremiah and he let a smile pull on one side of his face.

Chapter Thirty- Two: Parting

AS THE TWO MOUNTAIN MEN stretched out on their buffalo robes, they were satisfied with full bellies and tired bodies. The long pull through Mitchell pass between the tall rocky ravines by Scotts Bluff had been their most difficult day of the entire journey.

The animals had performed valiantly and by the time they cleared the pass, most were lathered up and deserving of the rubdowns and leisurely graze and watering they now enjoyed. The winding trail had several extended pulls that challenged the voyagers but all knew they were nearing the location on their journey that would be the deciding point for their future. Fort William was now just a long day's journey distant and the impending decisions were weighing heavy on many minds. The past four days since their confrontation with the Sioux war chief, Bear Killer, had been dry, hot, and tiring but the anticipated rest at this campsite promised relief.

Jeremiah remembered Caleb's reaction to the imposing sight of Chimney Rock and what he said, "That looks like the devil himself pushed his pitchfork up through the ground and was tryin' ta' git outta his hole!" He turned to Scratch and asked, "Did you hear what Caleb said about Chimney Rock, bout the devil?"

Both men lay with their hands behind their heads and looking at the emerging stars overhead as Scratch chuckled, "Yeah, that boy's sumpin' ain't he? Course what he said looks an' sounds like sumpin' the old timers would think."

Behind their camp came the lonesome cry of a distant wolf that surprised Scratch into reaching for his Hawken that lay at his side. The reassuring presence of the .54 kept him still on his bedroll. "Now, what's a wolf doin' out chere on the flatlands? He must be lost and lookin' fer his mate," he casually observed. As he relaxed and returned his hand to his other behind his head, he continued, "We might make it all the way to Fort William tomorry, if we make good time that is," and thoughtfully added, "several o' them pilgrims will be goin' different ways from there."

From beyond the trees to his right came the snarling cry of a cougar, followed by a low growl and cough. Scratch's hand clutched his Hawken and brought it to his lap as he sat straight up looking in the direction of the cry, "That there's a painter, them things is dangerous. Mebbe we better check the horses. Don't wanna lose any of 'em now." He stood with his Hawken in both hands and held at his waist. "Ya don't think that wolf and painter is circlin' each other, surely not, when there's all these animals around'."

He was still watching the edge of the trees with the ghostly shadows from the bright moonlight. His head swiveled from right to left and his feet moved as if he was in some fancy promenade. From behind him came a smattering of cries from a pack of coyotes as they added their soprano wails to the chorus of the night.

"What in tarnation!" he spouted in surprise," It's like all th' animals of the plains is circlin' our camp. Whatcha reckon caused that? They ain't smellin' no blood 'er nuthin' it don't make no sense," he rapidly exclaimed with confusion written across his brow. Now looking in the direction of the coyotes, he turned back to Jeremiah who stood with his Hawken at his side.

Responding to his partner Jeremiah said, "Don't make sense does it?" and turned his head away to look toward the trees. Suddenly the diving cry of an eagle screeched from the treetops and made Scratch drop to his knees anticipating the razor sharp talons of the hunter of the night to pierce his back.

Jeremiah couldn't hold it any longer and burst forth with a belly laugh that caused him to bend over and suck air. Standing upright and looking at his wide-eyed partner, the laughter boiled over again. Caleb had stepped to his side along with Charlie, both laughing and looking at Scratch who stood frozen and scratching his head in wonder. When Jeremiah gained some composure, he said, "All that came from the Squirt. He was out there with Charlie making the rounds and all those sounds."

"Him?" responded Scratch, "He made those sounds? I don't believe it."

At Jeremiah's signal, Caleb turned away and let loose with a very real cry of a cougar that sent chills through all the listeners. Then turning slightly to his left, the wail of a lonely wolf reached to the treetops and surprisingly elicited a distant answer. The answering cry startled the four but was answered by another round of laughter.

"Well, jumpin' Jehoshaphat, I ain't never heard the like. You did all those?" he asked for time to comprehend as much as for an answer, "How long ya' been doin' that boy?"

"Pretty much the whole journey, Uncle Scratch. Uncle Jeremiah told me ta' keep it a secret cuz he wanted to surprise you. Did we?"

"Boy, I'll say you did. You surprised me and skeered the dickens outta me! I thought shore we was gonna have ta' fight ever' animal on the plains in one night. Whew, don't ever do that to yore ol' Uncle again!" he smiled as he pulled the boy to his side and gave him a sideways hug as the chuckle emerged. With broad smiles and a few more chuckles that erupted in laughter, the four returned to their bedrolls for a good night's rest.

* * * *

WITH THE LATE AFTERNOON sun in their face, the scouting duo of Jeremiah and Caleb shaded their squinting eyes to make out the distant palisade of Fort William. This was the landmark fort established by Sublette and Campbell that would later be known as Fort Laramie. Several teepee lodges stood to the river side of the upright walls of the trading post that was the long sought and now welcoming sight for the travelers. Wheeling their mounts to return to the train, the duo that appeared as a man and his shadow, gigged their horses to a lope to quickly rejoin the travelers. When the news spread a chorus of cheers rose from the entire wagon train. Although not the end of their journey it was a prominent milestone for everyone.

Jeremiah directed the wagons to circle up on the West side of the fort to make their night's camp. They planned to have an extended rest, repair and resupply stop as well as a time to get answers to many long harbored questions. This was the final stop for the guides and all anticipated going their separate ways.

Jeremiah wondered about Scratch and his burgeoning romance with Charlie and how that would affect his future plans, but he was more intent on his own plans to resupply and not waste any more time in his return quest for the Wind River Mountains and his waiting Laughing Waters. With the horses and mules hobbled nearby and enjoying the abundant grass, the quartet of scouts had made their camp not too distant from the wagons. As the campfire blazed and sizzled the overhanging buffalo strips, Charlie moved the pan of Johnny cakes from the blaze then reached for the coffee pot to refill Scratch's cup.

A contemplative mood prevailed among the four but Jeremiah broke the silence with his blunt question, "Have you decided whatchur gonna do Scratch? Are ya' goin' to the mountains with us or ya' got sumpin' else up your sleeve?"

There it was, served up on a flat rock before them, the question that had lingered in everyone's mind for many miles. Clearing his throat with a scratching cough and looking straight at his partner, he said, "Partner, it's like this. Me'n Charlie there been thinkin' 'bout gettin' hitched and mebbe follerin' these pilgrims on West and settin' up our own place. I'm thinkin' it's 'bout time to be plannin' on more permanent terms."

The silence that followed was only disturbed by the muted clang of the metal coffee pot being set on the nearby stone. Scratch continued, "What with you'n Waters puttin' yore lodge together, 'n you goin' back to them Arapaho, it kinda got me ta' thinkin' 'bout home 'n hearth too." A smile parted his whiskers as he looked at Charlie's flushing face.

"Can't say as I'm surprised none. But one things certain, you will be greatly missed. We've come a long way together and I could'na done it without cha," answered Jeremiah. He thought how this reminded him of losing Ezekiel and his father before. The choking in his throat was cleared as he coughed and stood to his feet to turn his back to the fire and his face to the distant plains now seen by moonlight.

Scratch spoke to his back when he said, "Well, I didn't rightly want our trails to part, but I'll say this fer ya' my friend. You'll do to ride the river with, that's fer shore." As Scratch walked behind the taller Jeremiah, he dropped his hand to his shoulder and gave a brotherly slap on his back.

Sucking in a deep breath, Jeremiah said, "I can almost smell that tall timber of the mountains and the cool breeze off the snow-capped peaks. Gettin' anxious ta' get there."

The following day was busy with many crowding the sutler's for their resupply of necessities. Jeremiah topped off his supply order with additional powder, galena and coffee. He spotted some *foofaraw* that he purchased for Laughing Waters and her friends and settled with the sutler with the last of the gold coin in the one pouch. Before they'd turned into their bedrolls the night before, Jeremiah had shared some of his remaining gold coin with Scratch to help him on his way. Although he refused at first, Scratch begrudgingly accepted what he knew could make the difference in a good start and a failure at whatever endeavor they undertook.

Returning to the camp trailing the one pack mule, the two partners indulged in small talk concerning the other members of the train. Scratch shared with Jeremiah, "So, I guess most o' them pilgrims has made up thar minds about where they be goin'"

"Oh, so what'r they all doin'?"

"Well, several of 'em are stayin' right chere! Seems ol' Sublette talked Homer the blacksmith, Slim the wheelwright and Oscar Jensen, the harness maker, into settin' up shop together with the post here, an' take care of all the pilgrims that'll be comin' this away."

"Hum, that sounds like a pretty smart move. Tween the three o' them, they should purty well be able to fix anything. Probably even build 'em some new wagons and such," observed Jeremiah. "What about the rest of 'em?"

"That youngster, Benjamin Whipple, whut lost his wife in that storm, well, he'n that nigra, Freddie, they're gonna join up with that bunch with the American Fur Company. They was in here ta' get outfitted and got ta' talkin' to 'em and convinced 'em they was still plenty 'o plews fer the takin' so they done joined up," then with a chuckle he added, "And that Liberty girl appears to be smitten with the Sutler's son and I think she's gonna stay on here too."

"And the rest of 'em?" inquired Jeremiah as he continued with his resorting of the panniers and packs.

"The rest of 'em, let's see, that'd be the Barhams, Farmers, the preacher an' his wife, and that rascal Boggs, they'll all be goin' together and figger on joinin' up with another wagon train and takin' the South fork 'n see if they can't make it further West. There's word goin' round that Bridger and Vasquez are

224

talkin' 'bout settin' up a tradin' post down yonder on the trail and they're headin' thataway. Mebbe even try ta' make Californy."

"And you?"

"Well, me'n Charlie's gonna have the preacher marry us up proper, and then we might tag along with them pilgrims headed south aways. Who knows, we might have ta' just up 'n leave 'em and come up into the Wind's and see if'n you'n Waters gittin' along," he surmised.

Everyone with the train and a few others from the trading post had gathered for the big moment. Scratch and Charlie stood before the preacher and faced each other holding hands and repeated the vows as directed. With a loud "Hooray" from the crowd, they were now husband and wife and they held on to one another as the many friends passed by to offer their congratulations and good wishes. Jeremiah hugged both and Caleb imitated his tall Uncle with hugs and a few tears.

With their good-byes said, Jeremiah and Caleb mounted up and tugged on the lead ropes of the two pack mules, dug their heels into the ribs of their mounts and pointed them to the mountains. It would be several days of travel across sage strewn plains populated with antelope, deer and plenty of jackrabbits before the tall timber would welcome the broad-shouldered mountain man and his shadow image back home.

To The Tall Timber

Chapter Thirty- Three: Home

THE CLEAR WATER cascaded over the many rocks that sought to delay the progress of the snowmelt as it sought the lower elevations of the valley below. The stream wound its way between massive boulders that had lost their grip on the steep mountainside and found their rest and purpose amidst the cold waters that were home to the many brook trout that hid beneath an overhanging bank.

On a trail beside the stream, Jeremiah and Caleb led the sure-footed pack mules into a narrow cut that separated the two neighboring mountains. The Popo Agie originated in the higher elevations of the southernmost stretch of the Wind River mountain range. Caleb was amazed when Jeremiah pointed out where the stream was swallowed by an abrupt cliff face and reappeared a few hundred feet below and on the other side of the narrow draw. "I ain't never seen anythin' like that, Uncle Jeremiah. How come it did that, wouldn't it be easier to just keep goin' in the stream bed without disappearin'?"

"I suppose boy, but some things just happen and there ain't no figgerin' it out. That's one of 'em. But don't worry, you'll probly see a lot of other things in your life that you won't be able to explain or understand. Some things are a lot like believin' in God. Ya' just gotta take 'em on faith."

"Kinda like you and Laughing Waters, huh? I don't understand it but I just gotta take it on faith, huh? Jeremiah, do you think she'll be all right with me taggin' along?" said the boy, verbalizing a fear he'd harbored for some time. It was easy to picture Jeremiah and him just being partners like Scratch and Jeremiah were, but it was hard to put a girl in the picture. Especially one he never met or knew anything about.

"Caleb, what you need to get settled in your mind is we, you and me, are a package. Whatever happens, wherever we go, we are together. A package. And when Laughing Waters meets you she's gonna be tickled pink and happier than a new born coon on his momma's belly," he said as he smiled back at the boy and received a broad smile in return.

"Are they, the Arapaho I mean, gonna be up at the end of this here stream?" asked Caleb.

"Well, the Arapaho are like most Indian people, they are what some refer to as nomads, which means their home is wherever they are. They think of home, not as a place but bein' with their own kind, ya' know, their family. They move the village with the seasons, usually this village summers in the southern part of the Wind River range and that's where we're headed. But it's a big country, so it might take us some time to find them."

The clatter of the horses' hooves among the rocks of the game trail they followed, brought Jeremiah's attention to the sharp rise of the mountain in front of them. The stream cascaded down in a mad rush making all the water appear white. Through the tall Douglas fir trees before them, Jeremiah could see the series of waterfalls that marked the water's trek from the ridge high above. Taking a narrow game trail to cross the face of the timbered hillside, the duo turned away from the stream to pursue the zig-zag trail up the near mountain side.

As they crested the hill, the thick forest thinned to reveal a flat park-like setting. It was the natural valley of the stream-bottomed plateau that lay below the towering granite-topped peaks of the mountain range.

Following the trail that stayed just inside the tree line, they continued on their quest for the Arapaho village. Another hour brought them to the edge of the same Popo Agie that now appeared as crystal clear water that lazily traveled through the grassy meadow. Taking a noon break, the two travelers seated themselves to lean against a pair of Ponderosa pine that slowly waved their long needles in the slight breeze. They chewed on some slices of pemmican they made during the last days of their journey with the wagon train.

Dried currants, rose hips, cherries and blackberries mixed with the dried and powdered buffalo strips then mixed together with melted fat and stuffed into an intestinal casing, then sliced into edible size made a pleasant change from the usual jerky and spring water. Jeremiah was in a melancholy mood as he gazed across the small valley to the tree line on the far side. Caleb mimicked his uncle and chewed and stared at the waving grass before them.

"Ya might as well come on out, Shield. You never could put the sneak on me," stated Jeremiah loudly and startled Caleb, who said, "Who you talkin' to?"

Jeremiah smiled and whispered, "Wait and see," then pointed at the mules standing stock still with their ears forward and their eyes watching the trees behind them.

Silently, three Arapaho warriors stepped from concealment behind the kinnikinnick shrubs at the base of the trees. "Who is this white man that speaks my name?" said the taller of the three.

When the two friends parted company, Jeremiah had a scrubby imitation of a beard and now his face was covered with a thick black bush. With broader shoulders, additional height, and a more confident stride, he bore little resemblance to the childhood friend known as, White Wolf.

"Did you forget White Wolf so soon? I haven't been gone that long, have I?" implored the mountain man as he stood to greet the visitors.

A broad smile told of the recognition as the man stepped forward to greet his friend from his youth. "Is it really you? We were beginning to think you had lost your way and would never return. My sister has even spoken about searching for you. And who is this little bear cub you bring with you?"

As the group followed the trail to the village, introductions and explanations were shared and passed the short distance to the site of the village. Broken Shield conspiratorially told Jeremiah and the boy to wait near the trail within the trees and he would send Waters back to fetch the previously "bagged yearling buck".

As the warriors continued into the camp, Jeremiah and Caleb led the horses and mules off the trail and deeper into the trees. Then returning nearer the trail, they stood behind a cluster of spruce and waited. Within a short while, the muttering of Waters gave away her location as she walked with her head down looking at the trail and grumbled, "I don't know why he had to send me for the meat, they could have brought it easily." Jeremiah quietly stepped to the trail a few paces in front of her and said, "Mebbe so, but they couldn't carry me."

She stopped and without another move, she looked at the bearded mountain man now blocking the trail. Her hand dropped to the knife in the scabbard at her side and she took a stance to prepare to fight, and snarled, "Who are you that dares to stand before me?"

Jeremiah smiled broadly, moving his arms away from his body with his hands open at his side, he said, "I am the man who will share your lodge, if you'll have me."

Her recognition gave light to her eyes and with a spreading smile she reached for him as she ran to jump into his arms and wrapped her slender arms around his neck in a tight lovers squeeze. Squealing in his ear she said, "Where have you been?

230

I wanted you here long before this! Wait, you said you wanted to share my lodge, do you mean…"

When they rode into the village, word had already spread of White Wolf's return and many stood beside their lodges to bid him welcome. Waters sat behind him with her arms locked around his middle and her eyes peeking over his shoulder. Her happiness was evident, as she had made life miserable for all those near her in the recent months that harbored all her fears that this day would never come. As Jeremiah drew his mount to stop before the lodge of Black Kettle, he greeted the village medicine man and the father of Waters with, "Uncle, I have much to give you for a bride price for Laughing Waters. Can we speak?"

"It is good to see you my son. Show me these things you speak of and we will talk," replied the distinguished leader of the people.

As Jeremiah began to unpack the first mule, he handed a rifle to Black Kettle, whose eyes grew wide at this great gift. Few warriors had rifles and it was a significant gift. Then, when Jeremiah handed him the second rifle, he was amazed and even confused, "What will I do with two such fine weapons?" he asked.

Jeremiah smiled and continued to lay gifts at the feet of the respected elder. He knew the higher the price paid for a bride, the greater value and respect she had from the people and Jeremiah wanted everyone to know how much he valued his Laughing Waters.

The people had crowded around to see the array of gifts that now sat before the medicine man and they talked among themselves and looked from Jeremiah to Waters to the gifts and then to Black Kettle. The medicine man motioned for Jeremiah to enter his lodge for the promised talk and Jeremiah knew the price had been accepted and Waters would be his wife.

Walking Dove, the widow of Ezekiel, asked if Caleb, now called Bear Cub, could stay with her and her twin boys, Badger and Coyote. Jeremiah knew it was a generous offer and made so the soon to be wed couple could have their time together.

Bear Cub said, "Yeah, White Wolf, I think I should stay with them for a while so I can learn all about Arapaho things. That all right?"

"Sure," and then with considerable emphasis on the name, "Bear Cub, I think it would be good for you to learn *Arapaho* things. Mebbe then you'll make a good member of the village. But first, you hafta stand with me'n Waters while we get hitched. It shows everbody that you're a part," instructed Jeremiah.

"You mean like a package?"

"Exactly."

Waters refused to wait any longer for the ceremony to unite the two. Jeremiah thought he ought to at least get washed up and maybe shave and put on some new buckskins, but Waters would not let him out of her reach and had her friends spread the word through the village of the impending ceremony.

Happy for any excuse to celebrate, the village busily worked for the next few hours to prepare a feast to honor the return of White Wolf and the uniting of the two for life. With the short delay, Jeremiah was able to prepare himself and now stood beside Laughing Waters and before Black Kettle.

Laughing Waters wore the dress she had been preparing for the last several months. With fringe dangling from the sleeves that almost reached the ground, the pure white buckskin was adorned with a pattern of flowers in blue beads and colored quills across the yoke from shoulder to shoulder. A wide belt revealed additional matching beadwork that accented her slender waist and gentle flair of her hips. The floral pattern continued down the front of the skirt and appeared as if she were standing in a flower garden of brilliant blue blossoms. Peaking from beneath the fringe of the skirt were matching moccasins with miniature images of the same blue flower buds.

The hurried shave of his beard left a red face with a few small cuts and his hair had been pulled back into a single braid that dangled over the new buckskins prepared by Waters. With a small beaded blue flower on each shoulder, the fringed sleeves accented the well-fitting attire. Topped by the broad smile of the now bare faced mountain man, the "fancy get-up" as he called it gave him a special joy as he realized his long treasured dream.

The ceremony was short and the festivities began even though the new couple retreated to the lodge that stood away from the others and was barely visible through the nearby trees. Everyone watched as Jeremiah lifted Waters and stepped through the opening to their new home.

THE END

To The Tall Timber

A look at Star Dancer by B.N. Rundell

This is a story about a horse and a boy, but not just any horse: a wild mustang stallion and not just any boy, but a native American proud member of the Arapahoe nation on the Wind River reservation in Wild Wyoming. When these two wild hearts are knit together through unique circumstances and challenges, they become a championship team.

Chastised by his peers and often excluded because of his disability, Trey Standingelk is more comfortable enjoying the solitude of long rides in the mountain with just his horse, his dog and his lifelong friend and often companion, Skye.

The two companions find themselves as the captors and eventual trainers of a beautiful mustang stallion, but Trey's challenges lend an obstacle that must be faced. After learning about the opportunities in the realm of horse training and especially the competitive arena of Free-Style Reining, Trey and Star's world is rapidly expanded. The connection that develops between the horse, Star Dancer, and Trey goes far beyond man and beast, and becomes a heart to heart lifelong bond.

About the Author

Born and raised in Colorado into a family of ranchers and cowboys, B.N. is the youngest of seven sons. Juggling bull riding, skiing, and high school, graduation was a launching pad for a hitch in the Army Paratroopers. After the army, he finished his college education in Springfield, MO, and together with his wife and growing family, entered the ministry as a Baptist preacher.

Together, B.N. and Dawn raised four girls that are now married and have made them proud grandparents. With many years as a successful pastor and educator, he retired from the ministry and followed in the footsteps of his entrepreneurial father and started a successful insurance agency, which is now in the hands of his trusted nephew. He has also been a successful audiobook narrator and has recorded many books for several award-winning authors. Now finally realizing his life-long dream, B.N. has turned his efforts to writing a variety of books, from children's picture books and young adult adventure books, to the historical fiction and western genres which are his first love.

Discover more great titles by B.N. Rundell and Wolfpack Publishing at:
    http://wolfpackpublishing.com/b-n-rundell/

Western
Rundell
2018
(New
sticker)

$6.99

1739379

Made in the USA
Monee, IL
17 August 2022